TOWER HILL

"*Tower Hill* has the old 'small-town-plays-host-to-incred-ible-ancient-evil' set-up, an interesting background story as to where the evil has come from, and some very well done characters . . . sharp writing and genuinely creepy moments. . . . A quick enjoyable read. . . ."

—*The Horror Fiction Review*

"One of the best ones I have come across lately. Pinborough tells a great story, it's as plain as that . . . any-one thirsting for something new and exciting in the genre should definitely check out *Tower Hill*."

—Book Bitch

"Fans of Edward Lee and Bentley Little will relish *Tower Hill*. . . . Ms. Pinborough merges mystery, horror, and fantasy into a powerful, unique thriller."

—SF Revu

THE TAKEN

"*The Taken* has wide appeal, but what appears an entertaining ghost story and revenge tale ingeniously morphs into something much more complex. And as Pinborough deftly weaves the story lines together in the second half of the book, we learn that there is more to the residents of Watterrow."

—Bookgasm

"*The Taken* will be considered one of the top ghost tales of the year."

—Book Crossing

NIGHT PREDATORS

Silence buzzed in his head and then came the sound he dreaded: a soft tapping at the glass, gentle at first and then heavier, as whatever was on the other side sought out footholds to climb the side of the terraced house. It moved slowly. Harry's ears focused on its every tread, before another set joined it, scuttling up the far wall in fast-paced thuds. His heart pounded and in the sudden stillness of the room an irrational fear gripped him that the things outside would hear the rhythm belting from inside his chest.

No one moved and Harry knew that like him the others would be staring upward, mouths drying and yet unable to swallow, not wanting to make the slightest noise that might alert the creatures to their presence. More short-lived wails filled the night and outside a bin tumbled to its side, the metal clanging loudly in the street. A pack was prowling out there, Harry could feel it. . . .

FEEDING GROUND

SARAH PINBOROUGH

LEISURE BOOKS NEW YORK CITY

A LEISURE BOOK®

October 2009

Published by

Dorchester Publishing Co., Inc.
200 Madison Avenue
New York, NY 10016

ISBN 10: 0-8439-6293-3
ISBN 13: 978-0-8439-6293-2
E-ISBN: 978-1-4285-0742-5

The name "Leisure Books" and the stylized "L" with design are
trademarks of Dorchester Publishing Co., Inc.

Printed in the United States of America.

10 9 8 7 6 5 4 3 2 1

Visit us online at www.dorchesterpub.com.

FEEDING GROUND

And I will punish the world for their evil
and the wicked for their iniquity;
And I will cause the arrogancy of the proud to cease,
and will lay low the haughtiness of the terrible.
—Isaiah 13:11

What's that coming over the hill is it a monster?
Is it a monster?
—The Automatic

CHAPTER ONE

"I'm so hungry, man. When do you think they're going to feed us?"

There was a long pause during which the prisoner's cell mate didn't answer. Instead, Blane Gentle-King sucked his teeth quietly and peered out through the bars at the silent gantry. His eyes narrowed. He'd been in lockdowns before and knew the routine inside and out, but this one was different. It hummed through every molecule in his body. Someone had either done some serious shit like stabbed up a guard, or something was very wrong. But he couldn't figure out what, and that annoyed the fuck out of him.

"I mean, how can they only feed us once a day? That's got to be against our fucking human rights or something."

His eyes shutting for a moment, Blane drew in a deep breath. The Brixton nick governor must have some kind of sick sense of humor putting him in with a chubby nothing of a thief like Arnie Black. And word in the yard was that Black was a grass. That in itself had put Blane in a difficult enough position every day of the three months they'd been locked up together. People *expected* Blane to take care of it; just on remand or not. He had a reputation to live up to and maintain, even in a nick on the other side of the river to his own. And, if he was honest, most days he'd be happy to gut the man. Grass or no grass, Arnie Black was still a fucking pain in the arse. Some days, Blane was amazed at his own restraint.

His light brown fingers squeezed the metal bars. On second thought, maybe the governor wasn't so dumb. Maybe he just wanted to make sure he got Blane locked away for good whether for the murder outside, or for one inside. Either-or, the outcome for society was the same. Maybe the governor thought that Chubby Black was expendable if it got Blane Gentle-King off the streets for the next twenty years.

Irritated, he flashed a look over his shoulder at the pale man whose prison T-shirt carried too many under-arm stains to wash out, and where new ones were form-ing even though it was only ten in the morning. His nose wrinkled a little with disgust. His words were soft.

"Quit chatting your breeze or I swear I'll rip your fucking tongue out and feed it to you myself. You won't be so hungry then, fat boy." The last word drew itself out, filling every corner of Blane Gentle-King's Jamai-can drawl.

Arnie Black's swallow was loud in the confines of the cell. "Sorry, Blane," he muttered quietly, withdrawing into the shadows of his lower bunk. "I just wish we knew what was going on. That's all."

"Take it up with your fucking lawyer." Not that ei-ther Blane or Chubby Black had seen either of their lawyers for over a week. Flu. Stomach bug. All weak white-man shit as far as Gentle-King was concerned.

He turned his attention back to the gantry on the other side of the bars and forgot about Arnie Black, instead concentrating on seeing as much as he could of the prison. The top bunk would give him a better view and lithely jumping onto it, he pressed his back against the wall and tilted his head, peering down into the main thoroughfare of the old building.

He frowned. Right at the far edge of his vision was one of the screws' stations; two old wooden desks in a steel-wire cage. The table lights were on, but he couldn't see any part of any guards. Sliding farther down so he was almost horizontal, his long legs dangling over the side, he stared. Nothing. There was no one there. It was a two-man post, and Brixton had learned its lessons the hard way. They didn't cut corners. The prison riots of twenty years ago weren't out of working memory for some of the older staff. Brixton prison officers worked with old-school army thoroughness, no one wanting anything to go down on their shift. And yet here it was, a two-man post with no one on it at ten in the morning. It didn't make any kind of sense, no matter how he looked at it.

He came down from the bed and walked the three feet to the other cell wall, looking out from that angle. His vision was limited. He crouched down on his haunches, but it was no better.

"What are you doing, Blane?" Black crept forward on his bunk like an overweight, nervous puppy.

Blane ignored him, and standing up he tapped on the wall. "Hey, Jonesy. You awake?" The plaster smelled of damp and piss and the various frustrations of hundreds of men that had seeped into it over the years.

"Yeah. Too fucked off and hungry to sleep," a disembodied voice growled back. "Not like the lazy little twat underneath me. He'd sleep through a bloody nuclear war given half the chance." The man banged on the metal bedpost to make his point, and then paused. "What can I do for you, GK?"

"Can you see the left-side lower guard station from there?"

There was a heavy thud and the sound of shuffling feet, followed by a moment's silence.

"I can see the edge of the desks if I get down on the floor," Jonesy grunted.

"Any guards at them?" Blane wished he could slide through the paint-tatty bars and see for himself. A second ticked by, and then even from eight feet away, he heard Jonesy suck in a breath.

"Well, fuck me. There ain't no one there."

Blane rested his head against the wall joining the cells. "Same at the other end, bro."

"What the fuck does it mean, GK?"

Blane's brain raced in circles, each idea crashing into a black space of nothing.

"No idea," he said eventually. "But whatever it is, it ain't fucking good."

Divided by thick brickwork, neither man spoke, and even Chubby Black stayed quiet, his nervous eyes watching the tall figure of his cell mate.

"How many screws have you actually seen over the past few days?" Blane spoke to the wall, his eyes narrowed. "I mean since they started this lockdown shit."

"I dunno." A lighter clicked and the pungent smell of rolled-up cigarette tobacco drifted out into the empty gantry. "O'Halloran's been around a couple of times. Tight-lipped bastard. If he tells me to mind my own business one more time, I'll fucking have him next time they let us out in the yard."

Blane ticked the older guard off on his mental list. He'd seen him too. "Who else?"

"Munro brought the slop that passes as food around yesterday. And the day before. Sweating like a pig he was."

"Yeah, I saw that." Blane had. Munro was not a man designed to be a prison warden; word was that Brixton nick was his first job and Gentle-King figured it would be his last. No balls. Munro wanted to be everyone's friend, guards and inmates alike, ending up with no respect from either. Blane had no time for screws in general, but he hated screws that showed their fear. They made his teeth grind with a quiet rage that he knew was excessive but could do nothing about. There was one pussy guard in every nick, and Munro was Brixton's.

"Jackson and Morris were about, but I don't think I saw them yesterday. Maybe they're on night shift. That's about it. Can't think of anyone else."

Blane sighed and sucked in the ghostly taste of cigarette smoke as it passed his cell. He had enough tobacco for a couple of smokes left, but he was saving it. "Neither can I," he said eventually.

Someone coughed down on the lower level, which was enough to set off a few shouts and calls from angry inmates demanding to be let out of their cells. Under their indignation, Blane was sure he could hear the echo of their underlying fear. Soon the prison would stink of it; sour like an old woman's piss. He wasn't the only one sensing that something was going wrong.

"Four guards?" Jonesy's voice had lost its growl of street meanness. "What the fuck is that about? If some fuckers have fucked a guard up surely the prison would be crawling with them? How can there only be four?"

Blane said nothing, but understood the other man's incredulity. Without answering the question, he climbed back up onto the top bunk and stared thoughtfully at the wall. His mind wandered back through the memories of the past couple of weeks and things became clearer. They hadn't noticed how few guards there were because the numbers had been slowly dwindling for a while. If he hadn't been so busy trying to keep his head down and not stabbing up Arnie Black, then he'd have picked up on it. But why were things changing? What the fuck was going on?

From under his pillow he pulled the small cigarette tin that housed his remaining tobacco and small lump of Moroccan black. Maybe this was the right time for a smoke after all.

By six P.M. any buzz Blane's hardened system had got from the hashish resin was merely a lingering aftertaste. His head was clear. It wasn't just Arnie Black that was whining about being hungry, half the block had joined him, rattling their tin cups against the bars while demanding feeding and exercise, when underneath it all was that fear; its smell growing ranker and sweet. No guards had patrolled all day; not a single command had been barked at the inmates, and the lack of both echoed and laughed mockingly throughout the cells.

Blane clenched and unclenched his fists, needing to release some of his own tension, but not wanting it to show. The men could live without food for a day, but it seemed to Gentle-King as he listened to their catcalls, that the unwilling residents of Brixton nick were slowly realizing that without the guards to manage their lives they were completely powerless. And crazy as it sounded Blane wondered at the possibilities of them all eventually starving to death.

Down below on the first level someone shouted for insulin. The voice was weak. No response came.

"Do you think maybe there's been a nuclear war or something?" Arnie Black was snivelling, snot running down his chin.

Blane considered weaving his strong fingers into that greasy mop of hair and hammering the fat face to a bloody pulp against the solid brick wall, but restrained himself. If no guards had come around by this time tomorrow, there'd be plenty of cell mates killing the shit out of each other, and they'd all be able to get their lawyers to claim some kind of cause like self-defense. That was the kind of shit they paid their lawyers for. Blane would jump on that bandwagon and smash up Black then, but not before. It wouldn't look good to be the first to crack. Not with his reputation and while already waiting on a murder trial.

"If there'd been a nuclear war, we'd all be fucking dust." The purr in his even tone was heavy with menace. "We're in London, you thick shit. They'd bomb here first." He paused. "And who the fuck would bomb us anyway?"

"Then where is everyone, Blane? Where are all the guards? They can't just leave us here." The panic rose in his voice and the bottom bunk creaked as his rocking backward and forward became more intense, pushing the old springs into reluctant action.

"Just shut the fuck up, Arnie." Blane peered down over the thin edge of the mattress. "Everything you need to be scared of is right in here with you. Just remember that, you fat fuck."

Arnie Black lay on his side and curled up, having the sense to keep his mouth shut. The sound of his quiet, wet sobbing still irritated but it was better than listening to his pointless questions. How the fuck was Blane supposed to have any answers?

* * *

By nine o'clock the man calling out for insulin had gone into some kind of coma according to the shouts of his cell mate and that had pretty much quieted everyone else down. No guard came and the prisoners, Blane Gentle-King among them, waited with their breaths held to see if the man died. There was no concern in their anticipation; Blane didn't give a flying fuck if the man's head exploded or he got up and did an Irish jig, but if he died then they could no longer kid themselves that things were fine and that the guards would be along any minute, having just been held up with a minor emergency elsewhere. If the man died then they were all going to have to admit that things were seriously fucked up.

Somewhere along his line a toilet in one of the cells must have blocked and the stink of sewage slowly crept along the length of the gantry. Blane's eyes narrowed, his breathing shallow against the stench. His money was on insulin man dying. He didn't have a fucking clue what was going on in the nick, but the place was fucked up badly; every cell in his body screamed it.

The tense silence cracked as footsteps pounded up the stairs from the lower level, and as much as he prided himself on his cool, Blane Gentle-King's heart thumped into excited life in his chest.

"*Hey Munro! Where the fuck are you going? Come the fuck back here!*"

"*Hey fucker, stop! When are you fuckers going to feed us?*"

"*Let us out, pig!*"

"*Who the fuck's he got with him? They ain't no guards.*"

The calls were full of the righteous indignation of

the guilty, but Blane could feel the ripple of sweet relief every one of the prisoners felt at the sight of the guard.

"Oh thank fuck . . ." Arnie Black muttered behind him, and for once the sound of his voice didn't bring instant thoughts of violence to the fore of Blane's mind. In that moment, Arnie was inconsequential. The heavy footsteps were coming their way and Blane strained against the bars to catch a glimpse, but the figures were out of sight. Despite the protests and threats that poured from cells on every level, the men kept their strides even and didn't stop. Not until they came to Blane Gentle-King and Arnie Black's door.

Blane's grin widened. Things were suddenly looking up. On the other side of the bars, two large men in heavy leather jackets flanked Munro. Between them, short and insignificant, the guard sweated, his furrowed brow creating a network of tracks for the salty liquid to run through. Blane ignored him, looking instead from the almost–midnight black face on one side of the runt, to the white one on the other.

"You surprised to see us, boss?" Jude's large teeth shone out from his ebony face, and although Blane smiled back at him, it was the other man he spoke to. His right-hand man, Charlie Nash.

"What's happening, Charlie? I never thought I'd see you on the inside of no nick."

"I was missing you, man." Charlie barely cracked a smile. But then he rarely did. Charlie had been a serious kid and was a serious man, but Blane trusted him. And he didn't trust anyone else.

"So where's my money?" Munro looked up at Charlie Nash, his pink tongue darting out and licking his lips. "I need to get the hell out of this city. Get on a plane or something. Go somewhere where things are . . . normal. While they're still normal." His words erupted fast, his breath hitching between their gushes. He was scared, Blane knew the signs. But what of?

Charlie pulled an envelope from the inside of his jacket, lifting the flap to show the guard the thick wedge of notes crammed inside. "It's all here."

Munro made a clumsy grab at it, but Charlie Nash pulled his hand swiftly back. "Don't be greedy."

"Yeah." Whereas Charlie was an island of still, Jude hopped slightly from foot to foot. "Open the fucking door first." He grinned at Blane for approval, and from within the cell, Blane gave him a small nod. The boy was obviously fucking high, but he figured not too much, otherwise Charlie wouldn't have brought him along.

Munro fumbled through a ring of keys on his belt and Blane watched him. Why the keys? The doors worked on electric. Had the system failed? He looked up at Charlie.

"What's going on, man?"

Charlie raised an eyebrow and for a moment looked lost for words. "Fuck knows. You'll have to see it to believe it. But I thought it would be best to get you out of here while we still could."

"We're getting out of here?" The breathless voice cut in from behind, and Blane gritted his teeth. Charlie frowned.

"That your cell mate?" He paused, taking in the sight of the snotty, chubby man. "Must have been a long couple of months."

"You have no idea, my friend."

As Munro rattled the keys, finally sliding the correct one into the creaking lock, the calls of the prisoners surrounding them grew louder and more urgent. The metal door swung open and Blane stepped out onto the gantry. Finally smiling, Charlie Nash pulled a handgun from his jacket and tossed it to him. "Welcome back."

"And my payment?" Munro's voice had lost any hint of confidence it may once have held.

Charlie pulled a second gun from the back of his trousers, priming it swiftly as his arm rose. Munro didn't have time to move, his widening pupils and fallen mouth the only clue that his brain was desperately trying to compute the imminent danger to his frozen legs. Charlie Nash pulled the trigger and the gunshot echoed down the full length of the old building, ricocheting back at the men from the high ceilings.

The cells fell silent, just a few barked expletives chasing the ring of exploding metal. The thud of the bullet punching through Munro's uniform and into his untoned chest was decidedly less dramatic, but had far more impact. His eyes still wide, they lost their focus as his legs crumpled under him, his heavy body collapsing with a muted thump to the chipped floor. For a moment there was silence, and then Arnie Black appeared in the doorway to the cell, his double chin wobbling slightly as he shook his head from side to side.

"Shit, man, he shot a screw." He looked up at Blane, his breathless voice almost disbelieving the evidence in front of him. "He shot a screw."

"He fucking did, didn't he?" As he raised his own gun, Blane smiled. "And now I'm going to shoot you." The echo of the first gunshot had barely faded before the second rang out. Arnie Black's brains and part of his skull fled back into their two-man cell while his body toppled forward, landing softly on that of the dead guard.

Blane sniffed loudly. "Fucking bent screws and grasses. They do my head in." He looked up at the two men waiting for him. "Let's get the fuck out of here, shall we?"

"Hey, GK." Jonesy pressed his pockmarked and scarred face to the bars as if he could somehow squeeze his head through them. "Chuck us those keys." His hooded eyes glanced down to the heavy chain that lay next to Munro's lifeless body, and then back to Blane. "Go on. Be a mate."

Blane didn't like seeing desperation in a man like Jonesy; it didn't sit right with their lifestyle. And what did the other man really expect? That Blane was going to set them all free? Half of London's players were locked up in this nick. Why would he let that amount of competition back on the streets? He had his own empire to build and that was best served leaving the heavy ring of keys exactly where it was.

As he walked the length of the gantry the air filled with angry screams and shouts. He didn't look back.

CHAPTER TWO

London was quiet.

That was the first thing Blane Gentle-King noticed as the car slipped through the open gates of the Brixton prison. Whatever was wrong inside the prison, it was wrong outside it too. Charlie steered the Mercedes along the empty streets that normally throbbed with life. It should have disturbed him, but all Blane felt was relief. After Charlie had broken him out, he figured it would be straight to Heathrow with one of his dodgy passports to hide out in Jamaica until the heat had settled. With the way the world stood silent around him, he was reevaluating that prospect. Maybe he would get to stay in London after all. He sucked his teeth. Things might look bad, but there was always an upside.

Night was falling and although it wasn't yet dark, an eerie gray gloom filled the wide spaces between the dirty buildings of the inner city. A solitary black cab cruised past them in the other direction, its speed half-hearted. The orange light was on, but the driver looked half-asleep, with one arm hanging out of the open window trailing his fingers in the evening air.

In the backseat Jude rolled a fat spliff and passed it forward. Blane took it without a word, inhaling the sweet smoke deep into his lungs. This was proper sinsemilla, not the ordinary shit the prisons were filled with, and his head rushed, tingles flooding through his veins. His brain hummed like electricity, the buzz tickling his ears. He was out of practice. But as he felt the tension ease out of his shoulders for the first time in months, he smiled. The high felt good.

Charlie Nash took them over the river and headed along its curve back toward Newham, only three other cars passing them as they went. Two men stumbled along the embankment, one about a hundred feet in front of the other, and Blane peered out of the window at them as the car purred past. The first wore a suit and gripped his briefcase tightly as he weaved along the wide pavement, his frowning eyes focused on moving himself forward. He was drunk, that was obvious, but he wasn't a happy drunk. Just a blind drunk. Any fool could see the difference and Blane wasn't no fool. Raised in the hard life of the estate, he'd seen plenty of drinkers, back in the day before the crack took over those in need of serious mental and emotional wipeout.

The second man was in jeans stained with grease and oil, his yellow jacket declaring him London Underground staff. He was drunk too. And just like the first man, he didn't look pleased about it. Up against a black cast-iron City of Westminster bin a pile of unsold *Evening Standard* newspapers stood high, the top one fluttering its pages in the breeze. Blane sucked in another brain-rushing mouthful of smoke. The scenery was surreal. Were they even today's newspapers? How long had they been sitting there unwanted?

Jude sniffed. "Streets is even quieter than this morning." He'd rolled a second joint and more pungent smoke filled the car. Blane took another toke on his before passing it to Charlie. He'd had enough; his throat ragged and rough as sandpaper. Normally, they'd never even think to spark up while out on the streets whether it was day or evening; it wasn't worth the arrest risk, but it seemed that not even the police were out tonight.

"What the fuck is going on?" He finally organized his fuzzy thoughts into words. "Where is everyone?"

"Staying inside, we reckon." Jude leaned in between the seats and amid the smell of burning weed Blane's nose crinkled at the sharp scent of stale sweat. Jude needed to clean up if he was going to stay useful. "I'm telling you, man. London town is seriously fucked up."

Suddenly Arnie Black's whining didn't seem so outlandish. "Are we at war? Has someone dropped some kind of fucking germ bomb on us?" For the first time, Blane felt a brief flash of fear, or at least something close to it.

"Maybe." Charlie's voice was all North London mumble. "Maybe it's something like that causing it. It's all the birds, you see." He paused. "They started getting fat."

"Not just fat," Jude cut in. "Fucking American-style fat. Like those freaks you see on hospital shows that can't fucking walk. Charlie got most of them out of the block a couple of days ago. They was giving us all headaches."

"Fat?" Blane turned to Charlie. "What the fuck do you mean they started getting fat?" He wished that maybe he'd stayed off the weed until he'd got home. Maybe he was tripping out a little. "Women always get fat. It's what the bitches do."

Charlie shook his head. "Not like this, man. Something's happening. They're *changing*."

"Just wait and see, Blane." Jude sat back in his seat, taking his body odor with him. "Wait and see."

Pressing the small button by the gear stick, Blane opened the sunroof. He pushed his head through, his feet stepping up onto the bucket seat and standing tall, his torso fully out. Wind sent his dreadlocks flying backward and he squinted to look around him. Here and there people shuffled like zombies heading anywhere and nowhere. They didn't look like Londoners. Londoners walked fast, head up and focused on the next deal or on just barging past the people that were in their way and shouldn't be. These men just looked lost and tired. Something was wrong, and they all knew it.

Up ahead the gray tower blocks of the estate loomed high as they passed the graffitied sign that under all the tags and sprayed abuse had once said WELCOME TO THE LONDON BOROUGH OF NEWHAM. Blane had never cared that the words were barely legible. They were a lie. No strangers were welcome in his manor. Not unless they knew who the boss was.

Climbing out of the car, Blane paused to pull on his long leather coat. The night air was surprisingly warm, but his coat was his trademark, and he wanted the residents to know he was back. He looked up. London wasn't perhaps as dead as it seemed. Although many of the flats seemed dark and empty, several curtains and blinds twitched flashes of yellow electric light as occupants peered nervously out.

He stood in the full beam of the headlights for a moment before Charlie cut the engine. The outline of his coat and hair was instantly recognizable to anyone who lived in a five-mile radius, and to plenty who lived farther afield. Blane Gentle-King was back and he wanted anyone who was looking to be in no doubt about that.

Since the age of twelve he'd been working hard to

run this estate, no mean feat for a mixed-race kid with a yardie father and a white-trash hooker mother. Seventeen years on and with still six months to go before turning thirty, his dream was well and truly achieved. He'd been kingpin for five long years, and anyone that thought they could try and take anything from him had been dealt with severely, although not very often swiftly. Examples had to be made, and with Charlie by his side, that was something they did well. It wasn't very often that Blane was challenged—even during his brief stints inside. No one was ever that sure of themselves or whom they could trust. And Charlie was always there watching for anyone who looked like they might even be thinking about making a move. The estate may not be much in the eyes of the outside world, but it was Blane Gentle-King's kingdom, and he'll come calling for any fucker who tried to make it otherwise.

Behind them, past where the Thames Barrier rose its silver domes up from the river, the sleek steel and glass blocks of Canary Wharf had spread downriver to the Victoria Dock Road where they sneered down on Blane's small empire. In those buildings there were no flats, only *apartments*. LUXURY APARTMENT LIVING is what the banner that hung down the side of the newest block, erected only a few hundred yards but a million light years from the Crookston blocks, proudly stated. Those flats or whatever the fuck they wanted to be called were the pinnacle of Blane's dream. By the time he was thirty-five he intended to be running his business operations from there or even the wharf itself. No more cheap junkie hookers struggling to earn him a couple of hundred a night, and twenty-quid-a-night crack addicts that would happily rob him just to buy more gear from him. He had plans for an international operation. Big volumes shipped in and sold on. No more face-to-face dealing, and only top-class girls with first-class degrees working out of sleek offices in the West End where no one gave a fuck if the girls were taking Arabs three at a time as long as they were doing it in Park Lane and they were all paying their taxes. That, he'd decided, was the fucking life for him.

Tonight though, even the elegant apartments looked gloomy; not that many lights blazing from their vast glass windows and walls. If the people weren't on the streets then they must be inside, but why the fuck would they be sitting with the lights off? A bin lid clattered to the ground somewhere in the shadows to his left, and he crouched instinctively, his hand gripping his gun. No one appeared, and after a second or two he shrugged his jumpiness away. Must have just been one of the flea-ridden stray cats that hung around the recycling bins and the garbage room, scavenging when their owners in the flats high above them got bored of the litter trays and chucked them out once the cuteness of kittenhood was gone. A throb started at the back of his head, and he turned back to face the gritty walls of his own empire.

"Don't tell me," he said. "The lifts are out of order."

Jude laughed. "You guessed it, man."

Blane sighed. It was going to be a long walk up to the nineteenth floor.

They stopped on the seventeenth outside the door to what had been one of Charlie Nash's flats. He had two in the block and the council never complained. One was technically Charlie's mum's but her brain had long ago turned to mush from cheap vodka and too much weed and she'd moved in with some shit Glaswegian drunk on an estate on the other side of Newham. Blane doubted they ever fucked. They were too fucked to fuck, and that was probably the only thing that stopped Charlie killing the fat bastard who would never be good enough to replace Charlie's old man, who had been gone since Charlie was four but still occupied some sainted position in the man's head. And on a practical level, if the Glaswegian was dead then Charlie's mum would have to come back to her council flat and Charlie had spent some decent money making it his own. His other flat was used as business premises. Hence the heavy metal-reinforced door that faced them, having long ago replaced the not exactly flimsy council standard issue. The steel that now filled the space was almost a foot thick, impossible for the pigs to break through even with a battering ram. If Charlie or one of the other boys didn't want that door opened, it stayed shut.

Farther along the narrow corridor one of the encased night-lights flickered and buzzed trying to keep itself alight, and in its shallow beam Blane studied the door and frowned. It had been changed. Instead of the locks and bolts being on the inside, they were now securely done up on the outside.

He looked up. "And you're telling me you've got Janine locked up in there?" He stared incredulously at Charlie. "Because the bitch got fat?"

The white man nodded. "I didn't know what to do with her. She's your girl, so I couldn't kick her off the estate and I didn't want to put her in the flat along there"—he nodded along where the row was swallowed up by the dark indoor night—"with the other junkie girls we got working." He shrugged. "This made sense."

"You didn't get rid of the girls?"

Jude shook his head. "Nah. They still want the rocks, man. We figured they could run up a tab and work it all off when whatever this shit that's happening is over."

"I figure we got rid of maybe half the women. Some wouldn't come out."

"I can't believe you did that man." Blane shook his head. "Didn't any man fight back for his woman?"

Charlie reached for the small letterbox-size sliding hatch on the front of the door. It was normally opened from the inside to pass out packages of drugs to the skinny desperates that passed over their government benefits for just one more fix.

"Take a look for yourself. Then tell me I shouldn't have been worried."

The metal slid back, the sharp sound clattering into the night. Jude stepped away, his eyes shifting nervously from side to side. "All yours, man."

A sickly rotten smell far worse than the young black man's stale sweat poured thick from the small opening and Blane held his breath as he peered in. For a long moment he said nothing at all, before eventually his mind connected with his mouth.

"Jesus fucking Christ."

That thing was not Janine. It couldn't be.

CHAPTER THREE

Janine.

   Her name was Janine. She was . . .

   For a moment her mind fogged. Hungry. She was hungry. And she needed. She needed so badly it was making her whole body ache.

   Eighteen.

   That was the word. Her name was Janine and she was eighteen. For a moment happy with that, she shifted back on the pile of stained duvets Charlie Nash had thrown in with her before locking the heavy metal door. How long had she been here now? Time gone past blurred into an unimportant gray haze. She didn't know and she didn't care. Scattered around the darkened sitting room were empty packets of cheap meat. Not enough.

   She sighed and felt another loose tooth fall free under her tongue. She spat it out and looked down at the huge bloated thing that she had become. For a while, at some point in the vagueness that was the past, she'd been worried. No—more than that—she'd been scared. Now she could barely remember the shape of her thin legs and flat stomach. They belonged somewhere else. To someone else. Now, as she looked at the vast expanse of flesh, she felt simply contentment. Everything was as it should be. Soon this body would slough off and she would become . . .

   . . . What?

* * *

Eighteen. And not eighteen. So much older. Sometimes she was sure she could feel the soft sand of the ocean bed shifting and the icy chill of salt water pressing against the sack that was stuck so deep in the alien earth. Sometimes it seemed as if the spores had slept there forever. They weren't her memories, not Janine's, because however fucked up she'd got on the rocks, she knew for a fact that she'd never seen an ocean, let alone sat at the bottom of one, but the memory was real. It wasn't just her that had it. All the girls did. It was part of their changed memory.

WE NEED . . .

The thought buzzed into her head; the words carried angrily along the empty corridors of their minds from the women locked up in the other flat. In a flash she could see them inside her head: four fat women, age and looks unrecognizable, quivering in a dank, damp room. At first she'd had to think hard to see the others, but now . . . it came so easily. She smiled, feeling the sagging fat jowls of her cheeks jostling for space as her mouth stretched. Now she could feel all of them, everywhere. The network was endless.

Mainly though, she could feel the ones like her. The ones that needed. They were different, she knew that. Maybe, they were even BETTER.

Her skin itched on the underside. The need of the others was carrying into her own roaring addiction, and it made her angry. Her belly rippled. It was nearly time. The itch grew stronger and she frowned. When was Charlie coming back? Or Jude? Or any fucking one of them? She didn't care which, just as long as someone was there to feed her the sweet smoke she craved.

Her head tilted suddenly.

Outside. There were people outside; she sensed it even before the metal hatch rattled open. Was it her own ears that made out the three sets of footsteps climbing up from the ground floor, or was it her new collective hearing? It was so hard to tell. She did know the others looked to her. The others like her. But they always had, even when they were out on the streets. Janine got the best punters, the flashiest car drivers, and Janine always got her rocks first. Because after all, Janine—who at fifteen had been the prettiest girl on the block before the drugs and the fags and the fucks took that certain sweet glow—was Blane's favorite girl.

And that counted on the Crookston blocks. It counted for a lot.

Hauling her enormous frame to its feet, she lumbered out to the hallway, where a fresh breeze fought its way inward. It felt good on her greasy skin, cooling the strange slime that oozed from her pores.

Brown eyes flecked with hazel peered through, sparkling jewels in a golden brown desert, and for a brief moment what was left of her human heart paused. There was no confusion, the name burst into her rotting mouth. Blane. It was Blane. He was out. She tried to smile, staying a few feet from the door so he could see her properly. His Janine.

"Jesus fucking Christ."

Her toothless grin stretched. He could see her then. Something under her stomach shifted, more of whatever she would become adjusting itself as it absorbed her, and the ripple echoed across the once-baggy jumper that now stretched too tight over her torso.

"Hey baby." Her voice was low and guttural and she liked it. It was stronger. The man's eyes flinched against its gristly rattle. "I need a rock, baby. Just one."

What remained of her teeth clenched against her jaws, wobbling against their bleeding foundations. The eyes just stared back.

Inside, the new her writhed, her need its need, and it

made her angry. The men were nothing. Soon they would be just . . . just what?

She frowned. The fog wouldn't clear. It didn't matter. They would be unimportant, she knew that. But they had the drugs she and the others needed, and she hated them for that.

"I said I need a rock." She spat the bloody words out, the spray hitting the metal door like a gauntlet thrown down between them.

The eyes narrowed. "Sure, baby." The sweet tone rang false and the newer improved-and-so-much-cleverer Janine realized that it probably always had. She'd just been too fucked up and stupid to realize. The ghostly ache of every bruise he'd ever given her stung her throbbing body.

"Charlie." The eyes turned from the small opening. "How do you do this? She got a pipe?"

Voices mumbled and then those beautiful irises were back. She wondered momentarily how she could see the thousands of shades of brown in them so clearly given the shroud of night that wrapped itself around the unlit flat, and then her focus shifted to the small cellophaned package that fell through the door. The small lump of sickly yellow shone like a diamond in her mind's eye. A second thump delivered a fresh pipe and cheap lighter.

"Knock yourself out, baby."

She looked up, and smiled seductively, licking her thick lips with her black tongue. "You gonna let me out, honey? I'll be good to you."

A dry swallow.

"Not until you're better." The sweet voice was unsteady. "I've got a . . . a headache coming."

There was a brief glimpse of a white hand and then the opening slammed shut. Charlie. Charlie Nash wasn't stupid.

"*The others!*" *she shouted at the disappearing footsteps.*
"*The others are hungry too!*"

Leaning against the peeling wallpaper, her thick fingers
fumbled to free the rock from the stretched plastic. Eventu-
ally, she secured it in the metal head of the pipe and with
shaking fingers, lit it.

Her gummy mouth sucked the sickly sweet smoke in.

The anger faded a little and as both the monster inside
and out was soothed, the ripples stopped.

Just for a while.

CHAPTER FOUR

Craig's legs burned as he ran up the far stairwell, the heavy rucksack banging into his spine. The steps on the lower levels were rank with the cheap beer and drunks' piss that had stained them so often that no amount of bleach would shift it. Not that many had tried. He avoided touching the walls, a habit learned from early childhood. By the fifth floor the smell had weakened, and even inside the seventies structure, the air was cool against the cheaply council-painted walls.

The estate was never as quiet as it had steadily grown to be over the past week or so, and Craig couldn't shake the creepy feeling that followed him deeper into the body of the tower block. There was no laughter or arguments or mums screaming out the window for their kids to "come in right now, you hear me!" No music blaring from at least one flat on each level. Just silence and the occasional drip of water from a leaking pipe and the rattle of the breeze against the thin glass windows.

Some of the lights on the different levels still glowed, but in the main the corridors he passed hid themselves in darkness. They weren't all empty. They couldn't be. So what the fuck were the people inside doing? All he could see in his head was *fat*. Just like when he'd gone around to his own mum's, he couldn't see her or his sister anymore. They were lost inside the fat monsters they'd become. His dad's tired red eyes had been screaming something at him from the doorway as he'd mouthed the words "get away" from behind his wife's back. Craig Goldsworthy didn't have to be told twice. After ten minutes in the tacky sitting room of the low-rise council flat half a mile or so from the block, his head had been throbbing as if he'd sat in a petrol barrel all afternoon. Maybe Charlie Nash hadn't been so crazy when he'd cleared the women out of the two towers, despite their crying and screaming and saying they had nowhere to go.

Charlie Nash. He gritted his teeth. Charlie was the least of their problems now.

His feet moved steadily upward, taking the concrete stairs two at a time until he saw the number thirteen daubed in red paint on the wall above him, barely visible in the night that crept through broken windows into the south London tower block. His breathing ragged, he pushed the heavy metal door open as quietly as he could. Blane and his crew had been over by the right-hand open stairwell, but Craig didn't want to take any chances on them hearing his movements even if it was nigh on impossible. He let the door click shut before letting go of the handle.

The lift in the main corridor wore a neatly printed OUT OF ORDER sign, under which WHAT THE FUCK IS NEW? had been sprayed across the metal doors. Courtney had done that the day before yesterday and it still made Craig smile in the gloom. Courtney was like that. He was funny. And a clever fuck. He could probably go to university and all that other stuff that people on the estate didn't do, if he really wanted to. He was supposed to be getting straight As and Bs in his GCSEs. Craig felt a tremble of fear in the pit of his stomach. If they ever got their exam results. Somehow that big day didn't feel like it was coming. Exams had finished two weeks ago, just about when the world started to feel like it was really spinning funny, and things had only got stranger since then.

His sneakered feet trotted to the farthest door and knocked. Twice, then a pause, then three times. The lock clicked on the other side and a face appeared in the gap. Leke.

"You took your time, dude." White teeth flashed a friendly grin from the boyish ebony face, but Craig pushed past him.

"Let me in, and shut the door quick."

"What's up with you?" Leke pushed the front door shut, turned the bolt, and then pulled the chain across. People on the estate didn't take any chances with their security and Courtney's family wasn't any different.

The small hallway and lounge were well lit and cosy, but where the small rooms were normally spotlessly clean and tidy, empty takeaway and crisp packets reigned now on the sitting room carpet. Still, the boys had three weeks before Courtney's parents got back from Jamaica and that was plenty of time to get cleaned up.

Craig dumped the rucksack on the sofa. "We've got a serious problem."

Courtney appeared from the kitchen. Unlike Leke, who had the thicker build of a defender, and whose hair was pulled back in rows of plaits tight against the skull, Courtney was tall and slim; a fast runner, and always the goal-scoring forward in the under-sixteens school team all three played on. His skin was deep milk chocolate and his afro hair was cut short against his head, no designs shaved into like so many of the other boys had.

Once, he'd had the Nike tick carved into it, but that was only for the interschool final. Courtney was too cool for that shit.

He held a chicken-and-mushroom Pot Noodle in one hand and a fork in the other.

"More of a problem than whatever the fuck is wrong with the world? I tried my mum again. No answer. Same with my auntie in Pimlico." He shook his head. "And she was too fat and lazy to leave the house *before* all this shit started."

Craig shrugged. "This problem is more immediate." He looked over at Leke. "I just saw Blane getting out of a car downstairs."

"Blane Gentle-King?" Leke's eyes widened and he sank into the sofa, one hand gripping the rucksack as if it had some magical power to change what Craig had seen.

"How many other Blanes do you know?"

"Oh fuck."

"Holy shit."

Craig nodded. "We're fucked."

The Pot Noodle forgotten, Courtney leaned against the wall. "If he knows you're here, he'll kill you."

Leke looked up and let out a mirthless laugh. "No shit, Sherlock." He ran a hand over the lines of hair on his head. "Shit man." He looked up. "The police were supposed to tell me way before he got out. And how is he out? There hasn't even been a trial yet." He moaned slightly. "I wish I'd never seen that shit go down. And I wish I'd never told."

Not knowing what to say, Craig looked over at Courtney. What Leke had done was brave, but maybe also more than a little bit stupid. But then Leke and his dad lived on the other side of Newham in a nice semi-detached with a garden. They didn't really understand the estate, so when Leke had left Courtney's that afternoon all those months ago and seen Blane stab up that schoolkid over some drug shit, the first thing he'd done was tell his dad, who'd made him tell the police and the ball had well and truly started rolling. Blane Gentle-King had been arrested despite his protests and everyone on the estate knew he'd be coming for Leke if he ever got out, if he didn't make sure Leke turned up beaten or dead the day before he was due to take the stand. If it were up to Craig, Leke would have withdrawn that stupid statement and refused to testify, but Leke wasn't like that. Dumb, brave fuck.

"No you don't, man," Courtney said eventually. "You should. But you don't."

Leke stood up and stared unhappily out of the window before pulling the curtains tightly closed to cover the light. "Maybe with all this weird shit going on he won't be bothered by looking for me."

"This is Blane Gentle-King we're talking about. He's been on remand, not in the hospital having a personality transplant."

Courtney nodded. "Craig's right, but if he's just out tonight, he won't be looking for you now. He'll have all his own shit to catch up on."

"So what are we going to do?"

It came naturally that both other boys looked to Courtney for an answer. They always had. Craig was street-smart but he knew neither he nor Leke, who wasn't so dumb himself, would ever see things as clearly as Courtney did.

"We can't go to my house." Leke's normally open, cheerful face had closed in and pulled itself tight. "It's the first place they'll go."

"Your dad still away?"

Leke nodded. "Not back for another couple of days." His mum had died three years ago from breast cancer. Craig figured that they all had ups and down to their lives in one way or another. At least he still had all his family. His own thoughts darkened. *Fat*. Kind of had all his family.

"We can't go to mine either," he said softly. "Things are fucked up there. My mum and my sister . . ." He didn't know quite what it was he wanted to say. *Are wrong? Are freaking me out?* How could he describe it? *They've got my dad trapped and I don't want it happening to me?* ". . . are different," he finally settled on, before pausing again. "And it's not good." His own fear disgusted him a little. They were his family. He should be trying to look after them, but the idea of going back there revolted him. It wasn't home. Not anymore. "I'm beginning to see why Charlie did what he did."

There was a moment's silence after that. All three boys remembered the screams and shouts as Charlie Nash and the ten or fifteen other men with him had bashed at flat doors threatening all kinds of violence and murder if the women didn't come out. It had been less than a week ago, but the block had been quieter since then. And not just the block. There were delays on the tubes, the buses weren't running properly and the whole of London had become quietly sluggish.

"It was still fucked up." Leke's voice echoed dully. He would never see any good in Charlie, and Craig didn't blame him for that. If Blane wanted Leke found it would be Charlie that came looking and he would treat Leke with far more ruthlessness than he had done the fat women that were chucked out on the street and chased away.

"Yes it was," Courtney added. He rummaged in a small pot on the shelf behind him that held all his mother's tacky knickknacks from day trips to Brighton, and then pulled out a silver key and held it up.

"And that is?" Craig picked up the abandoned Pot Noodle and spooned a forkful into his mouth, dripping juice down his chin.

"The key to Mrs. Minster's flat downstairs. She gave it to me just before she got kicked out. To keep an eye on the place for her and her daughter. We can move ourselves into it. I can't see Blane looking for you there. It's too random. He'd have to be searching every flat and that's not his style. It'll buy us some time if nothing else."

Relief shone on the glow of his dark cheeks as Leke smiled. "Good plan, man. When do we move?"

Courtney shrugged. "No time like the present. We can stay there tonight and then tomorrow me and Craig can go to the police and find out what's going on and what he's doing out."

An hour later and they'd done two trips to the flat directly below, and as they'd finally locked themselves in all three boys' nerves were jangling. They'd seen no one else as they'd crept up and down the stairs laden with duvets and clothes and the various bits and bobs they were sure they needed: games console, magazines and Craig's rucksack of chocolate, crisps and Coke and a few microwave burgers that he'd nicked from the small corner supermarket on his way back to the flat. The shopkeeper had barely been able to keep his eyes open behind the counter, let alone focus on what Craig had been doing. It had been easy. Too easy. Normally when they went robbing from shops, sprinting practice came with it, but today he'd just strolled out, easy as pie. It had been that weird that he'd almost turned around and put all the stuff back. He didn't of course. He wasn't stupid.

Still in the dark, he emptied the contents of the bag onto the old-fashioned coffee table in the middle of the neat lounge. "Help yourselves, boys," he whispered. "Dinner is served."

Leke snorted out a giggle. "Where's the light switch? I can't see anything."

Courtney pulled open the thick brown curtains and let the moonlight in. "Probably best to leave the lights off. We don't want to draw any attention to ourselves."

As he tore open a packet of crisps, the crackling noise filling the room, Craig nodded. "It's only for one night."

Sitting on the floor, they munched in silence, the salty-sweet mix of crisps and various chocolate bars washed down with the sugary Coke. Leke let out a long belch before sighing and leaning back against the hard old-fashioned sofa. "It will all be okay in the morning, won't it?"

"Sure." Courtney kept his voice low. "The police will sort it."

Craig kept his mouth shut. He'd been out and about today, not just sitting inside endlessly playing PS2. He stared at his almost-invisible feet as the gloom nibbled at the tips of his trainers. The police maybe had too much else to sort out to worry about whatever Blane Gentle-King was thinking or doing. The world was fucking up. That was about the only thing he was sure of.

Eventually, listening to the water that gurgled through the old pipes of the tower block, the fits and starts of the grinding noise indicating the boys weren't the only people left despite how it seemed, Craig drifted off into a fitful sleep. His headache was coming back.

CHAPTER FIVE

London turned its back on the sun and night fell. On the nineteenth floor of the main tower of the Crookston blocks, Blane Gentle-King was getting quietly high on a mix of grade-A cocaine and sweet sinsemilla. Charlie had looked after things well while he'd been away. Maybe it was time to up his general's cut of the profits.

On the low leather sofa against the far wall, the only white man in the room pulled on a joint and let the smoke drift out before passing the weed on to the next fingers to reach for it. Blane thought he looked tired. But then Charlie hadn't done any coke. He didn't touch the hard stuff—that was part of Blane's reasoning for placing so much trust in him. When Blane had converted three of the kitchens on floor nineteen into crack factories, it was only Charlie from the whole crew whom he could trust not to take some of the product for himself, whether to use or to sell on the side. And it was only Charlie who knew where Blane kept the big stash, the haul from Amsterdam that had cost him everything he had, but was coming in with a nice return when the coke was cooked up to rocks. Blane felt a glow of satisfaction that wasn't entirely caused by the drugs. Charlie had been a loyal soldier since they were kids at school.

The rest of the boys weren't so bad either. Jude had stood by him when he'd had to knife the kid, and then offered to *track down the snotty brat that grassed them while Blane was inside, but he was too eager. Too young. He didn't understand that sometimes it was better to wait. Better to see how things turned out. If they needed the kid dead or scared they could wait until the trial started. And now it looked as if maybe there wasn't going to be a trial after all. Funny how things turned out. Still, at some point the kid would need to be taught a lesson, but Blane could wait till the heat was off.*

Underground reggae music played gently from the Bang and Olufsen system set up on the wall next to the small bar area and it seemed all the men were lulled into quiet by its soulful rhythm and the heady smoke. Normally, if Blane called a gathering the room would be full, but the posse was thin on the ground tonight. Aside from Charlie and Jude, there were only four others: the kid Brownie, Skate, Blinka and Leeboy. All tough men without families other than that which the posse provided. At least Blane had his strongest around him for now, and the others would be back when they realized that everything was back to business as usual.

Despite the drugs powering through his system, a headache beat at the back of Blane's eyes. It had started when he'd seen Janine and just wouldn't shift. Charlie said there'd been a lot of it going around but the migraines had eased when he'd got rid of most of the women. Blane frowned. He still found it hard to believe that Charlie had taken it on himself to kick out most of the women of the estate. What the fuck was going on with the bitches that would make him do that?

He didn't mind admitting he'd thought maybe Charlie had gone a little crazy, as if some of that shit he supervised the cooking of had got into his system and messed up his mind, but looking at the silent streets around them and then seeing Janine and the other girls for himself . . . well. Time would tell. One thing was for sure, those girls were going to have to slim the fuck down, and fast. He needed them out making money. And no one would pay to fuck them in that state.

Janine. He still couldn't believe that thing he'd seen was his baby girl. He didn't love her anymore—he wasn't sure he even knew what that word meant, but he knew enough to know you couldn't love some pussy that went out and sold her ass for you—but back in the day they'd had some good times. And man, her body had been tight. Not now though. Now she was well and truly mashed up.

His frown tugged between his eyes. The boys were quiet. Maybe he wasn't the only one with a banging head. His dreadlocks spread out around him, he leaned his aching skull on the soft leather and closed his eyes. Things would look different in the morning.

In the flat opposite Mrs. Minster's on the twelfth floor, Nathan Pelham shut his bedroom door and pushed his iPod headphones deep into his ears before pressing shuffle on the controls. He didn't care what was playing, as long as the music was continual. He turned the volume up so the first tune filled his head.

Scooter's "The Logical Song" cut right through his ear drums with its high-pitched, fast-paced remix of the Supertramp original. Nathan was the only boy at school who knew that Supertramp, a rock group of the seventies, had originally released the song in 1979 from their album Breakfast in America *and it reached number six on the US charts and number seven on the U.K. ones. He'd tried to tell some of the other kids but they didn't care. Nathan didn't understand that not caring. Details were important. He liked them. They made him feel as if the world made a little more sense. You could deconstruct and rebuild the world by its detail, like a jigsaw puzzle or a LEGO building.*

He pushed his thick glasses up onto the bridge of his nose so that they were touching his eyelashes. He bit his bottom lip. The music was helping but he still slid his chest of drawers against the closed door, before opening his battered English homework book and scrawling DON'T OPEN on a blank page. Inside out, the exercise book stood like an A-board on the surface. That might work. Just in case it didn't and at some point in the night he found himself needing to go back into the lounge, he unrolled the tea towel on his bed and carefully took out the large meat-chopping knife and the bread knife that he'd snuck out of the kitchen.

He took off his glasses and then pushed them back on again, careful not to knock the music away from his ears. The knives made him feel unsettled. But then so did the way his mum kept trying to get into his head and lure him into the lounge. She wanted him in there with her, but Nathan didn't want to go. Whatever was inside his head wasn't his mum. The details didn't fit. Nathan's mum had never got inside his head before, not in his whole sixteen years, and he knew that there were times when she wished she could, otherwise she'd never have sent him to the head doctor to try and make him "talk about things." So whatever was trying to get Nathan into the lounge now, couldn't be Nathan's mum. In some ways that made the idea of the knives easier. But not by much.

The cream duvet cover was cool as he sat down and let his hands clench and unclench on its surface, following the beat of the music. His shoulders slumped forward and his eyes squeezed almost shut. Nathan didn't cry much, but when he narrowed his eyes tightly that's what he felt like he was doing. His heart thumped with quietly contained anxiety. There were too many details to keep track of. The LEGO blocks of the world were being pulled away and no one was taking note of the order. He didn't notice as he started to rock backward and forward slightly. Blane Gentle-King was back; Nathan had seen him standing in the headlights of the car below. That detail was all wrong. His mum had said that Blane was arrested. He was going to prison for stabbing Leroy Jones. But now, just like his mum wasn't his mum, Blane Gentle-King was back and both were wrong.

Nathan wasn't scared of Blane—he was scared that the details were no longer making sense. And what were Courtney, Leke and Craig doing in Mrs. Minster's flat? He'd watched them moving in through the spy hole and had very nearly gone out to join them, but his feet wouldn't move. They were in the same class at school, but they never spoke. They thought he was stupid. Or odd, which was worse than stupid. He could see it even if he couldn't say it.

His rocking increasing, he reached over to the bookshelf alongside his bed and pulled out one of the Encyclopedia Britannica volumes that filled it. The side declared it "A" and he allowed himself a tight smile. Starting with "A" made sense. He opened the pages and started to read.

Janine watched her belly ripple in the dark. It wouldn't be long now. The air around her stank sickly and bitter from whatever oil it was that oozed from her pores, but she found that she liked it, her fingers sliding along one arm and enjoying the mucusy texture. Her head filled with the singing voices of so many others crying with the urgency of release. Their time had nearly come. She sighed and a fresh wave of foul air erupted loudly from her heavy body. They had traveled so far and waited so long but the waiting was over. The Birthing was starting.

CHAPTER SIX

His iPod headphones had dug hard into his ears all night and sitting up, Nathan yanked them out. His skin throbbed gratefully and he rubbed the sides of his head with cool fingers. He'd fallen asleep on top of his bed rather than in it, and shivering in the morning chill his young joints felt stiff. He stood up, forcing his legs to move and get his blood circulating again. His glasses sat neatly on the bookshelf and wedging them firmly on the bridge of his nose, taking three attempts to get them in exactly the right position, he checked the time on his watch. Six A.M.

Although it was almost June, condensation had formed on the inside of the badly fitted windows, but outside the sun was shining with the promise of a beautiful day. Nathan looked down at the silent iPod. Its screen was blank, the battery having died hours ago, no doubt not long after he'd fallen asleep reading. He pressed his eyes together and concentrated on nothing. Silence echoed around the caverns of his mind and he smiled. His head was his own again. The thing trying to get in there and claiming to be his mother had gone.

Something thudded against a wall somewhere in the flat and the cheap painted plasterboard behind his bed vibrated. If Nathan had been the kind of boy to adorn his room with posters or pictures then he was sure they would have visibly shaken on their hooks, but as it was he preferred the calm order of plain walls. Whatever had hit the wall had been heavy. The thing might have been out of his head, but something was still in the flat with him.

A low groan followed the thud. Nathan frowned and stood up, moving close to the chest of drawers.

"Mum?" His voice bounced back at him from the closed door. Something smashed quietly and was followed by another wail of despair. Nathan stared blankly at the painted wood. Was that his mum? He'd never heard her in pain. He'd heard her shouting at him and he'd heard her swearing when she'd banged her elbow or toe, but he'd never heard this kind of sound before. He fought the urge to push his fingers into his ears, block it out and return to reading his encyclopedia. The head doctor his mum had made sure the school sent him to once a week had told him that hiding behind dry information wasn't the best way to get by in the world, and despite every instinct humming in his body, he knew the doctor was right.

Remaining focused on the door ahead, he refused to even glance back at the book still open on his bed with its neat and tidy facts and figures and comforting details. There was no space in the encyclopedia for the kind of sound his mother was making. It was emotional. It made Nathan itch.

His feet shuffled helplessly beneath him and with his palms sweating, he slowly pushed the chest of drawers back into its place farther along the wall. The English book fell backward and slid down into the gap between the furniture and the plasterboard, taking its message of "Don't Open" with it. Glancing between the door and the chest of drawers, confusion raged inside him. In his mind he could see the lost book trapped in that space. It was untidy. Maybe he should get it out before going to see what was happening with his mum. His face heated until his pale skin glowed. It wasn't neat. It wasn't ordered. It needed to be retrieved.

In the flat beyond his bedroom, someone punched the wall three times before grunting loudly. Nathan closed his eyes. Not something. His mother. As he pushed the unsettling image of the stuck exercise book to the back of his mind, he picked up the meat knife. It seemed like a good idea and he didn't want to dwell on why. He'd go and see what was wrong with his mum and then come back and get the English homework book. He should have thrown it away after the exam and then he wouldn't be in this dilemma, but it had still had blank pages in it and even though he didn't much like writing, those wasted pages would have eaten at him long after the bin men had been. Still, he'd throw it away afterward. After he'd checked on Mum.

He stared at the door for a moment and the paint stared defiantly back, challenging him to stay in the safety of his ordered bedroom and away from whatever was waiting beyond its confines. Eventually, he reached out and turned the handle. He breathed. Ahead of him the small hallway was empty and calm, but the grunts and moans that didn't sound anything like his mother grew louder as they punched their way toward him.

The air smelled foul and his nose wrinkled. It was stale fart and cheap wine and something rotten. His senses tried to find the details and name them, but the bitter sickliness evaded his memory. It was a new smell. As he slowly crept forward, he peered into the small bathroom. It was empty, as was his mother's room on the other side. He was pretty sure she hadn't slept in it that night. The bed was the same untidy mess it had been the previous morning, one pillow half over the side of the double bed and the duvet tangled in a heap at the base. On the exposed sheet an oily stain, which didn't look as if it had dried out at all over the past twenty-four hours, spread across the center. Nathan turned away, unfamiliar emotions crawling over his skin.

He took a deep breath and moved on toward the lounge.

For a long moment he just stood in the doorway and stared. He should be in his bedroom. He should be fetching the book back from behind the chest of drawers. He should be somewhere where things made sense. He should be in Mrs. Minster's flat being the butt of jokes he didn't understand. In fact, he should be anywhere instead of here. His breath panted hard, hectically rushing in and out of his chest as his hand gripped the knife he'd almost forgotten he was holding.

"Mum?" The question slipped out of him and the thing on the sofa turned to look.

The fat, sweating creature that his mother had become over the past few weeks was on her knees on the sofa, her chubby hands pressed against the wall, several greasy prints already staining the paintwork that she was always so particular about not scuffing. Her hair was lank against her jowly face and the eyes that turned to see him were dark, piggy and mean. She groaned again and something slick and wet slapped against the leather, the noise coming from under the baggy dress covering her spread legs. A rose of red bloomed against the fabric and covered her vast rear before running in untidy lines down to the hem. Nathan watched the blood surge in a sudden rush down the outside of her thighs, filling the cracks between the sofa cushions, and with it came an eruption of foul gas that bubbled loud and long. Nathan's mind struggled to keep his bricks of order standing as he watched helplessly.

She almost smiled, her gums black and toothless, and then she gasped, her eyes widening in pain and for a moment from his place in the doorway, Nathan almost saw his mother still in them. His heart squeezed tight and his free hand went to his glasses, pushing them backward and forward hard on the bridge of his nose. Even with his vision slipping in and out of focus the mum-thing on the sofa was all too visible. His face grew hotter.

The skin of her massive body rippled as she began to convulse, her head twitching from side to side on her thick neck, her left hand hammering uncontrollably into the wall. Light streamed in through the open curtain illuminating every detail. His bladder suddenly full and his skin itching and burning, Nathan wanted to curl up in a ball and cry. He didn't understand this. And worse, he didn't think anyone would understand this, not even all the other *normal* people who weren't soothed by facts and figures, jigsaw pieces of information.

"Mum?" he said again, his grip tightening on the wooden handle of the kitchen knife.

"*Nugh nunununu ngh . . .*" Spit sprayed out from her trembling mouth, coating the back of the leather cushions, one long, thick string hanging from her rotten lips as if left over from puking. Nathan's own mouth fell open. Something was coming out of her under the bloody mess of her dress. Two slick, thin legs slipped out past the hem, jointed like insects' limbs, their sickly whiteness made pink with his mother's blood. They paused, before waving thin ends in the air, like antenna searching for something. With another wet slap and convulsion from his mother's wrecked body, two more stick-thin legs appeared, so pale they were almost translucent, coated with the same slime that oozed out of his mother's skin.

The four limbs wriggled and kicked and from under his mother's skirt, from the same place she'd been so proud to say she'd pushed him out from sixteen long years ago, something hissed angrily. She was pushing a new baby out now and it was killing her. As some part of her tore loudly under her dress, her hands slid down from the wall and her head flopped down heavily onto the top of the sofa's edge, her eyes open, but with no focus in them, the thick line of spit still hanging from her bottom lip.

Nathan swallowed, his throat struggling to complete the action as his brain tried to absorb what he was seeing. He wanted the English book. He wanted the encyclopedia. *He wanted his mum.* His eyes strayed back to the awful limbs that wriggled and writhed, trying to pull whatever they were attached to free from his mum's limp body. Strands of gossamer sheen oozed out from the four tips and latched onto his mother's fat limbs, wrapping around them and giving the monster leverage. The tiny ropes of webbing slid up the huge carcass of her body, creeping into the corners of her mouth, and Nathan could almost feel their sticky touch on his own skin. It *would* be sticky, he was sure of that. It would never come off. He watched as the shimmering threads wound themselves relentlessly around her head, her eyelids pulled back taut as one strand met another and meshed across her forehead.

Nathan barely felt the scream that was growing inside him. It rose up like a tidal wave against what he was seeing, until the torrent of emotions smashed through his carefully built internal wall, flushing the bricks away and destroying his order. The book was untidy. The lounge was untidy.

As the thing coming out of its mother let out an airy, inhuman shriek, Nathan stepped forward and shut his eyes, raising the knife high in the air. By the time he'd landed the third blow, both his mother's children were screaming.

When he looked at his watch again it was six fifteen A.M. It seemed much later. Sweat dripped down from his hairline and formed pearls on the light fluff that had yet to develop into even the hint of a mustache above his lip. He licked the warm saltiness away and dropped the knife, letting it clatter among the broken side lamp on the carpet. Blood covered the sofa and coated the lifeless bodies of his mother and the *thing* that had been coming out of her. Both were silent.

The book. He had to retrieve the book. His arms and chest soaked with his own sweat and his mum's warm blood, Nathan went back into the narrow hallway, gently closing the lounge door behind him. In his bedroom he carefully pulled the chest of drawers away from the wall and grabbed the orange exercise book. His fingerprints clashed with its color, and going into the bathroom, he dropped it into the wastebasket. He'd have preferred to use the pink recycle bag in the kitchen but that would have meant going back through the sitting room and his mind was trying very hard to rebuild his brick wall and pretend that everything back there was normal, or even just pretend normal as it had been yesterday. He'd settle for that.

His clothes peeled reluctantly away from his skin as he tugged off his blood-soaked T-shirt and jeans, throwing both items into the dirty washing bin and making sure the wicker lid was firmly on. The shower was hot, neither he nor his mum having used it the day before. Nathan stood under it until the water ran clear and only then reached for the soap and began scrubbing at his pale flesh and hair.

By seven A.M., when he was normally just waking up whether it was a school day or otherwise, Nathan was sitting on the edge of his bed, a towel wrapped around his slightly overweight waist. He picked up his glasses and pressed them firmly on his nose. It had been his favorite T-shirt and jeans he'd fallen asleep in last night. And now they were gone. Ruined. Tears stung the back of his eyes; real ones, hot and salty and blurring his vision. He tried looking into the colorful factual pages of the encyclopedia but the tears were getting in the way and it seemed that in every picture his mum's dead black eyes shone out.

In the end, he just closed the book and cried out long sobs that shook his naked shoulders. He sat like that until his skin prickled with chilled shock and his eyes were too sore to cry anymore. It was time to get dressed and go to Mrs. Minster's flat.

Brownie's brain was still fuzzy from all the blow he'd snorted the previous night, but at least his headache was gone. He could have used another three or four hours of sleep though. What the fuck Skate was doing dragging him out of his pit at seven thirty in the morning, he did not know. Not that he'd argue with the other man. Skate had been one of Blane's soldiers for way longer than Brownie had. If Skate told him to jump, he'd do it. He just might not like it, that's all.

"What are we doing, man?"

Up ahead, Skate didn't break his stride, his baggy jeans hanging down low enough to show a crisp, clean pair of Calvin Klein boxer shorts below where his over-size T-shirt fell.

"Going to sort out the birds." He looked over his shoulder as he reached the seventeenth floor. "Blane's going to want to see them later. Let's get them chilled and happy."

"But at seven thirty in the morning?" Brownie trotted down the last few steps, his own clothes almost identical to the older man's but his Calvin's weren't so new and his not-quite-so-designer jeans and T were crumpled from where he'd slept on the sofa at Charlie's place. Skate must have gone back to his own pad at some point in the night. Brownie couldn't remember. His own place was on the second floor and by the time the buzz from the coke had been subdued to a mellow hum by the weed, there was no way he was going to stumble all that way back. Not when Charlie's leather sofas were so comfy. He followed Skate down the hallway.

"Seven thirty ain't that early. Jesus, Brownie. How did you get yourself up to go to school?"

"Never went." It was pretty much true. He should have taken his GCSEs the previous summer but he'd known by the end of year ten that he wasn't going to get any passes, so he figured he may as well spend his last year of school making his connections stronger on the estate. He hadn't even turned up for most of his exams.

No one called his mum to find out where he was like they had with some of the other kids, and although he'd just laughed it off, that had stung. They hadn't called because they'd either known that his mum was a drunk who never had any credit on her phone anyway, or because they didn't think there was any point in him being there and either way it was just like calling him a piece of shit. Still. It was a long time ago. A whole year. And things had turned out fine. He was a proper soldier boy now.

"You surprise me." Skate's eyebrow raised above his dark eyes. "Well, if you want to stay running with Blane, you've got to treat it like a job. He likes people that stay sharp and put the hours in." Pulling back the metal hatch, he peered inside the flat, his face crinkling. "That's weird. At least one of the bitches is normally waiting by the door begging for some smoke."

From deep in his jeans pocket he pulled out a large ring of keys and started flipping around them. "And he likes you to be smart. So when we're done make sure you go home, shower and change before we go back."

Brownie nodded. Maybe he hadn't left school after all. Skate was only five or six years older than he, and yeah he had more experience running with Blane than some of the others, but it wasn't like he were Charlie Nash or anything. He'd done that six months in the nick though, and that had earned him his respect. Still, it irked Brownie to be treated like a kid. Even his waste-of-space mum had stopped doing that as soon as he could wipe his own arse.

"Anyway, you're going to want a shower when you come out of the flat. It fucking stinks in there." He slid the key into the lock but didn't turn it. From his other pocket, he pulled four cellophane-wrapped rocks, and handed them to Brownie. "They've got their own pipes and lighters."

"Can't you just chuck it through the hatch?" Even through the small opening, Brownie could smell the stale air that erupted into the corridor. It would be totally rank on the other side.

Skate stared at him. "Haven't you been listening? How would that be sharp?"

Brownie shrugged but didn't answer.

"Let's say we do just throw the stuff in and go back upstairs, what do you think Blane's going to ask us?"

His face prickling, Brownie wished he hadn't opened his mouth. "Don't know, Skate," he mumbled eventually.

"He's going to ask us how the girls were, and we're not going to be able to answer him cos we won't have fucking seen them." The older man's eyes were dark ice as he spoke slowly, laboring each point. "And then, instead of looking like we've taken care of things, we're going to look like a pair of dumb fuckers who can only do something half-arsed and he'll send us back down here to check on them again, while he sits upstairs and bitches about us with Charlie as if we're a pair of useless cunts."

He paused. "Now you may well be a useless cunt, Brownie, but no brother's ever going to call me that."

Brownie flinched against the word. It was the only taboo in a language in which every swear word carried a thousand meanings and each one depended on the nuances in the speaker's voice.

"Sorry, Skate. I wasn't thinking."

The older man stared at him for a long moment, and Brownie was suddenly very aware of how much taller and wider, and more *manly* he was. Maybe those five or six years did really make a difference.

"It's all right, man." Skate's voice had softened. "You'll learn." He tilted his head to the door. "I'll wait out here. These are fresh threads I've got on. Just go in, check they're still breathing and tell them to at least freshen themselves up. Tell them Blane'll be around later."

From somewhere across the estate came the sound of glass smashing and the echo of something that could have been a low wail. Skate frowned. "Seems like we're not the only ones up early."

"Or maybe it's just some drunk getting home late."

"Yeah, you may be right." Skate slapped him on the shoulder. "Now get this shit done, so I can get breakfast."

The rocks in one hand, Brownie turned the key and leaving it in the lock, pushed the door open. The stench rolled out like a thick tidal wave pouring over him. "Jesus fuck." Grimacing, he looked over at Skate and saw his own expression of disgust reflected there before the older man smiled.

"Those girls have got some serious wind."

"Oh, you crack me up." Brownie grinned despite the smell, happy that Skate's earlier anger seemed to have vanished.

"And speaking of crack." One dark eyelid dropped in a wink. "Go and deliver."

A shriek echoed up the stairwell and along the corridor as Brownie stepped into the dingy flat, and something in it made him shiver. Even before everything started going tits up, mornings in the estate had been quiet and in recent weeks the hush seemed to go on for most of the day. Now windows were breaking and people were screaming at each other and it wasn't even eight. The sun might have been shining but everything else still felt wrong.

Keeping his breathing shallow, he found his steps were small, his feet reluctant to take him farther into the flat. He still found it hard to believe that Charlie had locked them up in here, even after he'd kicked out all the other women. Thinking about that made Brownie feel funny inside. He'd felt weird sending his mum off with his auntie Pamela, both drunks stumbling in the direction of the tube, swearing at him incoherently over their shoulders, carrying a couple of carrier bags with a few possessions in and whatever booze they had in the house. He'd felt bad that he didn't feel bad. What he'd felt was relief. When they'd got fat, they'd changed, and he didn't want them around any more than Charlie did. Still, he'd tried texting her but not got any answer. She was mad at him and he could understand that. It didn't make him want her to come home though. She'd got meaner as she'd got fatter, and she'd been pretty mean to start.

He peered into the kitchen. Dirty plates filled the sink and on the side takeaway boxes grew green mold on what might have once been Chinese or Indian leftovers but was now just brown gunk. Maybe that was where the awful smell was coming from. It hung putrid in the still air, invisible but heavy and drenching his skin. He hated to think of that smell on the inside of him, sucked in by his lungs and absorbed into every cell of his body. Turning away from the kitchen, he shook the thought away. Fuck that biology shit. Maybe he should have started bunking school earlier than he did.

The front door was still ajar behind him and he fought the urge to just drop the small packets and run back outside. There was no need to feel so edgy, they were only four fat junkie bitches who were probably too fucked to get off their fat behinds and come to the door.

"Candy?" His voice trembled as it cut through the sludgy air, and he wished it didn't sound so nervous. No one answered. He took another step forward. A sharp hissing sound came from one of the rooms at the end of the short hallway, and then something thumped softly against the carpet as if maybe a glass had been knocked over. Brownie hesitated.

"You girls in there?" He took another two steps and peered into one open room to his left. There was a mattress on the floor and a few scattered sleeping bags, but it didn't look as if anyone was in them. A few weeks ago he'd have had to take a closer look to be sure, but with the size the women had grown to there was no way any of them would have fit in one of the bags, let alone looked reasonably flat lying down.

"I got some rocks for you. Come and get them." The awful smell had soured deeper in the flat, as if it had soaked into the walls and he thought if he breathed in too hard he'd gag. The pit of his stomach was already fragile from the drugs he'd taken last night and it wouldn't take much to make it turn completely.

The sharp hiss came again, this time loud enough to make Brownie spin around. His heart thumped hard as he stared at the almost-shut sitting room door. Frowning, he stepped closer. What the fuck were they doing in there? "Don't shit with me, ladies. I ain't got all day." He spoke loudly, wanting Skate outside to hear, and was glad at the hard edge of confidence he heard in the words. Maybe they were asleep. It was still the middle of the night for any self-respecting junkie anyway.

Something skittered against the door opposite, like light feet scurrying across the wood and upward, before soft thumps tapped rapidly across what he could only imagine was the ceiling. Brownie stared. It couldn't be right, because nothing could run around on the freaking ceiling, but that was where it sounded like the noise was going. Another hiss escaped the room and was joined quickly by a second.

Brownie looked at the wood, and then glanced back toward the reinforced front door that was slightly ajar. Skate was on the other side, probably getting more and more impatient with every second that ticked by. The cellophane on the small packages slid in the sweat of his palm. It wouldn't be good for him if Skate had to come and kick his butt to hurry up, so why did he suddenly feel so nervous about pushing open the door in front of him? The girls had been locked up. They couldn't have any guns or anything in there and even if they did why would they want to shoot him. He had what they *needed*. His internal argument made sense but did nothing to stop the nervous dryness inside his mouth. What was making those strange sounds? And there were four whores in here. Why wasn't even one of them answering him? He licked his lips. His brain was still too fried for this. It was too early in the frigging morning. If he'd just shifted his own lazy arse downstairs to the second floor last night, then it would have been one of the others that Skate had kicked awake half an hour ago.

He sighed. But he was here now. And there was nothing else to do but go into the room and sort the shit out. The strange pattering of feet seemed to have stopped, but his palms still sweated. Maybe they had a cat in there. A swift smile broke his grim face as a thought came to him. Yeah, maybe that was it. Cats hissed. They climbed things. He'd seen them down by the bins plenty of times yowling and snarling at each other and passersby. It was a couple of cats they'd picked up. And they must be hungry or something.

His heart thumped loud with relief as he pushed the door open. "You'd better be decent. I'm coming in." Doing his best to ignore the ripeness of the gloomy atmosphere, he stepped inside. "Jesus, you need to let some light in and open one of those win . . ."

The sentence drifted away as his eyes caught jaggedly on the images that screamed for his attention. There was blood. Four big pools of it, the edges splattered and spreading out from each crimson core, three that soaked deep into the far corners of the room's old carpet, and one that gleamed wet across the beaten-up old sofa that still held the sunken indent from one of the girls' fat arses, the cushions so heavy with liquid they shone almost black.

Brownie's jaw worked slightly, not sure exactly what it was his confused mind wanted it to do first: breathe, throw up or try to scream. It settled on letting his lips form a breathy word.

"Skate . . ." It was more of a wheeze than a full-fledged sound, swallowed up instantly by the room around him. He squeezed the rocks hard, the shape digging painfully into the palm of his hand as his eyes turned reluctantly to the four bodies slumped against the window wall, the ledge forcing their heads to loll forward.

This was fucked up. Badly so. And he wanted Skate in here and dealing with it. Bile burned in his chest.

The four women had collapsed in on themselves like deflated balloons, their torn, flabby bodies wrapped tight in something that seemed to have been wound around each one in a madly haphazard fashion. What was that? Not rope or wire. And string wouldn't hold. The strands had a pearly sheen to them, and for a moment Brownie fought back a giggle. Dental floss. It looked like someone had tried to tie them up with dental floss. As the urge to laugh subsided, the gag rose and he swallowed down the mouthful of bitter fluid. What the fuck had happened? Who the fuck had done this?

One foot finally took a hesitant step backward. He didn't care whether Skate came in or not. He just wanted to get out. Feet pattered above his head and something hissed; short and sharp. Frozen to the spot on the carpet, Brownie very, very slowly raised his eyes.

A bank of angry red pinpoints looked back at him and he let out a low moan. The shining white and purple skin on the creature trembled as another hiss escaped it. *Spider.* The mandibles below the awful eyes clacked harshly together. Brownie fought the urge to laugh and cry and curl up in a ball. He hated spiders. But spiders weren't that big. Spiders that big *didn't exist.* This was some weird drug shit fucking with his mind. It had to be. He stared despite himself, despite every instinct that told him to turn and run. The white bug didn't disappear; instead the pinpricks of red light that glared down at him from the raised white bumps on its surface seemed to come into a sharper focus.

The boy's horrified eyes drifted downward. The bulbous second section of the body was easily the size of a spaniel; supported on eight angular and segmented legs that held it to the ceiling in some way Brownie couldn't make out. Not that it was real. He was just tripping out, that was all. Blane's shit must have been too strong last night or some fucker slipped him acid. Have a laugh at Brownie. Yeah, it was something like that. Had to be. His bladder tightened. A flutter of feet tip-tapped across the ceiling, three more of the vast spiders scurrying out of the gloomy corners and joining the first. More eyes stared at him. There were four of them. He vaguely heard his own voice making some kind of sound that wasn't making any sense, just a low, moaning jumble that was trying to form words. *Four spidery monsters. Four bloody messes. Four bodies wrapped in weird webbing.* Tears pricked the back of his eyes. How could his brain make up this shit? He'd never been any good at making stuff up. So how could . . .

"What the fuck are you doing in there? Trying to get a free ride?"

Brownie heard the front door being pushed open and Skate's heavy tread tracing his own into the flat. The creatures above him hissed, the first prowling forward a few steps until it was right over Brownie's head. Tears pricked the back of his eyes. *There was no monster. There was no monster, no matter how fucking real it seemed.* The bitches were asleep against the wall and everything else was just made up in his head. That's how it was. That's how it had to be. Skate would see. Skate would . . .

"Jesus fucking Christ." The words were chased by a sharp intake of breath. "What the fuck . . . ?"

"Skate . . . ? Skate . . . I . . ." His voice finally found, Brownie took a step backward, bumping into the older man's chest right behind him. "I've still got the stuff . . . I've still . . ." He opened his hand, exposing the four cling-filmed rocks that it seemed like he'd been given a lifetime ago.

The room shrieked with high-pitched squealing as the four creatures flipped and dropped to the ground, their mandibles yawning wide. Brownie flinched and stumbled but there was nowhere to go, Skate's firm hands keeping Brownie between him and the things in the lounge, pushing the younger boy forward. Tears blurred in Brownie's eyes and for a moment in the gloom he could see the gossamer sheen on the strands of whatever that shit was that hung down from above. There was pink in it. Like blood. Suddenly, in the last moment, he was very aware of his own blood pounding hotly through his veins, and then the first creature crouched briefly before pouncing, leaping toward his arm. Although its awful mouth was stretched wide and ready to bite, it was the sight of the spider's underbelly that finally forced the scream from his chest as he felt the first touch of that awful slick skin against his.

The world slowed as he fell backward, landing half in and half out of the sitting room, the back of his skull vibrating with the dull thud of his head on thin carpet. He barely felt it though, his mind occupied with the dawning realization that maybe this *was it* . . . the end of the game . . . and it had all come so quickly.

He stared at Skate's trainers as they disappeared out the front door, bright sunlight flashing in for a beautiful moment before the older man took it with him back out into the tower block corridor.

Turning his head sideways, aware of something pawing at the bottom of his leg, he met Skate's horrified gaze through the hatch. They stared at each other for a long second and then the spiders leaped, squealing, onto his body. As one landed on his chest, the weight of its solid body knocking his breath away, he almost gagged on the foul, rotten smell that erupted from its slimy surface. The red eyes bore down into his, as out of sight something bit down into his arm. Burning pain flooded his body as the tugging at his shoulder became more insistent. His breath came in sudden pants as his eyes widened, the initial shock wearing off and the truth of what was happening finally settling in.

Behind his own scream he heard his flesh tearing as something ripped away his hand and leaped back up into the corner of the ceiling. It was, he realized, just before the creature on his chest bit down into his face, the hand that had been carrying the rocks.

Skate watched through the hatch as Brownie stopped convulsing on the carpet. A moment later the boy and the thing sitting on his chest that was pulling strips of flesh from the brown cheeks that were now just a bloodied mess, were dragged back by something out of sight, disappearing into the sitting room.

Skate stared for a long time, listening to the mix of his own racing heartbeat and the wet sounds of the squealing creatures ripping the boy apart. Eventually the flat quieted and one of the monstrous spiders scuttled into the hallway, its legs taking it on a haphazard journey up the wall, across the ceiling and down the other side before it stopped to stare back at Skate. There was madness in its movement, and madness in those red eyes, Skate was sure about that. It was the kind of insanity he recognized. He'd seen it in people on the estate all his life. These nightmare creatures weren't any different. It was junkie madness. Skate swallowed. His head hurt and he felt sick. Where the fuck had these things come from? The answer was obvious, but he didn't want to dwell on it. Too much too soon would be the path to his own brain crash.

On the other side of the heavy door, halfway down the short hallway, the spider hissed and jumped forward half a foot or so, its movement jerky and awkward, and then with a long, high-pitched squeal of sheer frustration, it opened its mandibled mouth. Skate just managed to pull his face out of the way before the first of the four wrapped rocks came flying through the small hatch, skimming his cheek. It was quickly followed by the others, fast as bullets fired in rapid succession. They hammered into the back wall of the corridor so hard he was surprised they didn't leave dents or chips in the plaster, before falling to the ground as little bundles of slime and blood. Somewhere beneath the foul shit that coated them the yellowish color of the rocks of crack was just about visible.

As he took one last glance through the open hatch, a second creature leaped over the first and launched itself at him, squealing madly. With trembling hands working more out of instinct than thought, he managed to barely slam the metal shut before the thing landed with a wet thump on the other side. He stepped back and stared at the reinforced door. Two more thuds beat hollow on the other side. Along the corridor, the awful shrieking sound was matched by another. Skate didn't have to turn his head to know that it would be coming from the flat Charlie had locked Janine in.

Without warning he bent over and dry-heaved a mix of spit and bile onto the dirty tiles below, one hand pressed against the wall for support. Something ate into his gut and it took a moment for Skate to recognize the feeling. It was fear. Real, soul-shaking fear; the kind he hadn't felt in a lot of years. Slowly he straightened up, his firm stomach muscles aching slightly, and he

swallowed hard. He had to get a grip. Outside somewhere, someone screamed, the sound cut short with a
surprised yelp. Skate did his best to ignore it. He needed
to get tooled up and then go and wake Blane and the
rest of the boys. Whatever they were going to do, they'd
do as a crew. Ahead of him in the corridor, just opposite
the stairwell, sunlight poured through the thin glass of
a cracked window. Skate headed over to it, pulling his
clean T-shirt off as he went, wrapping it around his elbow.

Despite being a large man, his footfalls were light in
his trainers, his whole body on alert. He peered over
the metal handrail and down into the stairwell. Nothing moved. Satisfied, he turned his attention to the
window and with a swift jab of his powerful arm, the
glass smashed, tinkling far down into the street below.
Skate wasn't worried about it hurting anyone. Right at
that moment the only person whose safety he gave a
fuck about was his own. It wouldn't have mattered anyway. From his viewpoint on the seventeenth floor it
didn't look like there were many people up and about in
Newham on this bright and glorious morning.

An eerie silence filled the square of grass that sat between the two towers. No cars moved in the narrow
road just visible before the low-rise flats farther back. If
he were looking out of the other side of the building,
Skate would be able to see the river, Canary Wharf and
the Thames barrier. As it was, he was looking into the
city. And it was too quiet. Far too quiet.

Glass smashed softly somewhere down to his right
and reaching his six-foot-three frame up on tiptoes,
Skate brushed away the jagged teeth of glass from the
rim and peered out. He squinted in the sunlight and

scanned the lower levels. Nothing moved, light winking brightly at him from the hundreds of windows he could make out on either side, and those that ran up the side of the building opposite. His eyes snagged on a dark space on the front of the other tower about three floors up. Was that it?

One ear still concentrated on seeking out any noises coming from his immediate vicinity, Skate stared at the space a hundred feet away and thirty feet down from where he was standing. Who'd broken the glass over there? Was it someone just like him needing to see what the fuck was fucking up the world today? Part of him, the part that was being swallowed up by fear, wanted to call out, to shout across as loudly as he could, just to be sure that someone else was alive out there, someone other than the crew he'd left sleeping upstairs in Charlie's flat. He licked his lips and then swore quietly under his breath. There was no way he wanted to do any shouting or banging on doors; not on his own and definitely not unarmed.

His brain was still fighting the image of those things that killed Brownie and he wasn't even ready to go near where they must have come from, not without losing his fucking mind at any rate, but he also knew what he'd seen, and he knew to trust his eyes, however much he might not like or understand what they'd shown him. For now, whatever he did, he was doing it quietly. Oscar "Skate" Johnson's mother, God rest her soul, hadn't raised any fools.

Deep in his trouser pocket a packet of cigarettes dug into his thigh as they pressed against the wall and he pulled them out, lighting one. He was glad to see that his hands had nearly stopped shaking. That was good.

Skate Johnson did not shiver like a pissing little girl when he was afraid. Through the long lungful of exhaled smoke escaping from his mouth and into the fresh air outside, Skate caught something moving on the other tower. He frowned, a chill settling in his stomach. Three pale, jointed legs slid out and clung to the wall, pawing it as if testing the brickwork for grip. Another followed, bringing with it the first section of the creature's body, the pinprick eyes visible as a mass of red rather than individual points. He forced himself to take another long pull on the cigarette, needing something to concentrate on, something that wasn't crazy, and something that might kill him but at least it would do it in an old-fashioned, traditional, cancerous way. The harsh smoke burned the back of his throat but it felt good.

Was it just his eyes playing tricks on him or was this one bigger than the ones in the girls' flat? The rest of the milky white body emerged along with the last of the legs, and for a few moments the thing just sat there on the side of the wall as if it had no idea what to do or where to go. Skate stared. It *was* bigger. And its awful white color was different too, purer and with no putrid-looking hues to it. None that he could make out, anyway. After a moment of watching, he realized what it was. This spider looked *healthier* than the ones in the flat.

Eventually, the creature moved, silently climbing up the side of the building and over onto the roof where it slid out of sight. It didn't squeal, and its movements weren't jerky or untamed. There was a precision to what it did that frightened Skate almost as much as the frantic aggression of the ones locked in the flat. He peered back over his shoulder at the lines of doors along the seventeenth floor. There was some bad shit behind two of them, that he knew, but what the fuck was going on behind the others?

His heart thumped as smoke clung to the walls of his dry mouth. It was time to wake Blane and Charlie. He took the stairs two at a time.

CHAPTER SEVEN

Nathan pushed open the door to the lounge. Neither Courtney, Craig nor Leke moved from where they hovered in the hallway, hands deep in their baggy jeans pockets.

"You need to see," he insisted.

Courtney licked his lips. "If you're fucking around with us, Nathan . . ."

". . . Then I swear I'm going to kick your head in." Craig finished the sentence, and Nathan found himself nodding. He didn't know why.

"You need to see," he said again. "It was coming out from inside of her."

Leke sighed. "Come on, let's do it. Just to shut him up."

A quiet sense of relief had been growing in Nathan since he'd knocked on Mrs. Minster's door at half past seven, just after the weird squealing sounds had crept down the side of the building from somewhere above. He wasn't stupid, despite what all the kids at school thought. He knew that none of the details of the world were working right, but he desperately wanted someone else to see that too; otherwise he'd be afraid it was just strange Nathan stuff going on in his own head.

He needed some people to see it that at least kind of

understood Nathan and wouldn't make him go away just because he was different. Nathan had always cherished his quiet time on his own with his books of facts and figures, away from all the communicating that he found so difficult, but for the first time in his life he didn't want to be on his own.

When they'd finally opened the door and let him in, he'd just sat on the sofa saying nothing while his mind tried to reorder the bricks. Courtney had got him a can of Coke and it was nearly flat by the time he took his first sip. He couldn't find the words to come out right, instead he just rocked backward and forward slightly, his spine straight while his brain worked on the puzzle. After twenty minutes or so, he adjusted his glasses and spat out the words, "You have to see." It was the best he could manage. But it had worked—eventually—once he'd got to his feet and literally dragged Courtney forward and shaken his head vigorously at Leke's edgy question of whether this had anything to do with Blane Gentle-King because if so he could take his weird, freaky ass back home right now.

And now they were here. Back home. Courtney peered doubtfully back at Leke and Craig and then shrugged. "How bad can it be?"

Nathan pressed himself against the wall so the other two boys could get by, and then he waited, his eyes squeezed shut, just in case he couldn't control his own urge to glance around the edge of the doorway, and then the bricks in his head that he'd manage to get into some kind of order would all be jumbled again.

"Holy shit."

He didn't know who'd spoken, the words barely more than a whisper.

"What the fuck is that thing?"

"It was fucking coming out from inside her. Look."

Another long pause.

"Shit. I think I'm going to puke."

"He must have killed it. And her. There's the fucking bread knife."

"Look at those legs, man. Shit. I really am going to puke."

Clothes brushed roughly past Nathan as Leke pushed him aside and dived into the bathroom. He heaved three loud times, each followed by a rush of liquid hitting liquid, before eventually he let out the low moan of someone who was done.

Nathan looked away from the bathroom door and straight ahead at his mother's patterned hallway wallpaper. "Can we go back to Mrs. Minster's flat now?" His skin tingled hotly but as he pushed his glasses back up on the bridge of his nose, the tips of his fingers were cold. He knew they needed to see, but there was something horrible about them staring at his mum like that, with that thing hanging out of her.

"Yeah." Courtney stepped back into the hallway, his smooth brown complexion slightly ashen. "Yeah, let's get out of here."

Leke appeared in the bathroom doorway wiping one hand across his runny nose, and he nodded vigorously. "Yeah. Come on, Nathan. Grab what you need and let's go."

As he followed Courtney down to his closed bedroom door, he frowned. What would he take? His encyclopedias were too heavy to carry and with a twist of sadness he realized that their facts and figures had somehow shifted into obsolete at some point in the night. His iPod was filled with music that he liked but didn't really understand. Only one thing came to mind.

His steps quick, he went into his bedroom and crouched by the bookshelf, carefully pulling out each of the small, blank notebooks that were piled up neatly in the far-left corner of the bottom shelf. Finally, he selected a faintly lined pad just smaller than A5 with a royal blue cover. Somehow it felt right. Next to the replaced pile of discarded pads was a row of pens. Having already chosen the book, the pen was easier. Two blue Bic biros would be fine. One to use and one as a backup.

Leke and Courtney stared at him from the doorway.

"Tidy room," Courtney said.

"Very . . ." Leke shrugged a little as if trying to find the right word. ". . . practical."

Nathan reached behind the door and pulled down the leather jacket that hung next to his dressing gown. He tucked the book and pens into its inside pocket before pulling it on. He felt better wrapped in its heavy flesh.

Leke stared at it, his eyes slipping away, and Nathan had seen the look often enough to know what it meant, even with his "communication problems" as his mum would call it. His jacket wasn't *trendy*. It wasn't *in*. Nathan figured for just those reasons it must suit him pretty well. Without looking back he closed his bedroom door behind him. If he could only find a way to say that to the other boys then they might even laugh with him. He didn't try though—he knew the words would just get tangled up between his head and his tongue. They always did.

At the other end of the corridor Craig was still standing in the sitting room, staring at the out-of-sight sofa and its contents.

"Come on, man," Courtney called down to him. "We've got to go. Stop staring at that shit."

Already at the front door, Nathan watched Leke elbow the other boy hard in the ribs.

"What was that for?"

"His mum, Courtney," Leke said. "His mum and sister got all fat like that. He'll be wondering what's happened to them."

Nathan watched, helpless. These conversations were beyond him. He just wanted to get out of this flat, which no longer felt like home, and back to Mrs. Minster's.

Courtney shrugged and sniffed. "I got a mum too. And she was getting fat." He turned his back on Leke. "Craig, man, come on."

Finally the last boy joined them by the door, but he didn't speak, his jaw locked and eyes glaring downward. Nathan felt relieved. There was only so much external emotion he could take.

Out in the corridor, they huddled together as Courtney fiddled with the keys, Leke's tapping sneaker the only external evidence of the urgency they were all feeling. It was only when the door shut behind them and they were safely in the stranger's home that Craig looked up.

"What do you think?" His voice was low as he looked from Courtney to Leke and back again, his eyes not even resting for a second on Nathan. "Do you think that's happened to all of them? All the fat women?"

Leke bit his bottom lip and glanced up at Courtney, before his eyes slipped somewhere past Craig. "Maybe not," he said eventually.

"Yeah." Courtney shrugged. "Who knows, man? Maybe it's only happened to the older ones. Your mum's not that old. Maybe her and Shannon are okay."

"I don't think so." Nathan shook his head fast, one finger keeping his glasses in place. They didn't seem to understand. "If they got fat like my mum and mean like my mum, then they must have had a thing in them like my mum." He paused and looked earnestly at Courtney. "Your mum too if she got fat. It's logical. Why would it only happen to one?"

All three boys stared at him in disgust before Craig took a step up and shoved him hard in the chest, sending him backward onto the sofa. "Just shut the fuck up, Nathan, or we'll lock you back up with your freak of a mother and that dead fucking monster."

Leke sucked his teeth and shook his head. As the three moved over to the other side of the room, talking quietly together, Nathan watched them and could only wonder what he'd done.

A gunshot rang out, all four boys' heads whipping around in the direction of the window.

"What the fuck?"

Courtney carefully pulled back the curtain's edge, flinching against the bright sunlight. "Can't see anything down there." Another gunshot exploded into the quiet. "Must be coming from the other tower or somewhere else in the estate." In the echo of the blast the square stayed silent and as the minutes passed no sirens wailed their way into existence. "Leke, try dialing nine-nine-nine on the landline." Courtney kept his eyes out the window. "Craig, you try the mobile."

"Won't work." Clasping his knees firmly, Nathan didn't even look up. "Won't work. I tried it before I came here . . . after I'd . . ." His mind almost wouldn't let him say the words, even though the details made sense. ". . . after I'd killed my mum," he finished softly. His glasses felt odd against his nose, unbalanced, but they had done all morning, more so than usual, and squeezing his knees he fought the urge to rearrange them again. It didn't work and his left hand shot up to push the frames backward. A sore patch of skin was forming on the small bump on his nose and it stung as the cheap plastic rubbed against it.

"He's right," Leke said. "No dial tone, only static."

"Same with the mobile."

When he finally looked up he saw that Courtney's soft eyes were staring sadly at him. "Shit, Nathan."

Another burst of gunfire broke the moment and the boys' eyes locked onto each others', this time even including Nathan in the round of worried looks.

"This is some serious shit," Craig said finally, and even for Nathan there was no problem hearing the tremble of fear in his voice.

"We're going to have to get some guns." Nathan's own voice was steady, the same monotone as always, no hint that anything was out of the ordinary with the day at all.

This time no one argued with him.

CHAPTER EIGHT

By nine thirty in the morning, Blane Gentle-King was just about getting his head around the shit that was being thrown at him. He stared out from the grimy top-floor window, his eyes drifting over the river and to the buildings of the south. One boat had chugged softly down the middle of the Thames, disappearing past the silver arched shapes of the barrier at nine, but since then the water had been quiet. Between him and Charlie they'd seen maybe three cars driving slowly through the streets even though there was no traffic, as if whoever was behind each wheel was terrified, just wanting to creep unnoticed out of town. As he lit a cigarette, blowing the smoke directly into the glass, Blane wondered if they had a point. From where he was standing it very much looked like something had badly fucked London up during the night.

Behind him, Skate sat on the soft white sofa taking long sips from a glass of whiskey. Leeboy was by the front door, and two more armed men were out front. No fucking monsters were going to be getting in here too quickly. Blane felt the cool metal of his own gun tucked into his waist. And even if they did, he'd deal with them.

Charlie picked his own drink up from the low glass table that, unlike the outside of Blane's windows which the council were never going to dig into their pockets to clean, didn't have a single smear. Blane liked things neat, which is why everything in his crib was either white, cream or chrome and glass. He figured it was the kind of shit the rich city boys in those Canary Wharf *apartments* had, and the soothing colors and sharp lines helped his thinking. Charlie had obviously made sure his place was kept well while he was inside. There wasn't a speck of dust anywhere and the sheets on his bed hadn't just been clean, they'd been new, the creases still visible even stretched as they were across the mattress.

Blane watched his oldest friend who was calmly sipping his whiskey. It seemed that Charlie had taken care of a lot while Blane had been away. He was a good man, Charlie Nash. One of the best. True through and through. No one had, or ever would come between them. Blane felt that stronger than ever today.

A short blast of semiautomatic fire echoed sharply up to the top floor, louder and with more bite than the earlier retorts. This round had come from inside the block. At least the boys were cleaning up.

"Is it how Skate says it is?" He turned his back on the window, leaving the city to sort its own problems out.

Charlie nodded. "I took a look through the hatch. I don't know what those things are, but fuck are they angry in there. Fighting amongst themselves. Squealing like pigs."

"Are there more?"

"Blackeyes, Chokey and Weights all turned up at mine from the other block about an hour ago. When I got rid of the rest I let them keep their women at home, cos you know"—he shrugged—"they're part of the crew. It was their business." He paused and took another sip of his drink, but his gaze was clear when it met Blane's. "They said these spider things came out of the women. Like they gave birth to them. Fucking crazy, I know. But true."

Blane chewed the inside of his mouth. He should be screwing at them for getting so high they'd tripped out. He should be laughing at their stories. He should be fucking tooling up and going to sort out whoever was firing weapons on his turf first thing in the morning and with no orders to. That's what he should be doing, because what they were saying sounded too fucking crazy to be for real.

But Charlie never touched any serious drugs, and Skate had been at it too long to let himself get too mashed up and Brownie was definitely missing. He thought about how quiet Brixton had slowly become over the past few weeks; in that time Charlie started to obsess about how the women were getting fatter and meaner. Blane was a street soldier and had been since he could walk. He could smell trouble, and the air reeked of it this morning. Eventually he shrugged.

"This is some motherfucking trippy shit." Blane took another long drag on the cigarette. What he really wanted was a strong joint, but that was going to have to wait until later. "What did they do when they got home?"

"Shot them. The women were dead. Blackeyes and Chokey got stoned last night and slept in some other geezer's place. Not one of ours. They got home and found these things there. Blew them apart. Weights did the same, but he got bit by his missus in the process."

"Bit?" Blane coughed out a short laugh. "That's why you and me have never been dumb enough to get married. Is he okay?"

"Yeah. It bled a bit, but he's bandaged it up."

"How many of these things do you think are left on our turf?"

"Hard to say. I got out a lot of women, but you know how it is, some hid. I left the old women here if they wanted to stay. Didn't seem right sending them out, especially those with no family."

Blane frowned, his head trying to cope with the enormity of it. As far as he could see, this shit had happened to all women. Otherwise, Charlie would have had some nice piece of ass from one of the clubs waiting for him when they got home. They'd all got fat. And if they'd all got fat, then maybe they'd all pushed out these fucking creatures that had got Brownie. And then . . . He snapped the thought shut. He had to make him and his own secure. They could worry about the wider picture later.

"Do you know which flats?"

"Mostly. That's what the boys are on now. Cleaning up where they can."

"One thing though." Skate stood up. "That one I saw coming out of the window from the other block? It looked different to the ones in the flat. Bigger. Still a scary fuck, but less . . . crazy. It was whiter too."

Charlie nodded. "I showed Blackeyes and Chokey through the hatch when they got here, cos to be honest, neither of them was making the most sense and it seemed the quickest way to see if they were talking about the same stuff. They said that the things that came out of their girls were like the ones we've got, but whiter and bigger. And they weren't doing any of that shrieking and mad crawling around the walls. It ties in to what Skate saw."

Skate looked from one man to the other. "So, there's two types of these things?"

"Maybe." Blane frowned, thoughtfully, before raising an eyebrow. "Or maybe ours are just angry junkie bitches. Maybe that's why they're different."

Skate's eyes widened. "Shit. That makes sense. The wraps. The thing spat them at me."

For the first time since he'd woken up, Blane felt the first trickle of a plan forming. "Let's go and take a look, shall we, brothers? And someone bring some rocks and a fucking pipe."

Blane came down the stairs inside the block with an easy swagger, despite his jangling nerves. Charlie did the same beside him, his gun free from his belt but hanging relaxed in the man's hand down by his side. It was important they looked calm. They had the crew to run and reputations to protect. If they started looking afraid the whole thing would turn to shit in front of them, and some fucker would no doubt stick a bullet in one or both of them, whether there were bigger issues to worry about or not. After all, that was exactly what he'd done when he was ready to take control.

He made a mental note to ask Charlie about the guns later, when they'd dealt with the immediate situation. Blane had always made sure his people were well protected, and there had never been a shortage of firearms. No one grew up on this estate without knowing someone that could get you a handgun, and once you were through that first door, guns were readily available for the right price and the right face, but it seemed that right now the crew were far more tooled up than they ever had been before. Blackeyes and Chokey had handguns on them at home, and in terms of rank they were way down. Still, as it turned out they'd been fucking lucky they'd had them. It still gave him a sense slight unease as if he was out of the loop. Which of course he was. He needed a proper sit-down with Charlie to catch up with things. A few months away was a long time in Newham, and he didn't want to look to anyone like he didn't have his finger on the pulse. Or the trigger.

He sniffed, looking both ways in the corridor. Squeals erupted at each end, a shrieking, hissing sound that set his teeth on edge. He forced his jaw to relax. "Did anyone look in on Janine?"

Skate shook his head. "I heard that noise, just like the things in here were making, so I figured . . ." His words trailed off and his shoulders sagged. "To tell it true, I didn't have no weapon and I just wanted to get back up here and tell Charlie to tell you what had happened to Brownie."

"What you did made sense, blood." Blane turned to his right. "But I think I'll take a look and see how my big fat baby girl's turned out this morning. Charlie, you're with me. Skate, you keep the stairs covered."

Outside the metal door on the seventeenth floor, Blane waited while Charlie dug out the right key to open the hatch. His head buzzed with a strange urgency. He knew what he was going to see would blow his mind, but he still felt a wave of excitement. If it was true, then all the rules had changed in one night, and where that might terrify some people, Blane Gentle-King found it exhilarating.

Charlie pulled open the grid and both men immediately leaped backward in unison as something squealed and threw itself against the small open space, landing with a wet, solid thump, before falling away. For a brief moment, Blane thought he saw gaping open suckers on its underbelly, deformed shapes, opening and closing as if trying to grasp something, a bitter stench belching out with each blind movement. Back against the wall, his nose furrowed, and then he let out a sigh. He'd dropped his cigarette and watching it burn out on the dirty tiles, he laughed a little.

"Jesus Christ, Charlie. I think I nearly shit myself."

Charlie was pressed back against the wall just the same as Blane and he smiled back. "I think we can safely assume the same thing happened to Janine as to Kelly and the others down the way."

"No shit."

The thing in the flat that had once been sweet Janine railed against the door again, but this time, rather than backing away, Blane walked toward it, watching it fling its strange body at the metal with no sense of restraint or sanity. Flashes of mottled white passed his eyes as the creature raged; the sounds coming from it diving into growls and then wet hisses before reaching back into the high notes of the squeals.

"You want me to deal with it, Blane?" Charlie spoke softly, holding up his gun.

"No, not at all, bro. This could be interesting." He smiled. "Just let her wear herself out a little, and then when she realizes she can't go nowhere, I want to try something. Give me those rocks and the pipe."

Charlie handed them over and Blane grinned. "After all, a junkie's a junkie right?"

The other man frowned. "Maybe. But I think Janine's past earning her rocks. Unless you know some sick friends."

"Who knows, Charlie. Maybe there's more than one way Janine can earn for me."

"You're the boss." Charlie stepped back, and slipped his gun into his trousers so he could lean against the wall, fold his arms and watch. "You're the boss."

Blane stepped up to the hatch.

CHAPTER NINE

It burned. Ever since it had emerged from the host its skin had raged with pain that roared and itched. Below its body, the eight legs twitched and scurried, needing to keep moving. Needing something. Its mind was still newborn and dulled but despite that there was a sense that something was wrong. It was different. Not like most of the others it could feel emerging from their birthing sacs and carefully cocooning the raw meat, softening it for food. They were connecting, their minds forming links and networks across this vast new planet, reassuring each other that all was well.

Exhausted from its attack on the door, the creature looked at the cocoon it had attempted, the strands of webbing leaving vast gaps around the sagging corpse It didn't care if the meat was softened. Its craving for something tearing into its every cell, it leaped on the thing it had so recently vacated and sank its mandibles into the soft belly, ripping free a chunk of bloody skin and flesh, flinging it madly from side to side before letting the suckers beneath its bulbous body start to eat. Within a moment, they spat the hulk of damp, warm food unwanted onto the carpet. That wasn't what it needed. The need, the burn, the itch; they came from something else. It screamed again, the sound pouring from its underbelly and its vibrating slick surfaces, its bank of eyes staring angrily at the small

*space in the door that the meat on the other side had opened.
It shouldn't be trapped. It should be free. It didn't think to
look to the window, its being driven by emotion and instinct,
without the rationality of the others, the ones it should be like,
but wasn't.*

*It reached out for those others it could feel, the millions
that had started to slowly creep out into their new home, but
a cool wall rose between them and itself. It raged again, and
this time it felt the rage of others like it, clear in its animal
thoughts. They were close by. It pushed its mind outward, its
range limited compared to the others, the normals, but still
felt their own needy screams coming back, an echo through
the empty air. It wasn't alone.*

*Darting its mottled body forward, closer to the door it
pawed angrily at the ground. Through its bank of eyes the
edges of the world shifted slightly, watery and infirm, everything coated with a red hue, no other clean colors existing.*

*A face appeared at the gap and it screamed again as it
scuttled sideways into the hallway, but this time didn't attack.
It had learned there was nothing to be gained and it was
tired, despite the heat that pulsed inside it.*

"Janine, baby?"

*It heard the words like bubbles underwater, dull and in-
sipid, without the potency of its own kind's communication,
which arrived straight into its conscious. Still, something
about the sound made the creature freeze for a moment, before edging forward.*

"Janine, baby, I got what you want."

*In a dark corner of its mind that was so different from
how it should be, a vibration of recognition trembled. A
clumsy word formed in its stream of thinking, which existed
without such codes; the shapes of it filling its confused mind.
Enraged, it launched itself against the wall, barely feeling the*

concrete against its skin, and then ran up to the ceiling, along to the end of the corridor and back, before dropping suddenly and hissing.

Blane.

The word itself meant nothing, but the creature felt a wave of hatred, a lingering echo of the host whose need had created its own and mutated it. Ghosts of memories it didn't understand filled it with vivid images, snapshots flickering and changing too fast for it to follow. Mating, rough and angry; beatings, dark bruises flowering in soft flesh; tears, warm and unhappy for the loss of what might have been more. And then something else: the dirty, hungry itch that overshadowed the rest like a pall of poisoned black smoke.

Blane.

All this was carried in the strange sound and shape of the word. The creature crept forward, snarling. It wanted to rip this man apart, to tear his limbs off and strip his flesh and leave him uneaten. It knew this in the pulse of anger that throbbed wordless in its core.

The man held something up in front of the gap and the need exploded in red, filling its vision. Before the objects had formed any clear recognition, no word like "Blane" eating alien into its mind, the creature scrabbled up the door and pressed its open suckers at the gap, wailing like a newborn, into the world.

Blane laughed, his long dreadlocks flicking backward as he winced at the sheer power of the noise coming from the thing that had pressed itself like a leech to the door.

"Man, she's a hungry bitch."

"Jesus, look at that shit." Charlie came up beside him and pointed to a strip of bloody skin hanging from one of the gaping, misshapen suckers. The black ink on it was unmistakable. "Fuck me," he added. "That's Janine's tattoo."

Blane nodded. He'd recognized the out-of-shape cheap rose too, but Janine and her body no longer interested him. It was clear that she was long gone, and if this thing had come out of her, then wasn't that what he'd read somewhere that bugs do? Eat their fucking mothers or mates or offspring?

"I guess we can say they're not friendly." Charlie sighed. "Jesus, this is fucked up, Blane. This is totally fucked up."

It was the first time since Charlie had woken him that Blane had seen the other man rattled and nervous. In some ways it made him feel better. He was still cool and Charlie was losing his. He was still the boss, and it was showing.

"Don't be too hasty, bro." Blane lifted the rock and lighter. "Blow some of this happy smoke into her. Let's see what happens."

Charlie shook his head. "You know I don't touch that shit. Don't want to start now. Not in the middle of all this."

Blane shrugged. "You don't need to inhale it or nothing."

"You need me straight, bro. I'm not taking that risk. I've seen what that shit does to people."

Watching his friend's straight back and steady gaze, Blane figured Charlie wouldn't be budged and didn't blame him. He looked at the suckers that opened and closed on the other side of the door, oozing that foul stink with every pulsating breath. Maybe it was better that he did it himself anyway.

The thing squealed, and the sound was echoed by the four of its kind farther down the corridor.

"Patience, bitch." The rock slotted into the head of the small pipe and Blane lit it. He sucked in hard, his mouth filling with the sickly sweet smoke. Slowly, he leaned forward until his face was only inches from the revolting suckers, and then blew it out, directing it straight into the rotten openings that still held a bloody trace of Janine.

The effect was immediate. Each of the suckers trembled, and the squeal that had been building to full force sunk into a hiss that was closer to a sigh. Blane repeated the action until the rock was burned to nothing and eventually the creature dropped to the floor, scuttling backward on slightly clumsy legs, its bulbous body almost bouncing slightly as if its insides were pure liquid.

Through the hatch they stared at each other, the hazel eyes evaluating the bank of pinprick red.

"Well, that's calmed her down, but she ain't fucked. Nothing messy in that stare."

He looked at Charlie, and then puzzled, his eyes went past the other man and thoughtfully ran down the corridor.

"Now, *that's* interesting," he said eventually. "That's very interesting."

"What?" Charlie looked over his own shoulder then back at Blane, who smiled.

"Those other ones. They've shut up." He peered back through the hatch at the monstrous spider that sat in the hallway. "This one gets some shit, and they all stop squealing."

"What's it mean?"

Charlie looked lost. He was too straightforward for this kind of thinking, but Blane didn't care. He had enough brains for both of them. Two clever fucks running one crew just wouldn't work.

"Maybe something. Maybe nothing." He slammed the hatch shut. "But we're going to need to make some bigger rocks, and find a way to pump the smoke in there without anyone having to get their faces so close." He wiped his mouth, the taste of the drugs still lingering. "Those bitches stink."

Heavy footsteps pounded up the stairs where Skate stood guard, and Weights came into view, holding something in his unbandaged hand. Skate nodded him through, and his solid frame lumbered toward Charlie and Blane.

"What's up, bro?" Blane looked up at the man who towered over both him and Charlie, his overtrained muscles making them both look like weak kids who had never smelled the inside of a gym. Sometimes Blane had wondered what he did it all for—the steroids, the endless workouts. Still, he wouldn't stop him. It never hurt to have a couple of tanks on side. Above Weights's thick neck, his ebony face was ashen.

"You okay? You don't look too good."

Weights shrugged. "It's been a long morning. My head is fucked and"—he held up his bandaged hand—"this bitch hurts like fuck."

"Maybe you should take it easy. Let the others do the work."

"Nah. It's better to be busy. Stops me thinking."

Blane wasn't sure how much thinking Weights had ever really been capable of, even before the steroids and the puff and the charlie, but he nodded anyway.

"I get you."

"We found this in one of the flats downstairs."

Blane took the jacket from the big man and turned it over in his hands. He didn't see what the point was. It was just an oversize Puma jacket like all the kids wore on the estate.

"There was a warm cup of tea and some half-eaten toast on the table. Whoever was in there, couldn't have been gone long. They survived the fucking night at any rate. When we found that, we thought you'd want to know."

As he pulled it open to examine the inside pockets, Blane froze. Along the inside collar, printed in biro in jagged letters, the words stood out against the white. "Leke Kudaisi's—fuck off!"

He looked up, his eyes sharp and angry. "Leke? Isn't that the little shit that grassed me?"

Weights grinned. "That's him."

"He's on the estate?"

"Must have been. Until about ten minutes ago anyway."

Charlie took the coat, looking at it thoughtfully. "Let's get the block clear and then we'll find him, boss. If one of those things doesn't get him first."

Blane stared at his best friend. "I want him. You find him, Charlie. You got that?"

"I got that, Blane." Charlie nodded, his face impassive. "I got that."

They stared at each other for a couple of moments and then Charlie's eyes slipped away. Blane smiled, glancing back at the closed hatch.

"This is the start of a new world, Charlie. And we're going to start a New World Order." He laughed. "I've got a plan, bro. I've got a fucking plan."

Still laughing, he wrapped one arm around his oldest

friend's shoulder and they strolled back toward the stairs, Weights alongside them, cradling his injured arm. Blane didn't miss the look that passed between the other two men, but he didn't pull them on it. They'd see. They'd learn.

CHAPTER TEN

In the six days since the world had gone mad, seventeen-year-old Harry Parker had lost any urge to join the army. His back pressed against the rough brick wall, pins and needles setting into his crouching calves, he made a mental note to mention this at his next sixth-form career interview. He then referred himself back to a previous mental note that pointed out that it was highly unlikely that any career interviews would be taking place in the near or even mid-distant future. But if they were, he had no intention of following up on all those years of army cadets. It seemed pretty apparent to him that the army wasn't all it was cracked up to be. Not in this present situation, at any rate. Where were the tanks? What were they doing coming out on the streets in soft-top trucks? Were they crazy or just stupid? No, whatever the future held, it definitely was not the army for him.

"Do you think we should go and help them?" Josh whispered.

Harry could feel the younger boy's body pressing into his on his right side. It was clear in the hollow dullness of Josh's just-broken voice that even he thought it was a bad idea, and neither Harry nor Mr. Green answered. Josh had asked that question every time they'd come across a situation like this over the past ten days or so since they'd started venturing out, and everyone knew it was just a guilty gag reflex. He didn't really mean it. And Harry didn't blame him. He knew exactly how Josh felt. He didn't have any urge to go out there either.

Sweat clung to his hairline, sliding down past his temple and tickling at his ear before disappearing into the neckline of his damp T-shirt. The air was heavy and hot, and soon it would start raining again; more warm downfalls of sweet-smelling water that seemed to have become routine over the past couple of weeks, even though they were completely out of place in the normal English climate. Harry sucked in a breath of humid air, unhappy at the taste of it. London air should be cold and leave an aftertaste of exhaust fumes, not this wet, sweet heat that he was inhaling. Sometimes he wasn't sure what scared him most, the mutant bugs or the changes in the weather. It was as if the world was changing and there was nothing they could do to prevent it.

"I wish it would stop." Beside him, Josh squeezed his eyes shut and moaned a little as another scream filled the silent street.

Harry wondered if maybe they should have left him back at the bed-and-breakfast with the other two, but Josh's tiny frame was too good at getting through small windows. The boy was fourteen but with his skinny chest and inability to crack the five-foot mark, he could easily be mistaken for ten. Harry glanced to his left. Mr. Green was staring straight ahead, muttering silently under his breath, his thick glasses steaming up with the humid air and their owner's panting, panicked breath. Harry's heart sank. Mr. Green, teacher of history, sociology and R.E., wasn't really cut out for this either. But then, none of them exactly were.

Forcing his cramped legs to work, he stood up and peered around the edge of the side street to see if what was happening to the army truck on Prince Regent's Lane was nearly over. They had heard its rumbling engine after coming out of the small corner shop on Sark Walk and had been running up to the main road to get its attention when they'd heard the sharp shriek of the brakes and the first screams of fear and agony amid sporadic loud gunshots. They'd stopped running then, staying safely behind the side-street wall and the shots had stopped soon afterward.

That was less than five minutes ago, and Harry had a pretty good idea that the soldiers had been overwhelmed, the screaming was a giveaway for that one, but he still needed to see for himself. Careful to keep himself hidden, he focused his nervous eyes. The skewed truck had veered across the empty lanes and come to a halt against the low barrier that separated the two carriageways, and the driver and passenger doors hung open, although there were no men in sight. Someone was still screaming though. The sound pierced through Harry's ears and into his soul. The fabric of the covered truck ballooned at one side for a moment, and then the shriek paused for a brief moment of silent bliss before starting up again. Harry flinched, watching the truck rock slightly, something heavy within lurching from side to side. It was hard to believe that it was a grown man making that awful high-pitched wailing sound, a man who had trained and fought and probably thought he was tough enough to take on any enemy. He probably wouldn't have believed it if he hadn't seen it before, but somehow the knowledge made it worse rather than better.

As the first two white legs clawed at the top of truck, Harry pulled himself back slightly so that only one eye could see, only a tiny part of his head visible. He blew his dark, floppy fringe out of his face. The bricks were rough as sandpaper under his fingers, but he couldn't stop himself gripping the ridge between them, digging his fingernails in hard, as the monstrous body hauled itself and the soldier it carried onto the soft top of the truck. Harry stared. He would never get used to the sight of the things, he was sure of that. Behind him, he could hear Josh sobbing quietly. Maybe it was Josh or maybe it was Mr. Green. Perhaps it was both. It seemed like they were miles away from Harry and he was miles away from the soldier who was still alive but in the grip of his own death.

His helmet must have fallen off inside the truck, and held as he was by two of the creature's spindly legs, wrapping themselves around the trunk of his body and pressing him into the mass of suckers underneath its own hideous body, his head lolled backward. It was a young face. Skin still firm, wrinkle-free and flushed. Harry figured that whoever the man was, he wasn't that much older that he was himself. Nineteen, maybe. Twenty tops. Perhaps he'd been fooled by all the years of army cadets too. He'd definitely learned his lesson now though. There were some enemies no amount of training could prepare you for.

The man's scream had thankfully stopped but his eyes were open, wide and conscious, filled with the dread of someone who knows with an absolute certainty that they are going to die, but is still hoping that perhaps some terrible mistake has been made and they'll be able to present their get-out-of-jail-free card. It wasn't going to happen though. And on some level, those agonized, haunted eyes knew it.

Harry didn't want to look at the young soldier any more. He didn't want to find him looking back. Instead, he lifted his gaze and watched the creature that held the limp khaki body. Even from a distance of fifty yards, Harry could make out the raised bumps on the front section of its almost translucent white body, from which the clear pinpricks of red eyes raged, angry and intelligent. It hissed, clacking its large mandibles together before rearing up on its spindly hind legs, displaying its trapped human trophy for a moment, before bounding from the roof of the truck and following the others of its kind back down the road.

Still watching the truck cautiously, Harry didn't move for a few minutes. Silence reclaimed the street. Nothing moved. Somewhere a bird chirped. Eventually, he let out a long breath. "I think they've gone."

Slowly, Mr. Green got up and then so did Josh, keeping himself close to the older boy and the teacher.

"Are you sure?" Josh didn't sound convinced.

"Yeah. I think they've taken them all down to the park." He squeezed the younger boy's shoulder. "It's okay. They really have gone."

"For now," Mr. Green added, and Harry fired him an angry glare. For a teacher, it seemed he knew very little about reassuring kids. He'd been pretty rubbish at it over the past two weeks. That much was for sure.

"I hate the park." Josh stretched his neck out so that his head could see around the corner but his legs stayed firmly in the side street. A shudder echoed in his words. Canning Town Rec Ground was about two hundred yards down on the left, and where it had once been lush green playing areas and well-kept tennis courts, it was now a network of long cables of thick, sticky webbing draped across every surface, an uneven pattern that stretched from the swings and slides to the trees and fences. Cocooned bodies hung from the branches of the thicker trees, above which the huge white spiders hid themselves in the leaves, trawling their prey upward when they wanted to feast and letting the empty husk of webbing fall bloody to the ground when done. The boys avoided the park, or any roads too close to it. The army truck had stood no chance really.

"I hate it too." Harry stared at the road. "You wait here. Me and Mr. Green will go and see what we can find." *While they're busy.* He kept the thought to himself. It wasn't as if the others needed it pointing out. He looked at the older man, whose Adam's apple bobbed manically in his thin and saggy neck. "You ready?"

Mr. Green nodded. "Yes. Yes. Let's get it over with."

"Keep an eye out, Josh. Whistle if you see anything suspicious." The small boy nodded, his fearful eyes still trained on the out-of-sight park. Harry nudged him.

"Keep an eye out *in all directions.* Okay?"

"Yes, Harry." Josh finally dragged his solemn face back to his companions. Harry ruffled his short hair.

"Good. We'll be quick as we can."

As he stepped out from the relative safety of the side street, Harry felt the surge of adrenaline whip through his body, forcing his heart somewhere up in his throat where it fought a fearful wave of nausea. The world seemed too bright as he sprinted over to the abandoned truck, taking the low barrier between the lanes like a hurdle. The thin material of his T-shirt clung to his back like a vulnerable second skin and skating to a halt ten feet or so from the brown metal of the truck, he dropped to his knees and checked underneath. The tarmac ran uninterrupted to the other side.

Mr. Green's feet had slowed down, but as Harry mouthed "clear," the middle-aged man caught up with him. They'd both been on the first recce four days ago when Christopher Watson had been pulled screaming under the white van they were ransacking. It wasn't something either of them were likely to forget in a hurry. Every night since then, when he could sleep, it was Watson's terrified face that drifted in and out of his disjointed dreams, his eyes full of accusation as if it were Harry's fault that the world had changed, and Harry alone should have had the sense to look under the van.

He got swiftly to his feet and jogged around to the back of the truck. There hadn't even been anything good in that van. Watson had died for nothing. He gritted his teeth. Maybe not nothing. His death had taught them all a valuable lesson. Harry never got too close to a high vehicle without checking underneath anymore.

Carefully, he pulled back the heavy canvas flap, its oiled surface slippery against his sweaty skin. An empty dark cavern waited in front of him, daylight piercing the gloom from the four bullet holes that cut through its side. He found a foothold on the tow bar and hauled himself inside. The sound of his breath echoed around the confined space and came back at him, loud and ghostly. Despite the humidity, he shivered as he scanned the area. The low wooden benches on either side were empty of any evidence that they'd been occupied, and so he scurried forward to the rear.

From the amount of yells and screams they'd heard,

Harry figured that apart from the two soldiers in the front cabin, there'd probably only been perhaps two more in the back. It was hard to be exact because one thing he'd learned since the world had turned into some kind of hallucinatory nightmare was that people had a whole range of screams, depending on just how much pain or fear was gripping them. Still, he figured four was about right. The attack hadn't gone on long enough for any more. Even with his newfound cynicism regarding the army's abilities, he figured that a truckload of men would have put up a longer fight. And who knew; they might even have won.

He peered into the dark corners, doing his best to avoid the strand of thin, sticky fluid that hung from the roof and clung in places to the curved sides. It glistened in the gloom, a miniature version of the thick, glutinous cables that stretched across the park. The slick threads came out of the spiders' feet. Harry knew that much. The memory of it lashing around Chris Watson's body while he stood and watched like a useless fool was all too vivid, burned into the back of his eyes. He blinked it away.

A dark shape protruding out from under the bench caught Harry's attention, and smiling, he crouched to grab it. Despite being blurred by shadow, he recognized the shape of the standard SA80 rifle. It even had a sight attached. That hadn't been needed when the spiders had bounded into the back of the truck. The action had all been a little too close range for the soldiers to cope with.

The weapon tucked under his arm, he looked around for any extra ammunition, but the truck was bare. Deftly removing it, six years of practice in various cadet training camps, Harry checked the clip. It still had more than twenty of its thirty rounds left. Good. He clicked it back into the butt. All those years of army research had at least paid off in his weapons knowledge even if they were never going to provide a career in this world where the word "career" was rapidly becoming redundant.

Back outside, he found Mr. Green staring some way down into the road that headed toward the rec, frowning slightly.

"It seems it wasn't all lost." The older man's brown hair sat in a slightly too long side parting across his head and where a thick strand had fallen loose down his forehead, he tucked it behind his ear with an elegantly tapered finger. His brow furrowed.

Harry followed his gaze. Lying in the road twenty feet from where they stood was a tangled mass of spider and man, both dead. A pool of thick blood had seeped out beneath them, and Harry thought it must belong to the man who stared wide-eyed toward them, a trickle of crimson dripping from his open mouth, his body barely visible under the full weight of the crumpled white monster. Harry wasn't sure where that dead thing was looking. The red light had gone from the bank of raised bumps that housed its vision, and its thin translucent legs stuck out awkwardly beneath the sheen of its bulbous body.

"I supposed one of the other soldiers must have shot them before getting taken themselves." Mr. Green's voice was soft and thoughtful.

Harry watched him carefully. Sometimes he wondered if their teacher was keeping it together quite as well as he made out, or whether it was all just a veneer over a cracking mind. Even back at school the history master had seemed delicate and arty to the point where most of the boys sneered behind his back that he was closet gay, despite having an equally strange-looking wife who rolled out for the classical recitals her husband played the organ in. They hadn't talked about Mrs. Green. Not since all this had happened.

As a soft warm breeze brought the first drops of hot rain down from the gray, sweating sky, Harry felt the ground shift a little beneath his feet. Maybe his own mind was snapping a little. School, the recitals, whether Mr. Green was really Gayboy Green or not—they all belonged in another world whose society and subtle nuances had been so important to him. A month ago he was stressing about his AS exams. Now the only thing that concerned him was surviving each day. What would he have done back then if he'd known what was coming? Maybe it was a good thing they didn't have foresight.

"He was probably the luckiest." Mr. Green stood still in the road, despite the rain that was building pace as it fell from above. "At least he didn't end up in the park."

"Yeah. Maybe." Harry shivered, despite the heat of the rain. There was an unpleasant slimy texture to it and he hated the feel of it against his skin. His feet itched. It was time to leave and not just because of the rain. The pack would be back soon. Unlike whatever was left of the human race, the giant white spider things seemed to love hunting in the downpours.

He nudged the older man bringing him out of his reverie. "I got this out of the back. It's still got some ammo in it. Was there anything in the front?"

Mr. Green looked down at his left hand, almost surprised to see a similar weapon in it. "Yes. Yes." He finally focused on Harry. "I got one too. And a grenade of all things."

Looking down, Harry could see the outline of the explosive device in the teacher's baggy corduroy trousers.

"Good." He grinned, tugging the other man away and climbing over the central barrier. "Just for god's sake don't pull the pin by accident."

Mr. Green let out the bark of a good-humored laugh. "No, that wouldn't do at all, would it? I shall take particular care not to blow us all up on the way home, don't you worry."

Home. Harry wondered at the word as they regrouped with Josh and began the jog back to the bed-and-breakfast at the heart of Forest Gate on Fords Park Road. How the hell had that become home?

CHAPTER ELEVEN

The curtains in the Sweet Dreams Bed and Breakfast lounge were closed, as they had been for days. Shutting the front door quickly behind themselves, Harry and Mr. Green ushered Josh inside before tipping the large desk up onto its side and pushing it back into place against the entrance. At least its heavy wooden top blocked the glass pane in the door. Harry presumed it was reinforced, but it wasn't worth taking any chances.

Peter's pale face peered out from the front room, which had been where breakfast had been served on neat old-fashioned tables complete with lace cloths and napkins, but now served as the small group's living and sleeping space.

"You were gone a long time," he said nervously. "We were getting worried." His clear blue eyes were wide and still fearful as they flicked from Harry to Mr. Green and back again and with his eleven-year-old girlish voice, he seemed very childlike. He didn't look at Josh. Although there was a three-year age gap, Josh and Peter were about the same height, and Peter didn't look up to him in the same way as he did the older boys and the teacher. He should do though, Harry thought. Josh might get scared, but he'd still take risks. Peter could do worse than learn from the young boy.

"I told you to put the desk back against the door while we were out."

"I couldn't do it on my own." He shrugged. "And James wouldn't help me."

"That boy," Mr. Green muttered under his breath as he put the grenade high on the cluttered shelf near the stairs, balancing it between a china milkmaid and a crystal swan. The teacher didn't need to say more. Harry knew exactly what he meant. James was . . . well, James was James.

Wandering into the lounge, Harry was immediately hit by the sweet smoke that lingered in the stale air, hanging visibly in the yellow glow of the overhead light. James grinned from his position on the mattress against the far wall where he'd made a kind of armchair out of pillows and duvets. "Welcome home, brave hunters." Waving with one hand, he chipped the end off the thin joint against the ashtray by his side with the other.

"Are you smoking another marijuana cigarette?" Mr. Green's indignant words came from behind Harry, and although he was equally annoyed with his fellow sixth-former, he couldn't fight the grin that grew on his face. Josh snorted and even Peter snickered behind his hand while looking away. Marijuana cigarette? Who the hell called them that?

James beamed his easy, handsome smile. "I certainly am. But have no fear, sir. It's the last one, more's the pity."

"Good." Mr. Green managed a tight smile of his own before disappearing to boil some water. His dislike of James's easy charm and natural arrogance, which came with being bred into the superelite of landed gentry and politics, had been apparent to most students well before the London history trip, and it was equally apparent to Harry that it wasn't abating. But then James didn't help. He was charming, yes, but equally selfish and lazy and lacking in respect. And that hadn't changed over the past week either.

"You got guns?" One eyebrow raised in James's tanned face.

"We saw some more army," Josh sniffed, his voice dull as he tipped out the rucksack he'd carried back from the small shop. Keeping one comic for himself, he passed another to Peter. "The spiders got them."

"We got two guns and a grenade though. So at least we can defend ourselves better." That was an understatement. So far they'd been relying on kitchen knives, and they all knew that if the spiders were that close then it was all over anyway. Still, the knives were better than nothing.

"Well, let me take a look then." James sat up, his curiosity engaged. "With one of those and my spliff I'll be like Martin Sheen in *Apocalypse Now*." His blond hair sat tousled stylishly on his head with no help from gel or mousse. Harry shook his own untidy and damp mop of lank brown.

"No way. You're stoned."

James shrugged and flopped back against the wall. "Sometime Harry, I think you're as bad as Gayboy Green back there. Although admittedly, he hates me more than you do."

Harry smiled. "You don't exactly do anything to help that situation, do you. I can't believe you bought some puff on a school trip." He sighed wryly. "No wonder the poor old bastard hates you."

"Well, bloody hell, Harry. He was dragging us off to see some god-awful foreign film with bloody subtitles, and the bloke did approach me, not the other way round.

What was a chap with my lack of willpower supposed to do?"

James had bought the weed on the night before the world went mad. Harry could remember thinking how quiet Soho was for early evening. Even at the history lectures they'd been attending during the days most of the rows of the auditorium had been empty. Two of the historians had canceled their talks, and looking back, Harry wondered why more alarm bells hadn't been ringing in his head. Still, St. Mark's was an all-boys school with a virtually all-male staff. They didn't see it coming in the way the rest of the world probably should have. So what if some of the weekly boarders had seemed freaked out by their mums getting fat? That's what women did, wasn't it? Worried about their weight?

The two younger boys already engrossed in their comics, chewing on Jelly Tots and Haribo, Harry and James examined the rest of what they'd quickly grabbed from the corner shop. There was a tub of powdered milk, some bottles of water, vac-packed cheese and cold meats that were still within their use-by dates, crackers, various bars of chocolate and some pasta and stir-in sauces. It was enough to keep them going for a few days at any rate, on top of what was left in the larder at the back.

"You didn't think to grab a good bottle of wine or some cans of beer then?" James scanned the items with a sniff of disdain. "Not even any fags."

"You bloody go and carry it all back then. And let's face it, getting drunk probably isn't the best idea in this situation."

"You think? I'm of the mind that drunk might be a bloody good thing to be."

Harry bit his cheek, refusing to rise to the bait. Half

the problem with James was that you could never be entirely sure when he was being serious or when he was saying something for the simple shock value of it. Plus there was the way he made Harry feel so bloody "straight" like he'd never done his own share of sneaking out of the boardinghouse and running down to the off-license to liven up a midnight feast. It was just that everything had changed. And even James bloody Mildrew must realize that on some level.

"No bread?" Having accepted that there was nothing in the way of light entertainment in their foraged goods, it seemed that James was finally taking a proper look at what they *had* got.

"No, it was all a bit green at the edges. It's too hot and in those plastic bags it's got no chance of lasting."

"That's a shame." James's voice had softened. "Would have maybe been nice to have had some while we still can." He looked up and smiled sadly. "Because unless you're planning on going all Nigella and taking up baking, bread must be off the menu for the foreseeable future."

Harry stayed quiet, a small patter of dismay echoing the rain that brushed against the windows outside. He hadn't even thought about bread. It seemed that every day something more was taken away from them. It wouldn't be long before the utilities stopped working if there was no one to service them, he'd been pretty sure about that straight off, but the smaller, petty, unimportant things like bread and milk and freshly baked cakes had slipped past his mind. Ridiculously, he suddenly wanted a cream-filled doughnut more than anything in the world. Tears threatened the back of his eyes and he bit their burn away. If there were fresh cream-filled doughnuts being made somewhere, then everything was really all okay and this was just a glitch. The idea was stupid. *He* was being stupid. There were no bakers. No ovens. No fresh flipping cream. He was lucky enough just to be alive.

"It's only bread," he muttered. "We can live without it."

"Of course we can." James looked up and in his eyes Harry saw past the flippant humor to the thoughtful young man underneath. Behind the arrogance his irises trembled. James was just as scared as he was. The moment flashed by in a second and then, grinning, James elbowed Harry in the ribs.

"Still," he continued, "at least beer and fags are better preserved. So hurrah for something at least."

By six o'clock they were eating pasta and tomato sauce with a healthy topping of grated cheese from plates balanced on their knees or on the floor. The small square tables that had filled the room were stacked up against the windows, some of the chairs balanced on top so that all the glass was covered. The rest of the chairs had been used to make a clumsy barricade at the top of the first flight of stairs once they'd dragged the bedding down. They wouldn't hold anything back for too long, but in theory would give them enough warning to get out through the back door. If nothing else it gave them a small sense of security whether it was justified or otherwise. Swallowing a large forkful of food, Harry glanced down at the gun at his side. At least they were armed now, and that gave them more security than a wall of tables ever could.

On the other side of the room Josh slurped a long string of spaghetti into his mouth, splattering red sauce all over his cheek. He wiped it away with the back of his hand. "This is good, Mr. Green."

The teacher smiled. "Glad you like it. Eat it all up and you can have some chocolate."

Next to Josh, Peter had spent a lot of time dissecting the long strands of pasta into one-inch pieces, but very little time eating them, instead forming small piles and mounds around his plate. Eventually, he lifted his fork and took a tiny bite of what it carried, chewing it listlessly. Harry sipped his sweet tea and watched the boy. He knew what was coming.

Focusing on a small corner of the wall, as if intent on not meeting anyone's gaze, Peter's shoulders slumped as he swallowed. James lit the last half of his joint and sucked in the sweet smoke. Mr. Green glared at him, but said nothing, and Harry was glad. They didn't need the row.

"Do you think our families are all right?" Peter's small voice cut through the quiet. Harry didn't answer and neither did Josh or Mr. Green, who were both concentrating on finishing their food. Their forks didn't even pause. Not that Harry was surprised. What was there to say? Peter asked the question at least once a day and the platitudes had got weaker as every day passed and were now so watery thin that even a toddler would see through them.

Beside him, James exhaled a long cloud of smoke, his eyes following it as it drifted to the windows, weaving its way through the mesh of wood and clinging to the curtains.

"No, Peter," he said finally. "I really don't think they are."

The small boy's face remained impassive, and the

group sat for a long moment of silence, even Josh pausing with the frankness of James's answer. Harry waited for Mr. Green to snap but no reprimand came.

"I didn't think so." Peter's voice was flat. He stared at the curtains and then picked up his fork, pushing food onto it with his finger. "I just wanted someone to say it. That's all."

Harry stared at James. The other boy raised an eyebrow. "Cruel to be kind, Harry. Always the best thing in the end."

On the other side of the room Peter swallowed the forkful and reloaded it. Within ten minutes his plate was clean, but he'd shown none of the enjoyment in his food that Josh had, as if he was merely refueling rather than eating. It disturbed Harry in a way he couldn't describe. The boy should be crying. Shit, they all should be crying.

"What about the others?" Peter looked directly at James when he asked his new question, as if the decadent sixth-former was the only one he could trust for an honest answer. "Do you think they made it back to school okay?"

The end of James's joint burned brightly as he sucked in a lungful, and for the first time Harry almost asked him for a toke, even though he'd never been into getting high. On both the occasions he'd plucked up the nerve to try the stuff, it had made him feel dizzy and sick, but that would be preferable to this. He didn't want to be having this conversation. He didn't want to think about the rest of the group. They were gone.

James leaned forward, examining Peter's earnest face. As night drew in outside, the bulb above them seemed to glow brighter, highlighting the sharp angles of James's cheekbones and perfectly balanced face.

Looking at that face made Harry feel strange. He was envious of James, that much was for sure. But that wasn't all that made him feel so uncomfortable around him. There was something else. Otherwise how else did he end up staying when the rest left? He'd wanted to go with them, but somehow found himself shaking his head when James said he'd wait it out and see what the police did. His face burned a little and he hid it behind his mug.

"I don't know the answer to that, Peter." James tilted his head, deep in thought. "Maybe they were right to go. That first day, well, we all know that was the quietest. That was probably the best day for leaving the city." He spoke slowly, and listening to the clipped lilt Harry didn't know if it was for the boy's benefit or a by-product of the potent smoke. Josh had put his fork down and was listening, and even Mr. Green watched to see what would be said next.

"On the other hand, although they might have got out of London on the first day, it would have taken them longer than that to get all the way back to St. Mark's. Surrey's a long way away. Even if they'd managed to get in a car or something, only Archer knows how to drive, so that would depend on him surviving the journey out of town."

James paused for a moment. Harry didn't like to think about Archer. He was the head boy, the year above both Harry and James, and he'd been the prefect companion on the trip, second only to Mr. Green. In the eyes of the boys though, he was well above. They all respected Archer far more than any teacher. Archer was just . . . Harry couldn't find the right words to describe him. Archer was just Archer. A god within the school and had been long before he'd reached his final year.

Archer was tall and handsome and witty, and succeeded at everything he did. Even James, with his devil-may-care attitude, looked at Archer with an element of awe. He was untouchable. Immortal.

The head boy hadn't looked so immortal when he'd left though, taking the other four boys with him, insisting that the best plan would be to get out of London and get back to St. Mark's. In hindsight, Harry wondered if maybe on a subconscious level that was part of the reason he stayed behind. Archer, with his bitten leg bandaged with torn-up sheets, hadn't looked too healthy.

"Ultimately, Peter," James continued, "there's no point in wondering about it. I like to think they got back to school, and maybe one day we'll find out. But until then, we need to concentrate on us." He paused. "They're gone. That's all I know for a fact."

Mr. Green unwound his long, thin legs and stood up, pulling back a tiny section of curtain. "It's getting dark. We should probably turn the light out soon."

Dread tinged his words turning them into little more than a whisper. Josh was on his feet and flicking the switch within seconds, his eyes wide pools of white in the sudden gloom.

"Bedtime it is, then." James crushed the butt of his joint into the saucer he'd used as an ashtray and sank down onto the mattress.

"Harry." Peter's small voice sought him out through the stale air. "Harry. Will you come with me and wait outside?"

"Sure. Come on."

He led the boy out into the hallway and down the corridor to the downstairs toilet. Farther into the house the darkness was thicker, clinging with the damp warm air to the wallpaper, fingers of dusk reaching into corners and claiming them for shadow. The floorboards beneath the thin carpet creaked as their two pairs of feet shuffled past the staircase whose railings seemed to grin at them, mocking their fear. Harry saw Peter's eyes dart fearfully upward.

"Don't worry. There's nothing up there. Not anymore." That wasn't strictly true, but Harry didn't like to think about the two dead bodies they'd left locked in the flat at the very top of the house. He opened the door to the small downstairs toilet. In a mug by the washbasin sat their toothbrushes and a well-squeezed tube of Colgate.

"Don't turn the light on until the door is shut, okay?"

The small boy nodded. "You won't go back without me?" His face was fearful.

"No, I'll be here. Now get on with it. And don't forget to brush."

The door closed, separating them, and a thin strip of yellow light bled under the gap. From the room at the front of the house, Harry could make out the sounds of chocolate wrappers ripping open, but no conversation. It seemed that once night started falling none of them felt the urge to talk anymore. Inside the small room behind him, liquid splashed in a noisy stream into the toilet bowl and Harry felt his own bladder squeeze. Despite himself, he glanced nervously up at the yawning stairwell.

He hadn't been up those stairs since day two, caught up in the midst of all the frantic activity of dragging down their stuff and building the barricades. He hadn't been right to the top of the building since day one, not since they'd all woken up to the awful sound of shrieking coming from the owners' flat. Since they'd arrived, three nights earlier, the only person they'd seen was Mr. Simpson, a tired, thin man with hollow rings around his eyes. His wife was ill, that's what he'd said. But on the third morning, it was he who was screaming, not she.

Archer broke in; Mr. Green, James and Will Harris alongside him. It was they who found the thing clutching Mr. Simpson's limp body, sucking at him, eating him while he was still alive. He wasn't alive for long. While the rest of them huddled in the doorway, Archer attacked, stabbing the monster over and over with a carving knife until it was dead. Simpson died moments after. No one had said anything for a long while, Archer's leg bleeding from where the spider had bitten him until it formed a pool on the sodden carpet. It was James who found the woman's wrecked body in the bedroom when he went to find something to bandage Archer up with.

Eventually, when they'd realized the phones weren't working, just like the TV and radio, and that something very, very bad had happened to the world in the night, they'd closed the broken door behind them, and left it.

Staring up, Harry swallowed. He didn't like to think about what was up there. The bodies would be rotting by now, bloating in this muggy air. Soon the smell would creep down to them, its greasy texture sliding easily through their pathetic defenses and they would no longer be able to pretend that everything upstairs didn't really exist. The toilet flushed and he jumped slightly, his skin and flesh separating momentarily, before pulling back together.

He lowered his eyes. It didn't really matter. It would only force the inevitable. Even though none of them had come out and said it yet, they all knew they couldn't stay here forever. At some point, they were going to have to make a break out of the city for themselves. The thought made his stomach turn slightly. Whether it was truly safe or not, the bed-and-breakfast had become their sanctuary over the past week. Maybe Mr. Green had been right. Maybe it had become home.

Sleep came in fits and starts as it did most nights. It seemed to Harry that he slept like a dog, one eye almost open, his ears seeking out any sound that might be a threat. London had become full of noise at night, and those when it rained were the worst.

Lying on his mattress, the glow of his watch declaring it was ten o'clock, he knew he wasn't the only one awake, despite how alone he felt. On the other side of the room, duvets rustled and noses sniffed, and over to his right, James sighed. He tried closing his eyes again, willing himself to sleep. It was hard though. Somewhere in the distance, a few empty streets away, a wailing started up, low and mournful for a while and then rising in pain and fear. It didn't last longer than a few minutes, cut off suddenly in midflow. It was rare that any human noise like that went on for long. Harry wondered why anyone would draw attention to themselves like that, especially at night, when the things were hunting.

Silence buzzed in his head and then came the sound he dreaded: a soft tapping at the glass, gentle at first and then heavier, as whatever was on the other side sought out footholds to climb the side of the terraced house. It moved slowly. Harry's ears focused on its every tread, before another set joined it, scuttling up the far wall in fast-paced thuds. His heart pounded and in the sudden stillness of the room an irrational fear gripped him that the things outside would hear the rhythm belting from inside his chest.

No one moved and Harry knew that like him the others would be staring upward, mouths drying and yet unable to swallow, not wanting to make the slightest noise that might alert the creatures to their presence. More short-lived wails filled the night and outside a bin tumbled to its side, the metal clanging loudly in the street. A pack was prowling out there, Harry could feel it. This time was always the worst. When the night was still young.

The house stayed quiet though, despite the creatures that had scrambled up its side. No glass shattered. No barricades came tumbling down. Finally, as the darkness settled outside Harry's eyes sank shut, his mind drifting. Around the room, the group's breathing became more even. As sleep claimed him too, Harry idly thought they were like rabbits in a warren, sleeping nervously as the foxes roamed seeking out easy prey. It didn't bring him comfort.

It was past two when he woke, his skin shivering and slick with sweat, the taste of a panicked dream still in his mouth.

"Why not me?" The disembodied voice rang hollow, the words followed by a sorry laugh as they cut invisibly through the window glass and hung in the middle of the room, taunting the boys who slowly sat up, staring at one another's dark outlines in the gloom.

"What the . . . ?" James kicked off his covers as if convinced he was still in a dream, and Harry grabbed his arm.

"Shhh!"

"Is that a—?" Josh's whispered question was cut off by another outburst from the street.

"Why the fuck not me? Can you tell me that?"

"It's a woman." Peter's voice was low.

The laughter from outside slurred and drifted, and then a bottle smashed.

"Everyone but me."

The voice was quieter but closer and Harry crawled over to the window, lifting a tiny edge.

"Don't let them see us. Don't let them . . ." Peter pulled his knees and covers under his chin as he whispered frantically, until Josh huddled in close, wrapping an arm around the younger boy's shoulder to calm him.

Body heat brushed Harry's back as James peered out through the small crack behind him.

"What's going on out there?"

Harry ignored Mr. Green's question and stared. Outside, the street lamps were still working, throwing down pools of light onto the cars and dark tarmac. The woman was walking up the center of the road, using the broken white line as if it were a balancing beam, her arms spread wide, one foot carefully placing itself in front of the other in that way that children do. A little farther back, shards of glass glittered like emerald stars against the midnight of the road. The neck of the wine bottle had rolled farther, separated from the rest.

Drunk, of course. She had to be. Why else would she be out wandering the streets in the middle of the night? It was crazy. Maybe she was crazy. Almost directly outside the house the woman paused, and Harry couldn't help but stare, drinking her in. They hadn't seen a woman in almost a week, not so very long a time, but enough to make Harry silently think that perhaps they would never see another again. Her long hair tumbled thick and free in auburn waves around her shoulders, heavy coils falling over her face as her head lolled forward, and with her arms still outstretched she spun around and around in untidy circles, her laugh hiccuping as her feet stumbled on their circular path.

"What's she doing?" James's whisper was harsh in his ear. "What's she doing out there? Why doesn't she get inside?"

Finally, the spinning stopped and she tilted her head back, letting the rain splash her face and neck. She wasn't young or slim or pretty. Even from the distance Harry could see the lines carved into her neck where the skin was no longer firm. She was blandly ordinary and reaching out for middle age; maybe in her thirties, perhaps even older. The kind of woman his own mother would call "attractive when she smiled," which Harry had long ago figured out she said when she didn't want to use the word "ugly." Kids were more honest. The woman out on the street wasn't ugly, but there was a nothingness about the way she looked as if life had long ago beaten out of her whatever glow she might have once had. Her hair was dramatic though, and watching it fall down her back Harry felt the urge to bury his head in its thickness and smell its life and femininity, despite its owner's age and dulled looks. He stiffened slightly in his jeans, the reaction involuntary.

"Should we get her inside?" James whispered again.

"No."

"We have to," Mr. Green hissed. "The poor woman . . ."

"She's making too much noise." Harry's breath made shapes on the window. "Let's wait. See what happens. We can look for her in the morning if it comes to it."

"She'll be gone by morning," James cut in, softly. "One way or another."

Her laugh had turned to sobs and as her shoulders slumped, she covered her face with her hands. It was eerie hearing her plaintive hitching of breath, out there in the dead street. Harry felt like a voyeur watching her; the curtain making a twisted peepshow out of her distress.

"I wish she'd go away." Josh sniffed. "I wish she'd just shut up and go away."

Watching her, Harry wished it too. For her own sake, if not for theirs. What was she doing? She must know. Surely she must know that it wasn't safe. Out in the street, her sobbing stopped suddenly and her head rose, a sound at the other end of the road catching her attention.

"Oh god." James's words were dry in his ear.

The next few minutes seemed to last forever, like a car crash with every detail unfolding vividly in slow motion and yet the brain still can't seem to find the will to react, left only to observe with mild surprise as the panels crumple and glass shatters.

Harry watched the woman's expression change with horrified fascination. Her shoulders shook with a couple of last sobs and then she wiped her eyes. Looking up, she sighed and then froze. Her brow furrowed, confused. She stared straight ahead and Harry could almost see her self-pity evaporate into the hot night air as she realized what she was looking at.

"What?" Mr. Green was on his feet. "What is it?"

"What do you think it is? For god's sake keep Josh and Peter quiet."

"Are they coming? Are they out there?"

Harry listened to the words that flew urgently

around him as if they belonged in a different world. He was locked in with the woman outside. He knew he should shut the curtain, get back into bed and tug the covers over his head until it was done, but he couldn't move. His knees ached on the hard floor, but he ignored them.

In the street the woman took two careful steps backward, no childish arm-waving this time. Her mouth fell open. In the corner of his eye, just edging past the tatty paintwork of the windowsill, Harry saw two white spindly legs creep forward. Even through the glass he could hear its inhuman hiss, the emerging pale body trembling slightly as the sound snarled from every surface. It raised itself elegantly up on its rear legs, its front limbs making jerky circles in the air, and it was only when the woman saw the revolting suckers of its underbelly that the true nature of her situation seemed to sink in.

Harry had never seen drunkenness slide away from someone before as easily if it were a discarded coat, but as adrenaline flooded her system, he watched a clear, sober light dawn in her eyes. She glanced from side to side as if she had no idea how she'd come to be out here, how she'd come to do something *so stupid*. Her feet stumbled backward with more urgency, her hands rising up in a poor imitation of the creature's legs as if her flabby flesh could somehow ward it off. Her lips moved as she muttered something under her breath, but Harry couldn't make out the words, even though some part of him felt that it was important they were heard, that someone at least would remember them.

The hardness that had been growing in his jeans retracted, disappearing into itself as a chill gripped the pit of his gut. The mutated thing in the street dropped

back down and took a few teasing steps forward, playing with the woman. Harry had seen enough over the
past few days to know that it could easily leap on her
from where it currently stood, the distance between
them barely a matter of ten feet. The woman and the
spider were so fixated on each other, that neither noticed what Harry could see so clearly.

A shudder ran through him and the back of his neck
itched. On the front of the house opposite, translucent
skin shone in the dark night as the thing emerged from
the gloom of the roof tiles, hanging over the gutter for
a moment before scuttling halfway down the front of
the building, its revolting slick surfaces glistening in
the reflected glow of the streetlight. Its myriad red eyes
burned, each tiny beam of light a shard of hungry anger. Harry's throat dried, watching it creep farther
down until it curled itself around the front window lin-
tel and waited silently for the right moment.

In the middle of the tarmac, still on the white line,
but Harry imagined wishing she was anywhere else but,
the woman shook her head. "No . . . No . . . No . . ."

Gripped by fear, her words were clear enough as the
spider in front of her advanced and Harry could make
out the rise and fall of her chest as she sucked in deep
lungfuls of panicking breaths. His eyes burned to
squeeze themselves shut but somehow his eyelids refused to comply. He thought of the gun lying next to
his mattress and the grenade out in the hallway. Maybe
if they went out now they might have a chance of saving
her. The idea faded as soon as it had come, the attack on
the army truck too clear in his memory. He wouldn't go
outside. He couldn't. Not for a stranger. Even if they
killed those two, there would be others. It was the

woman's own stupid fault that she was in this position. He couldn't let it be their deaths also.

His heart raced, bile rising up in hot, acid waves from his stomach. He just wished they'd do it. Get it over with. Get it . . .

The creature on the wall of the house sprang forward, on the woman in one easy bound, knocking any scream out of her on impact, her eyes and mouth both widening with shock and complete surprise. As it wrapped itself around her body, Harry watched that long auburn hair fling itself from side to side, only that and her booted feet visible.

The other spider hissed angrily but it was too late. The hunter and its trapped prey disappeared swiftly into the night, the woman finally finding her lungs and letting out a brief wail that echoed back through the street as if it could pull her back to safety on the road.

Finally, Harry let the curtain drop, the dull gloom of the room leaving black shadow residues at the back of his eyes, the shape of the woman and the spider lingering there until his sight adjusted. His breath came hard and rapid, and pushing James out of the way, he scurried onto his mattress and pulled the covers right under his chin, curling up in a ball.

It was only when his trembling eased twenty minutes later that he finally spoke.

"We have to get out of the city. We have to."

His words were quiet but sank with their own weight. No one answered. But then, he figured, as he straightened out and stared at the ceiling, trying to pretend that the woman in the street had just been part of some awful dream, no one had disagreed either.

CHAPTER TWELVE

"You know," Courtney said, his nose wrinkling, "at some point we're going to have to get out." He looked around at the other boys. "And not just out of this block. Out of the whole fucking city."

For a moment the small group loitered in the hallway. "It's okay," Leke said, pushing the door closed behind them. "The bodies are in the bedroom. The rest of the place is fine."

Courtney led the way into the small lounge where he dumped the rucksack on the floor. It held the few things they needed: personal toothbrushes, underwear and deodorant. Most of everything else they managed to scavenge from each new place they chose as their home for the night. Their original plan had been to try and get a couple of guns and then leave, but as things turned out, it was always too easy to stay put. Too many changes were taking place out there, and at least the tower was clear of the awful spider things like the one that had come out of Nathan's mum.

He looked around him. The lounge was clean but cheaply decorated. The old and tatty sofa had no armchair, just two wooden-backseats along the window wall next to a small folding table. Courtney sat on the sofa and felt the hard springs dig into his thighs through the thin velour cushion. He didn't like to think about those things that had come out of the women. Maybe that was why he was reluctant to leave the block. He didn't like to think that maybe, halfway around the world somewhere in the country whose mention always made his own mother smile softly, one of those things had slithered out of her warm body. Maybe in Jamaica everyone was safe. Perhaps they were just waiting it out there until the phones and the TV started working again and everything would go back to normal. As each day passed though, that thought became thinner, its substance a ghostly shadow in a corner of his mind. He still tried to cling to it though, wispy as his belief in it was becoming.

Nathan grabbed one of the wooden chairs and took it out into the corridor to wedge against the front door and hold it shut. Blane's men had done a good job of kicking in the doors of all the flats, either with sheer brute force or by shooting the locks off, but it now meant that none of the homes the boys stole each night was secure. Still, they did their best, and even if they left the doors wide-open, they'd be unlucky to get caught.

"Shit, man, that bedroom is rank." Craig's face was pale as he joined the others in the lounge. "I've shut the door and shoved a towel along the bottom of it. Can't we open a window or something?"

"The smell's not that bad." Courtney could hear the almost lie in his words. The stink might not have been unbearable but it was pretty grim, a heady sweetness that filled the air and left a bitter aftertaste in the back of his throat. If he thought about it too much, it would make him gag. "If we open a window someone might see and come looking."

"How many?" Leke asked.

"Just the woman and the thing. Blane's men shot its legs off. Looks even freakier."

Nathan sat on the remaining hard chair. "What are we going to have to eat?" He glanced at his watch three times in quick succession and then pushed his glasses up on his face. "We were late having lunch." His words came out fast and staccato. "Lunch is at one and we didn't have it until quarter to two, and tea should be at half past five but it's nearly six." He gulped. "So when are we going to eat?"

Sighing, Courtney looked over at Leke, who shrugged and then went to rummage in the small kitchen's cupboards.

"Tea isn't until after six these days, Nathan. That's when we eat. Blane's men don't leave the tower till about quarter past normally, you know that. We can't risk cooking anything until it's just the men left guarding the entrances. They might come looking."

Nathan nodded, the movement sharp and quick, but Courtney wasn't sure he really got it. But then, he wasn't really sure the way Nathan's mind worked was ever going to be clear to him. The geeky boy was cleverer than he'd ever given him credit for. That much had become clear over the past few days. Nathan was filled with facts and figures and random pieces of information, some of which had the other boys clutching their sides with laughter or staring blankly at him as he delivered them with his deadpan monotone voice.

Yeah, Courtney decided, watching the white boy Nathan was strange. But he wished maybe that they'd been nicer to him at school, or at least not treated him like he was invisible. It made him feel a bit bad inside. This moving every day was taking its toll on Nathan probably more than all of them. The one thing Courtney *had* figured out about the other boy was that he felt happiest when there was order in his life. Well, there wasn't much order happening at the moment.

He got up, went over to the windows and peered out. So far, they'd picked flats on this side of the tower that looked down into the courtyard and over to the rest of the estate, the second tower opposite and the smaller three-story blocks farther on. At least they could keep an eye on what was going on outside that way. And it wasn't as if they didn't have plenty to choose from. There were nineteen floors in the tower, and even without going near the top two, which was where Blane and Charlie had their flats, or down to the bottom two floors, there were still twelve floors, each with eight flats on each.

And that was part of the problem. The tower block was safe and the longer they stayed the harder it was to make the decision to leave. Not only would they have to get past Blane's men, they'd then have to survive out there in the city where no one was making the streets safe as far as he could tell. The nights were filled with the echoes of screams traveling through the city carried on the hot, wet breeze, and occasionally rapid shots would ring out closer to home, from either the bottom of the tower or somewhere farther away. It was strange that although they hid from Blane and he scared each of them almost as much as he terrified Leke, in the middle of the night it was his actions that made them feel safe. Weird.

Inside the block at least there was food and shelter. For a while, at any rate.

"I need to take a dump." Craig stood in the doorway, and Courtney stared at him.

"Why didn't you go in the other flat before we left?" Somewhere at the back of his mind, Courtney was vaguely aware that he sounded like his own mum and it annoyed him. "You know we can't flush." The toilets still worked but if they pulled the chain, the noise ran through the pipes of the building. They couldn't risk drawing any attention to themselves. So instead, they had become like rats or other vermin; moving from home to home, scavenging food and leaving their waste behind.

"I'll sneak across the way and go."

Courtney shook his head. "Wait till they've all settled for the night. You're going to have to hold it."

"Shit, Courtney! I'm only talking about going across the corridor."

"We don't split up. We made these rules, Craig. Let's at least try to fucking stick to them." The "never split up" rule had been Nathan's and as well as him being so adamant about it they had no choice but to adopt it; it made sense. They'd all seen those horror films where the kids get separated and then picked off one by one. That wasn't going to happen to them.

Craig scowled but didn't speak. Courtney turned his attention back to peering out through the small gap in the curtain. Down below, he could see Charlie Nash talking closely to a thickset bald-headed man. Even from the eighth floor, Courtney could see the lines of the dark tattoo that covered the back of his neck and part of his smooth skull. Both men carried guns over their shoulders, and Courtney was pretty sure they'd have handguns tucked into their trouser belts too. Even though it was warm, they both wore jackets and grimaced in the constant, steady rhythm of the hot rain.

It had been quiet around the block all day, and although the air had been filled with sharp bursts of gun-fire, it had been coming from the new flash apartment block, only a few hundred feet but a whole social class or three from the estate. Maybe Blane Gentle-King had got bored of his roots and was looking to move up in the world. Courtney didn't blame him. London was his oyster now; why would he stay in some shitty coun-cil estate?

The air had been cut with the sound of more gunfire too, but quieter and from farther inside the city. The boys listened to the ghost of that for a long time. Maybe there was hope in it.

"Anything going on down there?" Leke's question was laced with a hint of dread, and Courtney didn't blame him. On that first day, when they heard the gun-shots coming from the lower levels, they'd run panting to the roof and hidden in the small, unused generator room that stank of oil and old rags even though it was likely no one had even been in there for years. They'd waited there for hours, sweating as the gunfire and shouts vibrated up through the fabric of the building. Creatures had hissed outside the door, feet tapping against the metal that the boys were pressed against on the other side, before deciding that there were easier meals to have and disappearing down the side of the concrete walls. No human footsteps came up that far.

When they'd finally crept down the stairs in the night, the block was silent. They'd watched from the stairwell for a long time before Craig and Courtney darted inside Mrs. Minster's to grab their stuff. It was Craig who noticed that Leke's jacket was missing and it didn't take any of them long to figure out why it had been taken and to whom. They'd been more careful af-ter that and luckily it seemed that although maybe

Blane was keen to find the boys, the men he sent to do it were less so; their searches were cursory and now that the tower was so quiet, their heavy footsteps betrayed them early. Hence they'd come up with the rule about not using the flats on the bottom two floors. If they used those flats, then they wouldn't have time to get out and scarper up the stairs to play cat and mouse with Blane's crew.

It was a simple game. The men would search one corridor, while the boys ran along the one above, coming back down as the men went up. Courtney smiled just thinking about it. It was scary but it was also fun. And fun was something they didn't seem to have much of these days. His feet itched to get away from their self-imposed prison in the tower, despite the fear that gripped his stomach when he actually thought about being out in the world alone. How much worse could it be than sitting on their arses all day, going through other people's stuff and watching DVDs with the sound so far down they may as well not bother?

"No, nothing," he finally said quietly. "Just Charlie chatting to some bloke."

"Shit, I need a shit," Craig moaned, flopping into the sofa.

"Shit, you need a shit?" Leke snorted. "That's funny, man."

"Yeah, fucking ha-ha. Maybe I'll shit on you."

Courtney felt his irritation with the others rising in a hot flush in his cheeks, and clenching his teeth, he turned away from the window to face them. It wasn't just him. The tension between each of them and the others was rising. They'd spent a week trapped with one another, stuck inside with very little to do apart from stare at four walls and try to ignore the bodies. Even the thrill of rummaging through people's houses was wearing thin, and they were all starting to wind each other up big-time.

"What was there to eat?"

Leke grinned. "A whole cupboard full of Pot fucking Noodle and chocolate digestives." His eyes twinkled at Courtney. "You and this old woman must have been related or something."

Craig bounded into the kitchen and then came back laughing. "He's not joking. That's all she's got. Every fucking flavor. Chicken and mushroom, chow mein, beef. And biscuits and tea bags." He shook his head. "I always thought that the people that lived in this block were freaks, but now I fucking know it." He glanced up at Courtney. "No offense, man, but you've got to admit . . ." He shrugged to end the sentence and Courtney grinned.

"I can't argue, dude." He couldn't. Craig had a point. They'd found some weird stuff in the flats; old men with gay porn, one house had no food but shelves of classic literature with tiny scribbled notes in all the margins, caviar and food from Fortnum and Mason filling the cupboards of one flat that didn't even have a carpet and where the owner was using cardboard boxes for furniture. People were strange, that much was for sure.

Courtney wondered what Blane was making of the survivors. They'd watched from the roof as the straggly band of men had gathered in the courtyard while Charlie and his people had shot the shit out of the spiders in the opposite block before moving the men in. None of them argued. They looked like they were just shocked and happy to be alive.

Some nights Courtney would peer across at the

lights blazing from flats up and down that block and he'd think that if they didn't have Leke with them they could be over there, safe in numbers, not afraid to flush the toilet or play a computer game and with other people to talk to. People with guns. Sometimes thinking about it made his heart ache with wishing, but there was no way they could leave Leke. Leke was like his brother. And his mum would kill him if she ever knew he'd even thought about abandoning him. Leke was a *good* boy, that's what Courtney's mum would say. And she'd be right. He was. Still, sometimes, late at night, Courtney wished Leke had just kept his mouth shut about what he saw that afternoon all those months ago.

"At least she didn't have a cat."

Nathan's comment cut through Courtney's thoughts.

"Why would she have a cat in her cupboards, man?" Craig winked at Leke as he answered the autistic boy. "That would be weirder than fucking hundreds of packets of Pot Noodle."

"You know what he means, man." Leke rolled his eyes. "Don't wind him up. It's not fair."

"I don't like it when they have pets," Nathan continued, oblivious to the other boys' exchange. "They make me sad."

There was a long pause. The animal thing was weird too. In some of the flats they'd come across dead cats. Nothing obviously wrong with them apart from they were dead, most of them looking as if they'd gone suddenly. The one slumped in its food bowl was the freakiest. They didn't stay in that flat. For some reason they'd found it more disturbing than the ripped-up woman and the thing both dead in the hallway. There'd been a couple of dead dogs in the block too, but mainly cats.

"They're not all dead though, mate." Leke smiled

softly at Nathan and the kindness in it made Courtney feel bad for thinking of him as a problem. "Remember that one we saw on the stairs? He was alive."

Nathan nodded. "Tabby."

"That's right. And I heard something at the bins last night. Not something big either." No one needed him to clarify what he meant by that. "So I figure there's still plenty of cats out there in the world. Don't you worry."

Nathan's hand hesitated on the way up to adjust his glasses then dropped. "Is it time for tea now? We're late."

Leke grinned. "I think we can risk boiling some water." He clapped his hands. "And it's my turn to cook. Wicked. Kettle on, cooking done."

"We should shove some of those Pot Noodles in the bag. Just in case we have to run." Craig looked over at Courtney. "They're not heavy and they're easy food."

Courtney nodded, but wished they wouldn't all look at him for the answers. He didn't have any. He was a middle-of-the-ground kid. Craig was tougher than he, Leke kinder and Nathan—well, in some ways, Nathan was cleverer than he. The others might not see it, but Courtney did. Nathan knew stuff; maybe not street stuff, and maybe he didn't understand the way people worked on the inside, but he was full of facts and figures and bits of information that Courtney figured his own brain would never be able to hold. There were things inside Nathan that would be useful, Courtney was pretty sure about that. He listened to Leke whistling from the kitchen as the kettle boiled, and watched Craig squirming on the sofa. At least with Nathan, he couldn't predict what he was going to say next.

"God, I need a shit."

Staring at Craig, Courtney repeated his earlier words silently inside his own head. They needed to get out. Not least because if they didn't it wouldn't be the "Whites," as they'd heard Blane's men call the spidery things, that they had to worry about killing them. It would be one another.

At one in the morning he was still awake. Despite the strange noises that haunted the city, there was something he liked about the night. It was his *own* time, and although it brought with it dark shadows in the pit of his soul—black moments of harsh reality followed by waves of grief for his family that he fought to stem before the flow really got started—it also freed him from the company of the others, who snored, rolled on their makeshift beds, and if they weren't sleeping, at least made a good pretense of it. Maybe they needed their own time too.

At first it was the strange quiet that had kept him awake. The city always roared at night, a constant throb of engines and car horns and people out in the street. Londoners lived to the rhythm of a steady throb of traffic like a beating heart, day and night. But all that had changed over the past week. The car engines were as dead as most of their owners and the noises that echoed along the abandoned streets were either filled with terror or so unnatural that the squeals and hisses made his skin crawl.

If he did sleep then the gunshots woke him. The others made earplugs out of toilet paper, but Courtney didn't bother. Nathan neither. For Courtney, it was about needing to hear any danger. No matter how much Craig swore they were safe at night and that Blane and Charlie might go up and down to the top floor but they

used the outside stairs, not the inside because of the
smell, Courtney needed to keep his hearing clear. He
figured Nathan just didn't like anything papery in his
ears. Especially toilet paper. Maybe he was beginning
to understand Nathan a little bit after all.

The air in the flat was heavy with hot damp, the
steady rain outside creeping in from the stairwells and
broken windows, and it seemed to Courtney as he quietly uncurled in the armchair, that instead of freshen-
ing the air in the block it just added to the staleness,
weighing down the growing scent of rot and forcing it
into the fabric of everything around him. He didn't like
the new damp heat. It felt strange on his skin. His legs
shaking away the first tingles of pins and needles that
had crept into his muscles, he straightened up.

Craig had made himself a bed in the hallway by the
front door, and Leke and Nathan were in the sparsely
furnished second bedroom, top and tail in the cheap
single bed. They took it in turns with the bed, unless
they were lucky enough to be in a flat with no bodies.
The rule was that if they went inside and there were no
bodies in the kitchen, lounge or bathroom, then they
stayed. Sometimes that meant that no one got a bed,
but it also meant that they didn't draw attention to
themselves by looking for a really good flat every day.
Plus, in a weird way, it made it more interesting. Nathan kept a list of where they'd been. So far, it was pretty
short. Courtney hoped they'd be out of here before it
got much longer.

A pipe creaked in the walls and Courtney's ears
pricked up, his feet freezing on the thin carpet. Someone was in the block. A distant groan of metal teased his
senses. Was that an echo of flushing water? He strained
for more, but the sounds were coming from too far

away. It didn't stop his eyes peering fearfully upward though. There was only one group of people who would come into the block at night and that was Blane's men. Courtney had heard them before, both during the day and while it was dark, laughing and joking their way up to the top floors, but it didn't make much sense to him. From what he'd seen from the windows it definitely seemed like Blane was moving over to the large apartment block that stood sparkling and new between the estate and Newham and the glamour of Canary Wharf. So what kept him coming back to the flats on the top floors of the block?

Creeping slowly, as if the soft tread of his bare feet would somehow tremor up ten levels of concrete and turn into a deafening alarm signaling his whereabouts by the time it reached Blane, he crossed the few feet to the windows, and peered out through the edge of the curtain. The courtyard was still and silent below, the soft glow of a burning cigarette end all that immediately betrayed a man's presence. The figure leaned against the low wall of the courtyard. He smoked steadily, his hand barely falling to his side between drags. Courtney pressed his nose into the glass.

A stream of moonlight broke through the gray cloud that spat a constant spray of water to the ground, and tangled itself up in the man's blond hair. Charlie. It was Charlie Nash. What was he doing outside alone at this time in the morning? Blane's crew used to party all night and roam the streets of London dealing their business until the early hours, but even they didn't venture out much after dark now. They weren't the most dangerous things out there anymore and it seemed they had a healthy respect for that.

"Jesus fucking Christ, Blane." Charlie's quiet words

drifted up through the silent night, and although muffled by the closed window, Courtney could still hear them. His eyes strained, one hand against the glass he leaned into, its surface moist with his palm's warm sweat and the damp that crept in with the dark. A figure emerged from the gloomy entrance to the right-hand stairwell and Courtney quickly moved to the other end of the window to see better.

His breath caught in his chest and despite the constant unpleasant warmth wrapped around him, goose bumps prickled over his skin. Down below, dressed in his full-length leather coat, Blane laughed. It was a throaty, dangerous sound that owned the night. It wasn't Blane who chilled Courtney though. It was the thing that was beside him. The creature scuttled beside the tall, dreadlocked man, its movements inelegant and jerky, its mottled skin gleaming in patches on its bulbous body.

Courtney stared, his spit drying in his mouth. It was different from the others they'd seen dead in the flats. This one was smaller, its body more squat to the ground and it had that strange unhealthy coloring. His skin started to itch. Below, the thing let out a sharp squeal before darting a few steps toward Charlie. Courtney flinched, his eyes squeezing shut as if that would drown out Charlie's inevitable scream. But no such sound broke the night.

His heart thumped as he peered out again, his breath forming brief clouds against the glass. Charlie had retreated slightly, but the creature stayed by Blane, its front legs scratching angrily at the ground, the horrific body twitching.

"Fucking Squealers."

"Be nice, Charlie. That's no way to talk to Janine."

Blane turned. "Or her friends." His arm rose, pointing upward. "Aren't they all good bitches?"

Charlie's head rose following Blane's dark gaze, and for an awful moment Courtney was sure they were staring right at him. He couldn't move. This was it. They were going to come upstairs and kill them all for helping Leke. It was over. He stared back at the men and swallowed hard. If they were coming for him then he wasn't going to show his fear. Not yet, anyway.

Suddenly something thumped heavily against the glass, a mass of awful suckers and legs pressing against it as if lunging for his face and Courtney stumbled backward, yelping. His stomach rushed to his throat as his hands rose, waving in front of him as if he could somehow ward off the creature. Its feet scraped against the glass, and then it was gone, scrabbling down the front of the building, only a thick smear of mucus on the window left behind.

Panting heavily, Courtney forced his legs forward. What the fuck? What the fuck was going on? He bit back the revulsion that shivered across his skin and looked back out of the window. His heart hammered against his chest and his bladder tightened. He needed to see.

His mouth dropped open. Down below, Charlie Nash's expression was a mirror of his own. Blane's laughter rippled quietly across the courtyard as the four creatures gathered around him. "They're trained, man."

Charlie muttered something that Courtney couldn't make out, but his incredulous tone was clear.

"What do you think I've been doing up there? Just feeding the habit?" Blane's dreadlocks shook from side to side. "No fucking way, man." He spun around in the middle of the crowd of twitching creatures. "Welcome to the new fucking world, Charlie."

"What are you looking at?"

Courtney jumped, the words coming from right behind him, and spinning around almost punched Craig's white face. The other boy held up his hands.

"Easy! It's only me. Man, you're jumpy." He ruffled his hair. "Didn't you hear me getting up?"

Courtney couldn't speak for a moment, the air trembling as it passed in and out in shaky breaths. Eventually, he just pointed outside. Craig could see for himself. He watched his friend's face change, from confusion to shock to outright fear, before looking back outside himself. Blane was heading away from the block, strolling amid the four creatures as if he were out on a summer's afternoon walk with his favorite dogs. Charlie walked behind them, and it looked like he'd lit a fresh cigarette.

Both boys watched for a long time until even the shadow of the men's shadows had long disappeared. Courtney's eyes drifted up to the opposite block. Had any of the survivors over there seen what they'd just witnessed? What would they make of it? Would it fill them with the same sense of creeping dread that was itching up his spine?

"How the fuck . . . ?" Craig's breathless question trailed away and Courtney didn't even attempt to answer it. His own head spun. This changed everything. This made Blane . . . he couldn't focus his thinking into words that could cover it. Dangerous? Blane had always been dangerous. Finally he found it. *One of them.* That's what had just happened. Blane had become one of them. He tried to swallow, but couldn't, his throat too dry, his tongue like sandpaper against the roof of his mouth.

How much control did Blane Gentle-King have over those things?

His stomach turned to water as a thought dawned on him. How long would it be before Blane sent the spiders instead of the men into the block to look for them? A week? Less? They wouldn't be able to play cat and mouse with those things. The world, already in disarray, tumbled on its head all over again.

Craig stole his words before he could get them out.

"We can't stay here much longer. We're going to need a fucking get-out plan."

CHAPTER THIRTEEN

Charlie didn't smile at Skate as they paused in front of each other in the marble foyer of the smart apartment block on Victoria Dock road.

"How the other half fucking live, eh Charlie?"

Charlie shrugged. "Or die." He was pretty sure the tenants of these flats hadn't had time to do much living in them. The block hadn't been up that long.

Skate laughed as the lift pinged its arrival and a pair of tired-looking men in their forties wearing heavy boots and gloves wheeled a shopping trolley out. Bloody limbs hung over the side from the jumbled mess of human and White corpses that filled it, and a coil of thick webbing trailed behind the wheels. The stench of rot cut through the air and Charlie turned his head. "Jesus, they should have painter's masks on or something. That shit can't be good to breathe."

Skate snorted. "Yeah, right. I'll just pop down to home base and pick some up, shall I?"

Charlie saw his point. No one was that keen on wandering too far. His own nerves were on edge after the short walk from the estate to the riverside development, despite being heavily armed and with Leeboy at his back. They'd jogged most of the way.

"How's the clear-out going?"

"Not too bad." Skate shrugged. "Mainly just human bodies. Most of the Whites are long gone. We're burning what we find out the back. I've set the pile at the gates by the entrance to the underground car park. It'll work as defense for now as well." He paused, chewing hard on his gum. "There's a lot of windows that need boarding up, though." He shook his head slightly. "Fuck me, Blane likes to keep us busy."

Charlie nodded, but didn't comment. Not that Skate would have meant it in any bad way. All the boys knew better than to bad-mouth Blane to Charlie. They might as well just stick a bullet in the back of their own knees.

"You bring Weights over?"

"Yeah. He's upstairs in an apartment on the fourteenth." A cloud passed over Skate's dark face. "He's in some bad-shit way, Charlie. He don't look good at all."

Looking at Skate's jaw working overtime and the way his eyes trembled ever so slightly as he glanced a little to the left or right of the other man without ever really focusing on him, Charlie figured Skate had a little chemical help in holding himself together. He didn't really blame him. If he'd ever been into the coke, then this probably wouldn't be a time he'd choose to quit either. Still, if the world was going crazy then he preferred his own head straight. And maybe that made him as crazy as the world.

The block, although slightly taller than both of the Crookston towers, didn't have as many floors, the flats filling it having higher ceilings and many having more than one level. Charlie wasn't impressed by them. They'd lost three men clearing the bodies because of Whites hidden in those airy spaces and second floors. Most of the survivors who were checking the flats were just ordinary men. Their reactions were slow and it wasn't as if Blane had told Skate to arm them too heavily. And for what? They could have cleared the Crookston blocks much more easily.

The lift stopped at the fourteenth floor just below the penthouse and he stepped out onto soft white carpet, whose ocean of elegance was marred by the large bloodstain browning in a large patch outside the first door a little to his left. It spread in splatters up the wall. Charlie thought that maybe he liked that bloodstain more than the stylishly bland pale walls and bright spotlighting that illuminated it so well. There was something real and bold about it. A reminder that death could touch you anywhere and not to fucking forget it.

"Hey Charlie, man! Come check this out!"

Far down the wide corridor that curved slightly with the smooth circular design of the brand-new building that was never going to make its money back, Jude grinned impishly, childish enthusiasm brimming in his voice. "This is crazy shit, man."

Charlie sighed. What the fuck wasn't? He was getting pretty fucked off with crazy shit.

The other man's Nike trainer moved up and down on a foot pump that looked designed for blowing up air beds, but was now attached to some kind of homemade machine on the other side of which was a thick hose. Charlie's eyes followed it to where it disappeared into a cutout square of the apartment door, sealed in with thick brown tape. Looking at the pump and the thing in the middle and then the hose and the door, he figured Jude must have used at least three rolls of the shit.

"What the fuck is it?" he finally asked.

"Wicked, isn't it? I came up with it myself. Designed it and everything. That glass bit in the middle is kind of like a bong? The bottom comes off if you undo the tape, and then you stick a load of rocks on that metal gauze bit. That's held in place with—"

"Brown tape. I can see it."

"Yeah, and under there are loads of those little round candles in the tins. I pump the air in, which makes the candles burn the dope quick and then also pushes the smoke up the hose and into the flat." Jude's eyes danced. "Fucking brilliant, isn't it?"

Charlie was lost for words. "Yeah, I guess it is." He paused. "You know what's in that flat, don't you, Jude?"

"Course I do, Charlie. Fuck me, man. You think I'm stupid?" His eyes darkened with hurt pride and then his voice dropped. "The question is, do *you* know how many there are in there?" He tilted his head toward the door as if Charlie might need the extra clue.

Charlie frowned. "What the fuck are you talking about? There's four."

Jude's head shook with a quiet reverence. "No, man," he whispered. "There's ten in there." He frowned. "Where was you last night? Did you see Blane bring those four Squealers in? Walking in the middle of them like he was a fucking emperor or something?"

"I was right behind him." Charlie gritted his teeth. "I was there when he brought them out of the blocks. Then I went back to check on Leeboy and Chokey and the others guarding the estate. I slept over there."

"Then you wouldn't have seen. I was cutting the door up for this shit when six more turned up. Climbed up the side of the building and came over the fucking balcony." Jude stopped and swallowed. "It was freaking weird to watch, Charlie. They were mad, like really crazy angry mad, but they just went in the flat with the others."

Something thudded hard at the door on the other side, two discordant squeals raging, and Jude jumped. Charlie was sure the younger man also shivered as he forced his foot back into action.

"This is the third lot I've pumped in this morning, and they're still not chilling yet." He paused. "I think they're hungry." His eyes suddenly looked very young as he turned to Charlie. "I don't think they want the dead meat."

Charlie raised an eyebrow. "Then make sure your fucking fingers don't slip through that hole if you have to tape that hose up again."

Jude's laugh was hollow. "Yeah, too fucking right, Charlie. I'm on that."

"I'll catch you later. Going to see the boss."

"Yeah, man. Make sure you get a factory going over here soon though, man. I'm going to run out of rocks soon."

Charlie didn't answer.

The lift stopped at the penthouse level, but the doors didn't open. Instead, a voice crackled through the tiny intercom. "Yeah?"

Charlie leaned forward and pressed the talk button. "Charlie."

The lift door opened almost immediately. Charlie presumed there were stairs leading up here somewhere in case of emergency. If there weren't, then it was just another fuckup in his oldest friend's moving plans.

"He's on the balcony." Blackeyes moved out of Charlie's way, letting him down the three wide metal stairs that reeked of industrial chic, and into the vast open-plan main living area. The walls were glass from floor to ceiling, and even from far back inside the view out was pretty breathtaking. This glass obviously got cleaned, unlike the grime-caked smaller windows back at Crookston. The floor was dark wood, walnut maybe, and between the bottom of the stairs and the open doors onto the balcony a huge rug stretched out in an attempt to fill the space. It didn't succeed.

Lighting a cigarette, Charlie walked out onto the decked balcony. Sun-loungers lay under a vast awning that rose up from a glass table and large pot plants grew and thrived in the wet from their places against the glass waist-high barrier that separated the flat from the open air. This wasn't a balcony. It was a fucking garden up in the sky. It was probably the size of one of the flats at the blocks. He sucked hard on the cigarette.

"Check out the fucking view, Charlie. I can't get enough of it."

Blane didn't turn around but stayed where he was, both arms gripping the edge of the railing as he stared out. Saying nothing, Charlie moved up and stood alongside him. Just to their left the Connaught Bridge led over the river to Silvertown, and on the other side of that was London City airport, an island in the great workings of the river on the other side of which were the silver domes of the Thames Barrier. Charlie stared at the planes that sat unattended on the abandoned runway in the distance. So much technology. And for what? It wasn't helping them now, that was for sure.

To his right, as the river curved he could clearly see the circular O2 arena, once the much-maligned Millennium Dome, now just a bought-out and planned-to-be-successful venue for business conventions and rock concerts. He squinted as something shifted on its white surface in the gray streaks of morning lights. What was that? Something was climbing one of the circles of high spires that rose up from the dome's smooth white surface. Leaning forward he stared at the building until he recoiled suddenly.

"Fuck."

"Yeah I know." Blane's laugh trickled like rain. "I only just fucking noticed that. It's covered in Whites. White on white. Clever fuckers aren't they? I bet they've got a good fucking view from up there too."

Beyond the O2 arena the huge glass-and-steel empire of Canary Wharf rose up, whose style this block had so successfully imitated, if perhaps on a smaller scale. Charlie wondered if maybe there was someone standing out on a balcony over there, looking right back at them. He decided it wasn't worth wondering about. It may only be half a mile or so along the river, but Canary Wharf was an island of its own now. They had their shit closer to home to worry about.

"Jude says there's ten of them in the flat now." He flicked the butt of his cigarette over the side and watched it tumble. "Where the fuck did the others come from?"

"I figure Janine called them."

"Janine?"

"You know what I mean, man. The Squealer that used to be Janine."

From somewhere in the distance came the sharp retort of rapid gunfire. "You think that's the army?" Charlie wished the balcony faced the other way. What was the fucking point of being able to look out at the river now?

Blane ignored him. "I think they can do that fucking . . . telekinesis thing."

"Telepathy?"

"Yeah. Mind-speak stuff."

"Well, that's just fucking great." His sarcasm laid heavy on his words.

Blane finally turned to face him, his fine features betraying his half-white parentage beneath the heavy dreadlocks. "You've got to have some fucking vision, Charlie. She's brought us an army."

"You think you can control those things?" Tiredness tightened his nerves and Charlie's irritation grew. "What the fuck is going on with you, man?" He kept his voice low, not wanting Blackeyes inside to hear. "First you start feeding those things crack instead of blowing the shit out of them, and now this move over here . . ." He spread his hands, hoping the gesture expressed his concerns better than his words were. "It doesn't make sense. The blocks were easier to defend."

"I was tired of living in shit. The whole of London is our oyster now, Charlie. Why would you want to stay in the fucking Crookston towers?"

Charlie shook his head. "London isn't our oyster, Blane." He looked over to the O2 arena. "It's theirs."

Blane hawked, spitting over the side, a clear indication that he was pissed off. Charlie knew better than to push him.

"But you're the boss, man. If you want us to move operations over here, then I'm on it."

Blane stared at him and Charlie held his gaze. He was used to seeing the long streak of mean in the other man's expression—he knew how dangerous Gentle-King was, his lion-colored irises a good reflection of his character—but he was pretty sure that behind it now there was the first hint of madness. The edges of his wide pupils shook slightly.

"Yes I am the fucking boss, Charlie man." He grinned and stretched his arms wide. "Of all of this! I'm the king of the fucking castle, Charlie."

Charlie's own Irish blue eyes were clear as they stared back. "And that's some fucking empire."

"You got any guns with sights on in the stash, Charlie?" Blane looked out over the river, his voice calm again. "We could probably take some of those White fuckers out from here."

"Sure. Got a few in the lockup. I'll bring them over."

"You need to bring everything over. No point in having the stash over at Crookston, while we're here." He looked around. "I've been meaning to ask. Where did you get all the tools from anyway? We never had so many guns before."

"Replicas. I shipped them in from Amsterdam and then got a bloke I know to drill them out and convert them in his workshop. We still pick up a few from the dealers to keep them happy, but this way is cheaper and there's no police trace on any of them."

"Clever." Blane's eyes narrowed. "Why didn't I ever think of that?"

Charlie pushed his hands in his pockets. He'd never felt overly nervous around Blane before, but something was changing in his friend. Maybe he wasn't coping with all this shit as well as he thought he was. Fuck, none of them were, but maybe it was sending Blane over the edge. There'd always been a manic edge to him. It was part of what made him good at being the boss. It made him a scary fucker, and no one wanted to mess with someone like that. But Charlie had never thought that one day that manic touch would make him feel nervous.

"I guess because you're always too busy thinking about everything else."

"Yeah. I guess that must be right." Blane's face clouded for a moment and then cleared. "Hey Black-eyes!" Turning, he called back into the apartment. "Go get Weights. No, actually, fuck it. We'll go to him." He winked at Charlie. "Don't want him bringing that shit into my new crib."

"What shit?"

"Wait and see, man. He ain't good."

Charlie figured that for the first time in a few days, he and Blane were in agreement. Weights didn't look good. Not at all. From under his bandaged arm, thin strands of glutinous webbing crept out and wove themselves around and up his dark limb, embedding into its surface. Sitting on the stylishly low sofa his huge physique looked almost pathetic as he rocked backward and forward in tiny movements. His lips moved, muttering unheard words and occasionally spitting out a damp sob. There was a smell coming off him too; bitter and rotten. He smelled of the Whites and the Squealers.

"Have you seen his fingernails?" Blane whispered too loudly. "That shit is coming out from under them."

Charlie hadn't noticed it. He'd been too busy trying not to see the strands that seemed to be coming out of the corner of the big man's eyes.

"Am I going to be okay, Blane? Is there a fucking doctor coming?"

The helpless tone made Charlie shiver slightly. He

looked at his friend. "You want me to take care of this? Quickly?" It didn't take a genius to figure out that Weights wasn't going to be getting any better and even though he didn't seem in too much pain now, why prolong what was going to be inevitable? He was pretty sure that the webbing shit wasn't going to just shrivel up and disappear.

"I wanted to wait and see how it turned out." Blane pulled a joint out from behind his ear and lit it.

"I think it's pretty obvious how it's going to turn out."

"But is a doctor coming?"

Neither man answered Weights's plaintive plea, ignoring him as if he were already dead.

"Yeah, but I was still curious." Blane took three long tokes on the spliff and then tilted it toward Charlie. "You want some, man, before I give it to him?"

Charlie shook his head. Something about the sickly smell of the strong weed reminded him of the stench that was coming off Weights.

"Suit yourself." Blane grinned. "I think you're turning into some kind of old woman, Charlie Nash."

Charlie ignored the remark. "What's to be curious about? Don't let the fuckers bite you or they'll turn you into some kind of fucking mummy. Lesson learned."

"Where's your imagination?" Blane handed the joint over and Weights took it between shaking fingers, his eyes darting between the two men who continued to ignore him.

"I got plenty of imagination, Blane. That's why I don't want to see this at the end. My imagination tells me it won't be pretty."

"True." Blane shrugged. "Anyway, we won't be getting to find out." He turned away, tipping his head slightly for Charlie to follow him, and retreated into the hallway, leaving Weights pulling hard on the joint, still rocking on the sofa.

"So you do want me to take care of it?" Charlie felt confused. Why the fuck couldn't Blane just be clear?

"No." Blane's hazel eyes looked coolly into Charlie's blue ones. "I'm going to give him to Janine and the others."

The silence was punctuated only by Weights's ragged wet breathing as he dragged the drugs in and out of his lungs a few feet away. Charlie stared.

"What?"

"We stuck a load of dead bodies in the flat for them, but they're not biting." Blane smiled at his own pun. "Fucking literally."

"So you're going to give them Weights?" His harsh whisper rising, Charlie struggled to take it in. Weights was one of their own. He wasn't the brightest or the hardest, but he'd never put a foot wrong. Charlie had killed plenty of people in his time, but that was always purely business and nine times out of ten the cunts had deserved it. This was different though. There was something about this that chilled the acid in his gut. He didn't like where it was leading.

"He's dead anyway." Blane looked back at the large man, gripped in his own terror. "And yeah, I can keep the Squealers high, but they still got to eat, man. I can't keep them controlled without food, and it sure as fuck isn't going to be me they tuck into. That Janine could be a devious bitch when she wanted to. I doubt she's fucking changed that much."

Charlie leaned against the wall. "Jesus fuck, Blane."

He looked around his friend to the dying man in the lounge. "He's not going to keep them full for long. Who are you going to feed them next?"

"The people we've got in the block." Blane sniffed, leaning in, his low voice conspiratorial. "They wouldn't survive out there on their own. What are there? Forty, maybe fifty of them? I figure we tell them we've got a route out of the city but can only take maybe three at a time. Bring them over and when no one ever sees them again they'll figure they're living out their days in the fucking country, safe and sound." He grinned. "I'm a fucking genius, aren't I?"

"Sugarcandy Mountain," Charlie muttered.

"What?"

The words had drifted into Charlie's head from a long-forgotten memory dragged out of the cobwebs of his mind. "Sugarcandy Mountain. It was in a book at school. About the animals. They thought they were going to Sugarcandy Mountain but they were getting turned into dog food or some shit like that."

"Don't remember it." Blane's smooth brow furrowed and then he smiled. "But I like it. Sugarcandy fucking Mountain. I like it a lot." He turned back to Weights, the smile dropping. "So let's get this done."

"Wait." Charlie grabbed the leather sleeve. "What about when they're all gone? In a month or so?"

Blane looked at him as if he were stupid. "You think we're the only people left alive in London? Fuck no. You and the boys will have to go out on roundups. Find some more." He shrugged. "Same with the drugs and guns eventually, although we've got plenty of raw coke in the lockup and you done good with the weaponry." His dreadlocks shook a little with exasperation and he tapped his temple. "Jesus, Charlie. It's like you think I haven't given this any head time."

Charlie sighed. His head buzzed and spun. There was nothing about it that he liked. "No," he said eventually, "it seems you got it all pretty well thought out."

"Yeah I do. Now come on. Let's do this thing. You watch down the corridor and bring Weights when I signal."

"Sure, boss. I'm on it."

Standing in the open doorway, Charlie cautiously eased his handgun out from the back of his trousers and pulled the slide back. It clicked reassuringly. Weights was a big man, and he was also terrified. Who knew how the fuck he might behave? The temptation to stick a bullet in the back of the man's head was strong, but there was no way he'd fuck Blane off over Weights. If he had to use the gun, the shot would go in the back of the big man's knee. Enough to disable him but not take him out completely. Still, it would take more than his own strength to drag the fucker if he was down on the floor. But he'd figure out how to cross that bridge if and when he got to it.

"What's going on, Charlie?" Weights was up on his feet, peering out from the sitting room doorway. "Where did Blane go?"

Fuck, he was a big man. Charlie waved him back. "You stay there for a moment." He kept his voice calm and level. It was the voice everyone expected from him. No sympathy echoed in his tone. If it had, it might have alerted Weights, although he seemed pretty much wrapped up in the terror of his own head.

"Blane's setting up one of the flats as a medical cen-

ter. One of those men in the tower was a nurse or something, I think. They're getting set up to examine you."

Weights stared at him. "Really?" For the first time
Charlie saw a flash of hope hover nervously in his dark
brown eyes. "There's a nurse?"

"Yeah, really." The words stuck in his throat, but he
forced them out. Sugarcandy fucking Mountain. What
a fucking joke. "So you just stay there and finish that
joint. You're going to be fine."

Soft shoes jogged up the corridor and Jude's thin
frame appeared. "Blane's ready for you now." His whole
body twitched with nervous energy, the words coming
fast. "Shit, man, you should have seen it. I took the tape
and hose out of the door and those bitches slammed it,
but then when Blane looked in and started talking they
chilled, man, and then he just opened the door and . . ."

"Shut the fuck up, Jude." Charlie's words were ice
and he flashed his pistol at the younger man. "You want
Weights to fucking hear you?"

"Sorry, Charlie, it was just so . . ." Jude's words trailed
off under Charlie's glare. "Anyway. You can bring him
now."

Charlie nodded. "And why don't you make yourself
fucking scarce for now? One sight of your mug and
Weights'll know something's up."

"Sure, Charlie." Jude's cockiness had gone. He might
have seen Blane as some kind of god, but he had plenty
of healthy respect for Charlie. Charlie's reputation was
for being clear and cold. Watching the kid disappearing, Charlie didn't feel particularly cold. He had a fucking headache coming and for the first time since they
were kids he felt like he and Blane were moving in completely different directions. They needed to talk. And

soon. The gun tucked into his jacket pocket but still firmly gripped, he looked back into the flat.

"Weights? I think they're set up now."

As it was, Charlie didn't need the gun at all. Weights went as quietly as the proverbial lamb to the slaughter. He had no idea what was really planned for him until he'd stepped over the threshold, but by then Blane had slammed the door shut, the monstrous creatures creeping and scuttling out into the flat hallway to greet the big man. At least his screams didn't last more than a few seconds. Blane had been right. The Squealers were hungry.

When it was done, they went back upstairs. Charlie gazed out through the sliding doors to the patio and lit a cigarette, needing something to get rid of the bad taste that plagued his mouth. He was tired and his eyes itched. Normally, looking out over the Thames was something he found tranquil, a reaffirmation of who and what he was: an East End London man and fucking proud of it. But now the water was barely visible, a mist forming on the river from the damp heat that refused to leave the London air. From the penthouse its winding path just looked alien to him. An invisible shiver ran down his spine. Anything could be hiding in that growing fog and the idea made his skin crawl.

"Fucking bugs," he muttered eventually, breaking the silence and turning inward to face the problems he had closer to home.

Blane sat on a cream leather sofa, chopping out a large line of cocaine on the glass surface of the low table that sat elegantly on brushed metal legs. It made the similar one in Gentle-King's Crookston tower flat look like it came from some pound-stretcher cheap shop. Charlie watched as his friend shaped the drugs. The thick white strip of powder stretched at least two and a half inches and looking at it Charlie's heart sank further. How much of that shit did Blane need?

Blane snorted it in one breath and then wiped his finger across the residue, rubbing it into his teeth. He leaned back against the settee and rested his arms across its straight back, crossing his legs.

"Speak, brother. What's on your mind?"

Gunfire chased itself around the streets and buildings below them, and Charlie wasn't sure whether it was their own men defending their territory, or the army or police or whoever the fuck else was trying to return the world to some kind of normality.

"What's on my mind?" He almost laughed. "Jesus, Blane. Sometimes you truly fucking amaze me."

Blane grinned. "Always, Charlie. You'd get bored if I didn't." He gestured at the seat opposite and Charlie took it. If they were going to have this conversation then it needed to be on the level. He needed to look into Blane's eyes and see what was really going on with him, high or not.

"This story you're figuring on telling the muppets we've got stashed in the blocks." He sucked hard on his cigarette. "You know, about how we're going to get them out of the city."

"Sugarcandy Mountain." Blane smiled, rubbing his nose.

"Yeah."

"What about it?"

Charlie leaned forward, his arms resting on his knees. "You don't think maybe we should be thinking like that? About getting out?"

Staring at him, Blane snorted. "You want to save those wankers? They'd be dead already if it wasn't for us."

"No, not them. Fuck them." Charlie shook his head. And he meant it. All those people knew what Blane and Charlie and the rest were like. If they chose to trust them, then they deserved to be treated like dumb sheep.

"*Us.* I'm talking about us maybe getting out of London. You and me." Unable to stop himself, he chewed his bottom lip. It was a nervous tell and Blane would probably see it. He was on dangerous ground here, but he'd always spoken his mind within reason and he wasn't going stop now.

Blane stared for a long time before a puzzled frown rippled between his hazel eyes. "Leave London? What the fuck for?"

"Look around you, mate. This isn't . . . this isn't our London. The world's changed. We're sitting in a city of fifty thousand or more people. If what we've seen is anything to go by then half of them have changed into these fucking bugs and are intent on eating the other half. What's wrong with wanting to be somewhere with a smaller population?"

Blane sat still, his expression unreadable, white dots of powder decorating the edges of his nostrils. Eventually, one hand rose and he wiped it away.

"No way, man. I'm going to build a citadel. An empire." His words were pushed out between clenched jaws and Charlie was pretty convinced that although it was still pretty early, that line of coke was far from being the first of Blane's day.

"A what?" Charlie stubbed the cigarette out and fought the urge to light another. He was trying to ration himself. Everything was precious. Even if most of the crew seemed to think the stuff they found in the flats was going to last them forever, he wasn't that fucking stupid.

"You know. A citadel." Blane leaned forward, mirroring Charlie's pose. "Get some fences with barbed wire up around the block; maybe even electrify it. someone will know how to work that shit. We've got the Squealers." He shrugged, oozing smug confidence. "The Whites will learn to keep away. There'll be easier prey than us. And as soon as we've figured out ways to move around the city, it'll be ours, man. All ours. It's survival of the fittest."

Charlie shook his head. "I'm not sure we're the fittest anymore, Blane."

"Don't go fucking soft on me now, Charlie. Not after all these years. We're the strongest. We always were. And we're clever." His hands gestured wildly, the coke hitting his system. "Soon as we're set up, I'll get the boys out raiding supplies. With the Squealers to guard them it'll be easy. We'll get all the tins and fucking long-life supplies and then we'll be like a beacon for all the survivors. They'll want our protection. Don't you see it?"

Charlie wasn't sure that he did, but Blane didn't wait for an answer. His face shone with a light coating of sweat as his hands stretched wide. "Then we'll expand our safe zone." He pointed a slim finger. "And don't tell me all the fucking women have changed because I've seen all those fucking films and there's always some small percentage that's immune or some shit."

He grinned. "It'll be ours. Everything that counts anyway. We've got the muscle. And more than that we've got *the Squealers*."

"You really think you can control them indefinitely?"

"Don't you? We've got the gear. They need it. And when it runs out"—Blane raised an eyebrow as if he thought he was preempting Charlie's next question—"then we go and raid the stashes of our late colleagues. I wouldn't be surprised if those bitches could smell it out."

Charlie sighed. "I fucking love London, man. You know I do. Farthest I've ever traveled is Harlow and that was just to visit my uncle in the nick. I love the sounds, the smells, the traffic . . ." His words drifted away. "But they're gone. It's just the buildings left. It's like being in the tomb of a dead thing."

"Are *you* dead, Charlie?" Blane raised an eyebrow. "Am I?" He sniffed hard. "It's just change, Charlie. That's all. Nothing to be afraid of."

Staring into the face of his oldest friend, Charlie's heart felt heavy, and it had been a long time since his heart had felt anything at all. Yes, things were changing. And the way he looked at things was changing too. He glanced away.

"Yeah. I guess you're right."

"You sure?" Blane's eyes narrowed. "You wouldn't do anything stupid like leave me, would you Charlie?"

"No way, Blane. It's always been you and me." The words rolled uncomfortably out of his mouth. Lying to Blane didn't come naturally to him. "That's not going to change now."

Blane Gentle-King grinned, and for a moment Charlie almost saw the ghost of the kid he'd once been dancing in the relief in his hazel eyes. They were wide and open and almost innocent.

"London's everything to me." His voice was soft. "If

I left London I'd be nothing. No one." He shook his head, the thick dreadlocks tumbling into his face. "I can't do that, man."

Eventually, Charlie nodded. "I get it, Blane. I really do." And he did. Could he really leave without his friend? He wasn't so sure. Maybe Blane Gentle-King was the only person left alive who really knew him. His head throbbed.

"Our block over at Crookston is starting to stink pretty bad." Running a hand over his short blond hair, he changed the subject. "You want me to get some guys in there clearing it out?"

Blane shook his head, and the brief mist of youthful naïveté that had settled on him for a moment dispersed. "Nah. The block's done. Burn it."

"What?"

"You suddenly deaf or something? Get your shit out of there and burn it down."

"But won't that . . . ?" He let the question fade. Won't that draw too much attention? The Whites, the army. Whoever. That's what he'd been going to ask. But of course Blane didn't give a shit about any of that. If Blane wanted the block to burn, then that's what would happen.

"It's symbolic, man. The end of one era and the start of something better." Blane spread his arms wide, gesturing to his surroundings as if somehow he'd earned them. Charlie stood up. Maybe Blane had, in his own way. He'd survived and he'd taken what he wanted. There weren't many who could act with such clarity in the midst of this madness. Unless of course there was a touch of insanity to Blane's clarity. Charlie wouldn't be surprised. Not after Weights.

"And it'll flush that fucking kid out."

"What kid?"

"The fucking grass." Blane's eyes hardened. "He'll be Squealer feed. I'll fucking enjoy that moment."

Charlie said nothing.

"Make sure you get those kids, Charlie. Take Skate and Jude with you when you set the fire. If those shits are still hiding in there, then they'll catch them when they get out."

Charlie nodded. There was no point in asking him if it was worth risking good men to catch a few boys who would likely be hunted down by the Whites after a few hundred feet anyway. Blane's face was set, thinking it all through.

"And then when the block's down and you've brought that boy back, empty the lockups. Get that shit over here. The guns and all of it. We're going to need to get a factory set up here."

"Jude said."

Blane grinned. "He's a good kid. If only he'd learn to fucking wash. Shit, he has some bad BO."

Charlie snorted despite himself. "Yeah, you got that right. Why do you think I'm always smoking in the car? Someone needs to show that boy a can of Right Guard."

"You think that would do it?" Blane shook his head and laughed. "I reckon we might have to stick him in a washing machine first. He's like my fucking cell mate in Brixton. Some of that stink on him is *old*, man."

"Ninety-fucking-degree hot wash." Charlie shook his head. "That would work. The little runt would come out whiter than my arse."

Both men laughed and for a second or two they were just Blane and Charlie again, as they had been since kids, now grown men who would take on the world and win, side by side. Except the world had changed. And that was something Charlie couldn't hide from. Their humor subsided and Blane wiped his eyes.

"Shit, man. It's good to laugh."

"Yeah." Charlie nodded. "Yeah, it is." Shaking his head, he turned toward the stairs and the waiting lift. "I'll go and organize torching the block. It'll take a while to get going and we'll want it blazing before dark. Those fuckers are still braver at night. And they're not exactly shy in the daytime."

As if to emphasize his point a rattle of gunfire sounded somewhere beneath them, followed by a shout and then more gunshots. When the air fell silent, the atmosphere had changed. Charlie's legs felt heavy as he climbed the steps.

"Hey."

Charlie turned. Blane was reclining once again against the sofa, languid as a dozing lion whose flicking tail was the only small sign of danger. He peered up from under hooded lids.

"You won't try to leave me, will you, Charlie?"

"I told you no, Blane. You trust me?"

"Yeah, I trust you." Blane watched him until Charlie felt the skin on his face crawl. "But I wouldn't let you leave anyway, Charlie." He sniffed. "Just so you know."

Charlie shrugged. "Well, now I know."

Blane nodded.

"So can I fuck off now and get on with your business, your highness?" Charlie's tone was light and even, no hint of the tension that ate into his shoulders in its steady rhythm.

"Yeah. And make sure when you come back you pick the best of these flats. I want you close by, Charlie. Where I can get you fast if I need you."

"I'm on it."

It was only when the elevator pinged and the doors slid shut, working perfectly as if no one had bothered to point out that the world was truly fucked up, that Charlie finally let out a long breath. He thought about hitting the alarm button and freezing the machine just to have a quiet cigarette in peace. He didn't of course. Not only because Blane would go fucking mental at him, but also because he had a sneaky suspicion that if the lift got stuck it would take them a very long time to get him out. Maybe he'd start taking the stairs.

CHAPTER FOURTEEN

Peter watched Harry gripping the butt of the gun tightly in his sweating hands as he peered around the side of the van and into the next street, the barrel of the weapon leading the way. As much as it reassured him that they were armed, he wished Harry looked less nervous. From the way Mr. Green's thin throat was working, the Adam's apple bobbing up and down eagerly in his neck, Peter figured he wasn't too comfortable about carrying a semiautomatic either. He looked like he was trying to swallow a small lump of vomit that had risen up into his throat.

"I'm so pleased I ended up with the handgun. Thanks for that." The heavy sarcasm in James's voice rang out in the quiet street and Peter jumped slightly.

"At least you got a gun." Farther back, Josh sounded glum.

"Yes, but by the time I get the bloody thing armed we'll all be dead." He paused. "Or I'll have shot myself in the foot. Neither of which option appeals to me very much."

Peter wished he could have some of James's easygoing attitude. The sixth-former didn't seem to care about anything—the school, their friends, their *families*. A dark cloud settled in his soul. He didn't want to think about his family. Not yet. Maybe not ever. Shreds stripped themselves from his heart. Maybe if he were older it would be easier. Maybe then he wouldn't have this awful ache of terror constantly eating him up from the inside. He peered back again at Mr. Green who was bringing up the end of what had once been a short line, but was now a huddle of warm, sweating, scared bodies. The gun in the man's hand shook. Perhaps being older wasn't a cure for fear. Somehow that thought terrified him almost as much as the spiders did.

"Is it safe?" he whispered.

"I think so." Harry lowered the gun, and Peter wished he wouldn't. The windows of the houses that surrounded them glared down, reflecting the watery sunlight that broke occasionally through the damp clouds. He didn't want to think about what might be behind that glass. He just wanted to get away from it.

They trotted into the middle of the street that lay silent ahead of them. If there were other survivors around they were staying indoors.

"How far to the river?" James finally lowered his voice as he looked over Peter to Harry. It made Peter feel like he wasn't there at all. And maybe he wasn't. Maybe he was dead already. *Just like his mum.*

"Can't be far." Harry shrugged. "Maybe half a mile or so?"

"Why are we going to the river anyway?" Josh's voice rose and fell between the high pitch of Peter's own youthful tone, and the lower one of the older boy's, as yet not fully broken. It would sound strange when it was. Josh was fourteen but smaller than some of the boys in Peter's class, who were three years younger.

"I figure if we keep to the river then we can follow it until we get out of the city. Plus, it'll leave less to look out for. At least on one side."

"Yes," James added. "And there'll be more space down there. Those embankment streets are always wider. These ones"—he glanced up and around them—"are so bloody hemmed in."

Mr. Green was staring farther up the road, and peering past the older boys Peter followed his gaze.

"Hey look . . ." he breathed, but couldn't finish his sentence. His eyes widened. It was the closest he'd felt to anything near wonder in what felt like forever. The others turned and fell silent.

Josh giggled. "That looks so weird."

The red double-decker bus lay on its side, stretching at an angle across one side of the long road. Smashed glass sparkled around it. In silent agreement to move, the whole group trotted forward. Peter stared. The bus looked to him like a felled elephant, shot dead in the jungle, its side rising several feet higher than his own head. He peered cautiously in through the cracked glass. The pairs of seats were empty and he could make out wedges of chewing gum stuck randomly underneath on the gray metal where the padded cushions ended. It looked dirty.

"No sign of life." Harry's words drifted around to him.

"That's a relief all things considered."

Peter followed James's voice around to the front. Rain started falling in thick drops and somewhere in the distance thunder rolled heavily across the sky. Mr. Green sighed, but no one added to it. The rain was something they'd come to expect. It poured endlessly with lackluster energy from dark gray clouds hanging constantly overhead, soaking the ground every day for hours on end. Water streamed down the back of Peter's collar and glancing upward, he grimaced. For the first time there was a hint of wind in the air. Maybe this bout was going to be more than the rest. Maybe it was finally going to storm and let the air clear and go back to normal.

He licked his lips and immediately regretted it, the strange hot, oily taste staining the inside of his mouth. This wasn't fresh English rain. Normality was gone. Tilting his head, he peered at the large white letters in the bus's destination box.

"Plaistow." He pronounced it slowly, the place unfamiliar.

"I've never really known how that's supposed to sound." Harry frowned. "Plaaaastow. Plastow. Which is it?"

"I don't suppose it really matters much anymore," Mr. Green muttered. "The buses aren't exactly running. It's all just London now."

Peter felt the chill that sometimes made him wonder if he were almost dead already settle just under the surface of his skin. Places shouldn't just stop existing. Were the signs around them just grave markers for places that used to exist, that had only been kept alive by all the people who lived within their shelter?

The moment of fascination with the fallen bus passed as the rain pelted them harder.

"I hate this bloody weather." James turned away from the carcass of the vehicle.

"I hate this bloody road," Josh added. "I keep thinking about the park back there. And I'm sure I saw another one signposted down this way. I don't want us to go near those, Harry. I don't even like passing these trees."

He nodded over at one of the large trunks that rose up from its dug-out place in the pavement, evenly spaced away from the others that grew at even intervals along both sides of the street. They'd been placed as if someone somehow thought their presence would distract from the grimy shop façades that screamed rundown inner city from their cheap signs and the dirty paving slabs in front of them. Peter followed the line of knots in the rough bark up to the heavy canopy. The branches hung like curious fingers over the edge of the curb, dragged down by the weight of the lush green leaves.

"There's no parks at the river, I don't think."

Peter could hear the uncertainty in Harry's voice, but his words were enough to get them moving again. They left the bus to rot and rust in its own good time.

His feet trudged forward, his head down against the rain. It seemed the only things *other than the spiders* that were flourishing happily in this new world were the plants and trees. Everywhere he looked small shoots of grass pushed up out of tiny cracks in the pavements, weeds fighting to reach for the moist air. How long would it be before the city was just a damp jungle, the ghosts of buildings peeking out from behind the thick vines that trapped them? He'd seen films like that, old sci-fi ones, where people escaped from domes to find the wreck of the modern world. He'd always thought that might be fun. He'd been wrong. But then in those worlds there were no monster spiders hiding in the trees to leap out and get you. And in those films, the good guys always made it out alive. Did he count as one of the good guys?

The thought sunk like a stone in his heart. James probably did, with his devil-may-care attitude. There was always one of those in the heroes. And Harry too. Everyone looked to Harry for answers. He was clever and sensible. He wasn't Archer, but he was close enough. If this were a film then Harry would probably be the leading character.

Pushing a stream of water out of his face, he squinted over at tiny Josh and skinny Mr. Green. He was like them, weak and afraid. If it had been just the three of them, they'd probably have been dead already. And they'd never have left the bed-and-breakfast, no matter how much the bodies upstairs had started to smell. He picked up his pace, ignoring the dirty puddles that seeped into the bottom of his overlong jeans as he splashed through them, and jogged until he was just behind the two sixth-formers, leaving Josh and Mr. Green lagging behind. He felt safer there among the heroes; it didn't matter if Mr. Green had a gun or not.

They walked in silence for five minutes, the occasional sniff punctuating the steady patter of water on concrete, Mr. Green nervously watching for any movement behind them and Harry and James checking in front.

The end of the long road was in sight when Harry stopped. "Look."

The large window to the double-fronted shop that declared itself CYCLE KING was already smashed, a jagged sheet of glass lying across the pavement, surrounded by shattered fragments.

"We'd get out of the city much faster on bikes."

Peter followed Harry and James inside, careful not to snag himself on the sharp edges. He didn't know if the spider things were like sharks and could smell dripping blood, but it was probably best to presume the worst. The air inside retained the damp but at least they were out of the downpour and the two smaller boys huddled in the display until the other scouted the aisles for any danger. It seemed that, for now, there was none.

"Take your pick." Harry smiled.

The light was gloomy, and between the racks of bikes and all the associated equipment the walkways were narrow and cramped, the owner having obviously filled every available inch of his premises with stock. Their feet shuffled loudly as the boys moved around, squeezing past each other to examine the different colors and sizes and gear options. Finally, they'd pulled the ones they wanted from the racks and were rifling through the waterproof-clothes section, throwing anything discarded to the floor.

Tugging a lightweight Gore-tex top over his own clothes, Peter stared at them. The dropped tops and jackets were like the bus. Just another sign that the world was over and they were already dead. No one was going to come in through the door and complain about the mess. Nothing needed to be neatly ordered. There were no more customers. A pang of something like pain but emptier gripped his insides. He wished they were back at the bed-and-breakfast. At least there he could pretend, if only a little bit.

"God." James looked down at the brightly colored waterproofs he'd pulled on. "I look like some spotty geek going on a geography field trip."

Josh giggled and Peter almost smiled. It was funny seeing James looking so uncool.

"We all do." Harry didn't look so keen on the bright yellow stuff that he'd found that fitted either. "At least if there's anyone else out there, they'll spot us."

"Great." James looked up. "Just what I want while I'm dressed like this. To be seen by strangers."

Mr. Green passed him a safety helmet. "That looks like it should fit you. Try it." His own was already done up tightly under his chin.

"You must be joking."

The teacher checked the inside of each one to size it and then passed them around. The boys just stared at them.

"No one wears bloody safety helmets." James shook his head.

Peter fiddled with the strap under the shiny blue surface. He wore a safety helmet when he went out on his bike at home, but maybe this wasn't the best time to mention it. His eyes wide he looked between teacher and student. For once, Mr. Green didn't seem nervous. He shrugged.

"Suit yourself, Mr. Mildrew." The teacher began wheeling his bike to the window, and then stopped and turned back to face them all. "But just remember. If we have to cycle fast away from something and you take a tumble and crack your head open on the pavement, there's no ambulances and no hospitals coming to save you. All we've got is one very poor excuse for an emergency medical travel kit." He smiled. "A couple of aspirin and some plasters. So you'd end up just lying there bleeding to death with your brains spilling out around you and maybe if you're lucky one of the spiders will come and put you out of your misery." He lifted his bike up onto the dais. Peter swallowed hard and no one spoke. This wasn't the Mr. Green they knew, nervous and arty. This was someone else.

"We couldn't carry you. This isn't the movies. There'll be no makeshift stretcher running behind the bikes. That doesn't happen. In the real world you just get left to die because everyone else wants the best chance to survive." There was no love and very little like in the glare he gave James, even Peter could see that. "So wear it or not. It's up to you. But don't say I didn't warn you."

"Mr. Green . . ." Harry sounded shocked.

"I know what I'm talking about, Harry. I was in the forces a very long time ago. I did my active service and I've seen how people react when it's a matter of survival. And it's never how you think it's going to be. It's invariably nastier."

"You were in the gulf?"

"No. The Falklands. Before you were even born."

The gun over his shoulder, he took his bike out into the street. After a long pause, Peter was relieved to see Harry slide the helmet onto his head and strap it tightly. He glanced at Josh and then put on his own. The other boy followed, and then headed over to the window and the outside world.

James stared at the helmet in his hand for a moment, a cloud gathering between his eyebrows, before eventually he tossed it to the ground. "Sod that. There's only so far a chap can go. And my hair's wet already."

The somber mood lifted once they were back in the road. The rain didn't seem so bad with the waterproof clothes on and there was something liberating about cycling, and for the occasional moment the awful knot in the pit of Peter's stomach almost unwound as he giggled at James and Harry weaving their bikes around each other's up ahead. Plus, there was the added concentration involved in actually staying on his own machine. He'd realized pretty much as soon as they'd started pedaling that his seat was about three inches too high, and his short legs were only keeping the wheels moving by stretching his feet to his tiptoes on the pedals. It made him wobble. He'd slipped behind; even Mr. Green, who was supposed to be keeping an eye behind them, had overtaken him. He bit his bottom lip and pressed slowly.

It was a relief when a few minutes later, Harry braked and the group came to a halt.

"There's a fire." Shielding his eyes from the rain, the boy pointed ahead of them and a little to their left.

Thick black smoke rose, fighting the rain for its existence and claiming a small portion of the sky.

"We should head that way."

"Why?" James didn't sound keen. "Something's on fire. Big deal. It was bound to happen eventually."

Leaving the group ahead to the discussion, Peter clambered down from his bike. This would be a good time to adjust the saddle. With one hand holding the light frame steady, he crouched down to examine the workings of it. The model was only two up from his bike at home and he was sure there should be a catch under the seat somewhere and then it would just slide down to the next setting. Maybe he'd drop it two notches. Just in case. His hands fiddling under the seat, he half listened to the words that drifted back to him.

"But maybe someone started the fire."

"Maybe the army are there."

"Or maybe something a whole lot worse."

His small fingers found the catch but damp had made them slippery and he fought to grip it enough to pull it out. He frowned, his face tight with concentration.

"But if there are people . . . it's got to be worth checking."

Something glinted in the window of the shop opposite, and Peter looked up for a moment, his hand still fiddling with the seat. What was that? Red smears trickled and sparkled as they ran down the glass, the light carried in the tracks of the rain. He squinted, puzzled. What was inside that shop? A stain of white flashed into view and his heart froze.

"Okay, we'll go. I'm curious now anyway."

It wasn't anything on the inside of the shop. Something was being reflected from the outside. From *behind* him. The knot in his stomach tightened, pulling all his organs into it. Maybe he was wrong, maybe it was just . . .

The angry hiss stopped all thought. His mind blackening with slow-rising panic, he struggled upward, the bike tumbling to the ground. Slowly, he turned. A sob gulped into his throat and as the knot in his gut unwound in sheer terror, it released itself in a steady stream of warm urine running under his waterproof outer layer and into the gutter of the road.

The thing was barely three feet away, its bulbous body waist-high and crouched between its bent spindly legs. He stared at it and the sickly bank of translucent bumps stared back from their tiny red centers. If he ran his hand over the creature's front section he was sure it would feel scaly like diseased skin. Below the angry eyes, the four mandibles clacked together.

The world grew brighter, glittering at the edges of his vision, and as his breath raced in his chest trying to force out a cry, his feet stuck in a puddle of his own piss, Peter wondered if he was really there at all. Heavy drops of rain hit the white spider's back, sending vibrations across its slick, pale skin and making it wobble slightly as if it were a huge water balloon. The water clung to its surface though, sliding all the way around to the hidden underbelly. From somewhere deep inside, where he was pretty sure that this wasn't real and couldn't possibly be happening to him, Peter wondered if maybe the sickly hot rain and the terrible spider belonged together. Maybe this was their world now, and the remaining humans were merely an irritation. Or worse. Just *prey*. The thoughts raced hotly around his brain while his body stood immobile.

"Come on then . . . let's . . ."

"Oh shit."

"Oh . . ."

The moment of stillness broke and too many things happened at once. The others started yelling, their words incoherent and just a mash of sound. Another white creature emerged in the corner of his eye a little farther down the road, and from the hissing coming from behind him, Peter was pretty sure a third was scuttling down the front of the building. The spider in front of him crouched to leap, and in the center of all this action, in a tiny silent moment inside his head, it dawned on Peter that all this was real. There never had been any question about it.

He turned, not knowing where to head but instinctively flinching from the spider flinging itself at him. His foot tangled awkwardly in the barely used wheel of the shiny new red bike, which lay useless in the road, and he tumbled forward, for a moment in free fall, before something punched him hard in the spine and gripped him, pulling him back. The wind knocked from his lungs, he turned his head openmouthed to finally face the others. They seemed a long way away, their wide eyes staring back.

He wished his words would come. He wished he could scream and shout and make sure they got this thing off him, because he was alive and he wanted to live and he didn't care if everyone else in the world was gone, he was still here and that was really all that mattered. Instead, his mouth hung open as he felt something awful and cold grip his spine from the inside. The two angular legs wrapped around him, a poor imitation of a mother's embrace, and squeezed over his chest. Even through his clothes he could feel the sharp, almost-invisible bristles that grew like needles from the thin, hard sections. They stung his skin.

It was enough to finally set his voice free.

"Help me!" As the words escaped him the awful inner hold on his spine tightened, pulling him closer into the belly of the beast, and Peter's eyes filled with hot tears. In the bleary distance Harry scrambled with his gun and a volley of shots shattered the air randomly around them.

"Don't hit him. Don't . . ."

Trying in vain to push the limbs that held him away, Peter saw Josh running toward him, screaming back at the others. "Don't shoot at him!"

More bullets fired and the creature behind him staggered farther into the road and then crumpled. He ignored it, his own captor gripping tightly and twisting to his right, preparing to flee.

"Shoot, Mr. Green! Bloody shoot!"

Through hazy eyes, his mind trying to ignore the awful, unknown thing that was going on around his spine, that felt like it was going *into* his spine, Peter could just about see the teacher standing frozen in the street, one hand still on his bike and the gun slung uselessly over his shoulder. He was in the perfect position, directly in front of them. Peter wished he could scream to him that this was real, even he knew that now, and Mum was dead or worse and the world was ruined but he still wanted to be alive and he knew he should have kept up with Harry and James. His spine ached, an awful, unforgiving pain that screamed damage, and more hot tears gagged into his throat.

Warm hands gripped his own cold fingers as Josh reached him, tugging at the alien limbs imprisoning him. The creature fought back, tossing Peter from side to side, each movement wrenching at his insides and turning the world vaguely black. His head hanging low, he could see blood running with the rain. His blood. The mandibles above him snapped and Josh cried out, a chunk ripped from the arm of his jacket, and more crimson joined with Peter's in the road.

The bite didn't stop Josh from trying to free him though, and trapped as he was, a strange sensation flooding his system and making his tongue too thick to work, his legs growing numb underneath him, Peter sought out the other boy's gaze. He suddenly felt tired, his arms flopping forward uselessly as whatever the spider was pumping into him took effect. Josh needed to get away. He couldn't help. He couldn't stop this. The futility of his situation still seemed unreal. He was eleven and until last week he'd never really thought about death at all. And now here it was, paralysing him from the inside out.

Using the last drips of his adrenaline, he raised his heavy head and found Josh looking right back. His eyes were too angry to be afraid, his face flushed with the exertion of trying to pull Peter free, jaw set in such determination he probably didn't even feel where he'd been bitten. For a brief moment, Peter wondered if he'd got it wrong and maybe Josh was one of the heroes too, and then a single shot fired out, lightning in the thunder of the bursts of semiautomatic.

With his own vision growing dim, Peter wasn't sure what he saw first. Whether it was the anger fading instantly from Josh's eyes, or the way his mouth dropped open with surprise, or whether it was the small explosion at the side of the blue cycle helmet that punched his head to the right and sent a mist of hard plastic shards and soft pink brain into the air.

No life left in his grip, Josh's hands fell away, following the rest of his body into an untidy heap on the ground. Peter could no longer hear the gunfire and the screams and yells of the others, or maybe he just wasn't listening. The world was fading. Josh's dead eyes stared into his one last time, and in the last moments before unconsciousness drew him down into the darkness Peter wished he could have told the tiny older boy about the heroes and the extras. Maybe then he'd have thought twice before trying to save him. Too late now.

Air rushed past his face as the monster holding him leaped at the side of the building, carrying him up to the sky and away, and as the light faded he wished he'd never put the stupid safety helmet on. He'd like to have felt that last breeze.

And then, at least for a while, it was gone.

CHAPTER FIFTEEN

Charlie stared upward through the heavy rain at the thick black smoke bellowing out from what had been the top floor of one of the Crookston towers. Behind him, across the green square, a few of the survivors had crept out to take a cautious look, peering out from the shadowy undercover areas that led to the stairwells.

They'd have been better staying indoors. If they were seen Skate would send them off working on something and the risks were far greater outside than in. But then, human curiosity was often the cause of stupidity in action. After one quick look over his shoulder, Charlie didn't give them any more attention. They didn't really exist to him, and he hadn't even bothered with their names, one face blending in with the next. It came naturally that he'd always seen ordinary people like that, as something different to men like himself and Blane and the crew, and now that *everything* was different he had a feeling that most of this straggly band of weak men wouldn't be around that long. Either the Whites would get them or Blane would feed them to the Squealers. So what was the point in really *seeing* them?

A last few fragments of blown-out glass tinkled onto the concrete in front of where he stood with Skate, safely back on the edge of the square lawn.

"I only told you to blow the bloody doors off," Charlie muttered, one eyebrow raised, the joke meant purely for himself.

Skate snorted. "Ain't that from that film? Mark Wahlberg? *The Italian* something . . . ?"

Charlie didn't smile. "*The Italian Job*. And it was Michael Caine." Blane would have got the reference and he wouldn't have tagged it to some shite remake either. Most of the classic Caine films were a bit old even when they were growing up, but Charlie had loved them, and Blane had watched them with him. Blane had understood. Charlie Nash had needed a father figure when he was growing up, and Michael Caine had been it. *Get Carter*, *The Ipcress File*, *The Italian Job* and even *Alfie*. More than twenty years on from watching them, Charlie could still quote lines from them all. Classic British movies.

"I thought we sent Jude and Leeboy up there with fucking petrol cans."

"Yeah, but I told Jude to try the gas." Charlie watched the occasional red tongue of fire licking the building through the black pall.

Skate grinned. "Hope Jude's still got his eyebrows, man. They'd have to have got off that floor in a hurry."

"He's a fast little fucker. He'll be all right."·

Charlie lit two cigarettes and passed one to Skate. He took a long drag behind a cupped hand to keep the burning leaves dry. There was no sign of any movement around the building. Chokey was watching the left stairwell and Leeboy would have come down to guard the bottom of the right one. If the boy who had grassed Blane up was still inside, he was going to have to come out one way or another. It was a pain-in-the-arse job though, and as far as Charlie could see, a waste of time.

Who really gave a shit if the kid lived or died anymore?

"Did you notice there were more Whites around here this morning?" Skate's voice dropped, as if perhaps the spiders could hear him from wherever they disappeared to.

Charlie shrugged. "I heard some shots, but I wasn't out here."

"Well there were." Skate paused. "But there don't seem to be many coming near that new block." His words were slow.

"What's your point, Skate?"

"I'm just thinking about the Squealers. They were over here and there were less Whites. Now they're gone it seems the Whites are showing themselves more. But over there"—he nodded in the direction of the out-of-sight building—"we haven't seen any Whites all morning."

"Maybe a coincidence." Charlie's voice was even, but his heart thumped. Maybe Skate had a point; maybe the Whites didn't like being around the Squealers. They were different from the rest, that was for sure. Perhaps they were outcasts from their own fucked-up society.

"Yeah, maybe." Skate shrugged. "But now that Blane's tamed the Squealers, I'm thinking that he should send a couple with us when we have to come over here. You know, like extra protection?"

Charlie laughed, loud and hard, the suddenness of it making his belly ache.

"What's so funny?" Skate's dark eyes clouded.

"Oh, nothing, man." Charlie pulled his face back into line, the odd twitch betraying him at the corners of his mouth. "It's just that if you think those things are tamed . . . well, you're fucking tripping." He shook his head. "That's not tame, Skate. That is, at best, a very uneasy truce. And don't kid yourself otherwise."

"A truce is still a truce."

"Maybe. But I'd still feel happier with you at my back than one of them."

Skate gave a half smile and Charlie felt the tension of the moment go. He checked his watch. It was nearly two already. "You go and check Leeboy and Chokey are where they should be. I'm going to go and start sorting the stash to move over."

"You not coming to catch the kid?"

"Nah, setting this fire has taken up too much time. I need to get the shit moved today. We've already had to move it to here from the main stash. Now I've got to shift it again. You can handle the kid. I trust you."

As Skate strode away, Charlie looked up at the burning block. It was home and it was going up in smoke. After clearing out the cook room, lugging the chemicals to safety outside where Skate organized a couple of men to ferry them over to the new block, Charlie had taken a long look around his own place. Even though it was done up to a pretty good standard, the decor and furniture suddenly looked tired and cheap after spending the morning over at Blane's new citadel or whatever the fuck he wanted to call it. Still, the flat had been his place for a long time. It was familiar.

He'd stood in the lounge for a good ten minutes, an open holdall at his feet, wondering what the hell he should put inside it. As it turned out, he didn't have that much he wanted to save. Just his clothes and shoes. He left an old framed picture of his mum on top of the telly. He'd kept it there more out of guilt than any affection and he figured the guilt could go up in smoke now.

There were no photos of Lucy. He'd quietly burned them when she left. The only personal possession that he in any way treasured was the silver necklace she'd given him, and that was still around his neck. He'd never quite found the will to take that off. His fingers had almost risen to touch it but he'd kept them down. Lucy was long gone, and maybe given the way things had turned out for the world, that wasn't such a bad thing. Even if she'd stayed they'd have just fucked each other up some more until one of them snapped.

He was in and out of his home within twenty minutes, and when he'd left, he hadn't looked back. Staring up at it burning now, he ignored the hollow ache somewhere beyond the pit of his stomach. It was only his past that was going up in flames and most of that hadn't been all that good. He'd taken only one picture from his house. It was tucked between some papers in the shoe box under his bed that held his passports, three of them each in different names, his birth certificate, driver's license and his mum's rent book. He'd left all of those documents behind but he'd slipped the photo into his pocket.

Dropping his cigarette onto the muddy grass, he pulled it out. The square of paper had the grainy faded color of any picture taken before the computer revolution, its image a frozen moment of time twenty years past.

Two boys sat on the wall at the back of the garages that Charlie now used as lockups and stashes as and when required. The sun was shining and each boy had an arm around the shoulders of the other, both wearing "Frankie Says Relax" T-shirts proudly over their jeans. Nowadays, Blane would kick the living shit out of any gay fucker that came close to him, but back then, when they were eight or nine, that song was just the coolest thing, because whether it was real or not, all the kids on the estate and countrywide believed that the strange sound at the end of the song truly was the sound of some bloke shooting his load, slowed down by a million times, and that made Frankie Goes to Hollywood the hippest band in the charts in everybody's book.

Charlie's fingers seemed thick and large as they trembled slightly, wiping drops of stinking rain from the shiny surface. They were a pair of scrawny fuckers back then, both grinning toothily from ear to ear, Charlie's blond hair still carrying the strawberry tinge that coated it through his early childhood until, eventually and thankfully, it faded to the dirty sandy color of his adulthood. Not that the change had stopped Blane calling him Ginger whenever he wanted to wind him up. He'd kept that up until they were about fifteen and something invisible shifted in their lives and Blane realized it was important that people respected Charlie too. It made them stronger.

In the photo his hair hung slightly too long over his eyes, thick and unkempt and a far cry from the short cut he wore these days. His thin shoulders were leaned inward, as were Blane's, the two boys so close their heads were almost touching. Despite inheriting his mother's pale skin, Blane's hair was pure Jamaican afro before he grew it long and dreadlocked it, and in the time frozen in the picture, when Frankie was cool and both Charlie and Blane had yet to reach double figures and touch their first gun and scar their souls with everything that came after, the man who now inspired terror across the estates looked like a young Michael Jackson, his skin clear and cheeks full under his laughing eyes. There was no menace in them. Not a trace.

Both boys' smiles were open and full of the fun to be had when you weren't yet ten and the future wasn't filled with dirt and blood. They were going to be best friends forever. It was set in stone. The only solid in their fluid lives where adults came and went and their growing eyes couldn't much longer stop seeing their mothers for who and what they were.

Charlie stared at the picture until a window cracked loudly above him, the heat and flames spreading down to the next floor, no doubt lapping at the petrol trail Jude would have left. His eyes burned slightly and he wasn't sure if it was from the dark smoke, the rain or the itch of betrayal. Yeah, he thought what Blane was doing with the Squealers was wrong. Yes, he thought the situation was completely fucked up. Yes, he thought they should be leaving this gangster shit behind and heading out of town to somewhere clean. But could he really leave Blane? After all these years? Blane was all he had left and crazy or not, they needed each other. They always had.

Ignoring his own doubts, he carefully slid the photo back into his pocket. Glass above him fractured, splinters tumbling to the ground. There was less energy to it than the explosion of earlier, and Charlie watched a jagged section glitter as it twirled slowly downward. Maybe Blane was right. Maybe it was the start of a new day. Try as he might to convince himself, the words felt hollow in his head. And, he thought, as he finally shifted his feet and headed down the side of the building and around to the back, the rain still tasted like shit.

As the glass on the top floor had blown out of the front of the building, it had done the same on the back, sheets of dirty glass scattered haphazardly across the gravel. Charlie skirted around it, past where he'd parked the car after his journey over to the main stash. His skin itched just thinking about that; how many times he'd had to turn and find a different route because of smashed-up cars and webbed wreckage in the streets. And then there'd been the Whites. Maybe Blane should have come with him on that run rather than Skate. Maybe then he'd have understood that the citadel wasn't such a great idea, and that the Whites would be coming. Eventually.

He scanned the roofs of the line of tatty garages, keeping well back until he was sure nothing was crouching on top, waiting to spring. He shivered, scouting for any sign of translucent legs or red eyes housed in insipid white bumps. When he was sure it was clear he moved in closer, jogging toward a tatty black door in the middle of the row. Beneath his feet, weeds sprouted from any tiny gap in the uneven ground, the leaves and shoots green and strong as they weaved upward like ivy, clinging to the walls of the garages that surrounded them.

Crouching to unlock the first of three heavy padlocks, he grimaced at the strong scent coming from them. He'd never smelled plant life so strongly, as if the rain was giving them something that it never had before. He pulled the lock free and moved away to the other two, working quickly. Newham was starting to smell like he imagined a jungle: hot and sweet and lush. The door slid slowly upward, creaking and rattling with every metal inch until it came to a halt, hanging half down, creating an awning over Charlie's head. The room smelled dirty and dusty and damp. It smelled good, like a garage in the inner city should smell. There was nothing natural in it, just grease and metal and sweat. He could understand that.

He cautiously stepped over his makeshift trip wire, which was stretched across the entrance, hidden only in the shadows of the concrete room. If someone broke that wire then they'd be in for a shock. The gun balanced high on a box at the back and pointed in the general direction of the doorway did not have the safety on and its trigger would fire if the wire was tugged.

The world may have changed, but Charlie figured while there were still men alive, there were still treacherous, greedy fuckers out there. If they tried to rob the stash, then odds were one of them would end up with a hole in him somewhere, and if not, they'd be long gone empty-handed before the smoke had faded. In Charlie's experience treacherous men tended not to be brave. All the ones he'd come across had cried for their whore mothers in the final moments, at any rate.

He moved farther into the darkness, resisting turning on the lights. Reaching into one of the holdalls closest to his feet, he pulled out an automatic handgun and tucked it into his belt. After a moment's hesitation he took another and shoved it into his jacket pocket along with several clips. He didn't question why. Something about the weight made him feel more secure and Charlie had long ago learned to trust his instincts. He sighed, running his hands over his short hair, not liking the damp rain he felt there. He wanted a shower. Long and hot, and while they were still working. Surely all those water-processing plants and electricity centers would pack up soon enough without workers to keep them all running smoothly? His head throbbed. Blane would probably have an answer to that one too.

He turned, scanning the room for the bag with the four two-kilo packs of untreated cocaine wrapped up inside. He'd get them over first. Blane had freaked that he'd brought so little of the drugs over from the main stash in the warehouse, but Charlie had figured that the weapons were more important. Skate had agreed and in the end Blane had come around. It did mean that they were going to have to make another trip over there at some point. Maybe he'd let Skate go alone with some of Blane's eight-legged Squealer guards. How comfortable would the big lad feel then, he wondered.

Something white snagged in the corner of his eye, and all defenses immediately alerted, he dropped to a crouch and spun, peering outward under the low hood of the rusty garage door. What was that? A White? One of Blane's Squealers? The gun already out of his pocket and gripped easily in his hand, he stared, his heart thumping hard.

A thick white coil hung down the side of the grimy building, but it wasn't a spider's webbing or whatever that weird shit was the Whites had covered most of London in. This was something different. Something ordinary. Adrenaline flooded his system as he relaxed. Sheets. Fucking sheets tied together. He stayed where he was until a pair of dark trainers came into view, and then as they were followed by baggy jeans, he darted over the trip wire and out into the open space. He looked up. A pair of terrified dark eyes met his as their owner struggled to haul himself back up the knotted rope that swung and twisted as he wriggled. Shoving the gun back in his jacket, Charlie grabbed the legs, wrapping his arms tightly around the trainers that kicked out at him.

"Not so fast, mate." With a grunt he tugged the boy down, sending them both tumbling to the hard ground, Charlie underneath, the black kid on top. The wind knocked from his chest and with sharp pieces of grit and shattered glass pressing into his back through his coat, he gripped the boy and lay still, taking a moment to get his breath back. His eyes followed the trail of sheets upward to a broken window on the third floor. They must have smashed it just after the top floor blew.

They.

He frowned, staring at the three faces that looked back, eyes wide with shock and terror that for a moment sent them back to being the children they were on the cusp of leaving behind. One dark face peered out from between the two white ones and Charlie recognized him instantly. Leke whatever. He'd caught the wrong kid. The one Blane wanted was still inside. The boy above looked almost in tears as a white boy with a harder, older face pulled him and the kid fiddling with his glasses on the other side of him, away from the window. Charlie stared at their frightened faces for a moment longer. Shit, they were just kids. A misfit bunch of fucking kids not so different from the two trapped in the photo in his pocket. Fuck.

The kid on top of him wriggled and Charlie rolled him over, straddling his back.

"Get off me!"

"Shut the fuck up," he muttered, enjoying the freedom of breathing space in his lungs again, before letting out a long, low whistle.

"Skate! Chokey!" The boy struggled under him as he called out for the men, young elbows digging into his thighs, and gripping the boy's head with both hands, Charlie slammed his smooth, good-looking face into the gravel. Blood rose in tiny spots, marking the grazes running up his skin.

"Just stop fucking moving. You're starting to piss me off now."

Charlie had to give the boy his due—he fought back, squirming uselessly beneath the large man's weight, determined to try and free himself. He didn't go limp until two sets of feet charged noisily around from inside the building. Only when Chokey had a grip on the boy's arm ready to haul him up did Charlie push himself to his feet.

"Be careful. He's a little fighter."

"This the one Blane wants?" Skate looked the boy up and down.

"No. It's not him."

The boy's chin came up. "There's no one else here. The others left days ago. I was too scared . . . I . . ." Chokey slapped him hard across the face.

"Save it for Blane."

"And you save it for when Blane tells you to hit the motherfucker," Skate growled.

Charlie peered up at the window, ignoring their spat. "Chokey," he said softly. "Go and check the third floor. Maybe there's someone still up there." He shrugged. In his heart he knew he should send Skate. Skate was tougher and cleverer. If there were kids up there, they wouldn't get around Skate. Chokey though, Chokey was different. He was all muscle and no brain. If those kids were smart, they'd find a way around him. So why was it Chokey he was sending? The next words came from somewhere so deep inside they seemed to be those of a stranger.

"But I think maybe he's telling the truth. I didn't see anyone up there lowering him down."

Chokey nodded. "No worries, Charlie. I'm on it."

Flashing Skate a glare as he shoved the boy into the other man's hands, he sauntered back around to the side stairwell, slowly disappearing into the gloom. Skate was younger than Chokey, but Skate would have run those few steps. Why the hell hadn't he sent Skate?

"You all right, Charlie?"

Charlie fingered the photo that sat snug against the cool metal of the gun.

"Yeah."

Was he all right? Maybe. Maybe not. But one thing was for sure, he needed to *seem* all right. He looked over at Skate. "Let's hope this one will keep Blane happy." Taking the boy's other arm, he hauled him forward, his grip rough as if the action could somehow counter his thoughts. They were just kids. And there'd been enough dying already. He just hoped Blane never found his lie out.

"I didn't see anyone up there lowering him down."

Shit.

He didn't look back. He didn't think about the lockup, the door still half open, the guns and drugs inside for anyone to take. He didn't think about those things until later.

CHAPTER SIXTEEN

"Shit, shit, shit."

Craig's brain raced so hotly that he barely heard Leke's sharp exhales of expletives as he pulled him away from the broken window.

"They've got Courtney. They've got Courtney." Leke's eyes filled with a slow tide of dread. "What are we going to do? We've got to . . ."

"Get out of here." Craig kept his voice low, one hand tight on Leke's arm, the other gripping a handful of Nathan's jacket. "We need to move. Now."

Leke licked his lips. "That's Charlie Nash. Shit, that was . . ."

"The bin cupboard."

Nathan's monotone cut through the panic. Craig stared at him. Large drops of sweat formed against the boy's flushed skin and one finger frantically worked at the bridge of his glasses. Despite sounding so calm, Nathan's whole body betrayed the fear that his voice couldn't release.

"What the fuck is he talking about?" Leke's voice rose an octave, his own terror forcing him back to his childhood. Craig ignored him, his brain twisting around the suggestion. He knew what Nathan meant.

Not taking the time to explain, he pushed Leke out through the hallway toward the door of the flat.

"Down by the right-hand stairs. The bin room. Go."

Leke didn't need telling twice and the three boys sprinted out into the empty corridor. Even though the fire was several floors above them, the air tasted of gas and the grit of smoke, dirty and poverty-ridden. Craig felt it clinging to the soft flesh of his lungs as he dragged air in and out, his taut legs pushing past Leke and taking him to the front of the small group by the time they reached the stairs. He paused, peering over the side, his eyes quickly seeking out any shadows or movement that might betray someone's presence. There was nothing. Not visible in the small area he could see, anyway. He charged down the narrow stairwell, his feet slipping slightly on the damp stairs. Leke ran alongside him, his speed and movement equally as agile as Craig's own, even if the black boy didn't have the solid power. They moved in parallel with the ease they'd always shown on the football pitch. Behind them, Nathan was a different story. He was fast enough, fear keeping him close to the other two boys, but as Craig peered back to check he was okay, the geeky boy was all gangly arms and awkward legs, one hand clinging to the handrail as he threw himself down the stairs.

Craig turned his attention back to his own feet. At least Nathan wasn't trying to fiddle with his glasses as he ran. That was something. He spun around the final turn, his feet barely touching the flat area between floors, before deftly traveling down the last flight of steps.

He held up a hand to keep the others back and peered

around to the covered area that led from the outside of the blocks to the stairs. The gray walls bore the scars of battle with too many graffiti artists to count, but in the gloom away from any natural light, the damp concrete floor was empty. He flicked his hand, signaling the others to come forward. They had about two minutes maximum to get hidden in the bin room before Blane's men started ripping the block apart looking for them. Leaving the block was out of the question, Charlie was outside and they'd be caught for sure, but if they could just hide somewhere for a few moments, somewhere no one would think of, then they had half a chance of getting away before being found or the burning building collapsed in on their heads. And no one would think of looking in the bin room. No one but Nathan. That's what he hoped, at least.

Staying close to the wall, the three boys trotted toward the back of the building. Rain drifted at them from the open sides, and Craig found himself clinging closely to the rough surface in order to avoid its touch. The voices were louder now, footsteps coming toward them from the area by the garages. They reached the tatty wooden door to the refuse cupboard, and with nervous hands Craig tugged at the black bolt, housed too tightly in its casing. Paint flaked away from it, coating his hand. His heart raced, pumping heat to his already flushed cheeks. The footsteps were getting closer. Spitting angry sounds that had no meaning, he pushed the metal free and yanked open the door. The stench of rotten food flooded out at them as if the storage room had been holding its breath, waiting for someone to come and release its sigh. His stomach churning, Craig grabbed Nathan first and shoved him into the small space between the lines of large green overflowing waste carts and where the door would close.

"No, I can't . . . the smell . . ."

Craig ignored him. "In. And for fuck's sake, shut up."

Leke didn't need any encouragement, sliding alongside Nathan and squashing him up against the wall to make space for Craig. "Come on!" he hissed.

Craig pulled the door closed behind them. The world fell into cloying darkness, his fingernails almost invisible as they gripped the narrow edge of wood panel holding the door shut. The stench was almost overwhelming. Normally emptied every Thursday morning, the large green Dumpsters had been left full and forgotten for at least two weeks as the world had slid into its quiet Armageddon. Along with the sickly foulness of rotten food were other stomach-churning odors: soiled diapers, stale beer and the vinegary dregs of wine, vomit and other richer, oily odors that coated the air and eased themselves on the boys' clothes, settling in the delicate membrane on the inside of their noses. Craig felt sick, trying to breathe more shallowly despite the adrenaline that rushed through his system.

Behind them, something moved in the mountains of rubbish. Foil rustled and paper shifted in the dark recesses overcrowded with waste. The hairs on the back of Craig's neck quivered as all three boys froze. The sounds came again, loud in the quiet gloom. Light feet scuttled, edging closer.

"What the fuck is that?" Leke's words were barely more than breath.

"Something in here." For the first time, Craig heard an edge of something close to emotion in Nathan's voice.

The rubbish rustled again, more insistently this time, and Craig was sure that whatever was moving back there was coming closer to them. Vomit rose in his chest and he swallowed. They couldn't run. There was nowhere to go. Outside was just as dangerous as in.

"Shh. Stay still. Just a few minutes."

Outside, one set of feet rumbled past and disappeared up the stairs; Craig was sure he could feel the vibration of their weight through the ground beneath him. They were trapped. There was nothing they could do but wait it out and hope the men didn't linger too long at the block.

"I want to get out of here." Leke sounded close to tears, and Craig gripped his arm.

"Stay still."

The rubbish behind them fell silent for a moment. Craig wasn't sure whether that was better or worse and he fought the urge to try and turn to look. What the fuck was it? The obvious answer reared an unwelcome image of pale legs and a swollen body behind his eyes. He tried to blink it away, but it wouldn't go, teasing his fear from the inside of his skull.

Beside him, both Leke's and Nathan's breathing had risen to rapid pants, the same mental picture no doubt plaguing them, and he knew it wouldn't take much to make either of them panic and run. Shit, he was pretty close to it himself. He squeezed his eyes shut. Just a few minutes. That was all they needed.

On the other side of the door deep male voices made soft conversation, long pauses punctuating their exchange as they too waited, shifting from foot to foot under the shelter of the concrete. One of them spat, the hawking clear even if their words weren't.

The thing in the waste behind them shuffled closer,

loud in its menacing intent. Craig bit down on the inside of his cheek. It was right behind him, whatever it was. He gripped the wood panel tighter. He would not run. He wouldn't.

Heavy soles hammered back down the stairs and Craig's ears followed their path until they stopped by the others, so close and yet invisible.

"Nothing. I checked the whole floor. Jude's on the fourth laying the petrol trail and I just scanned the second. No sign of anyone."

"I told you . . ."

Craig flashed a sideways glance at Leke and found him looking back. They both recognized that voice. It was Courtney.

"I told you they all left. Days ago. I was too scared so I stayed behind."

His voice sounded flat and small. Craig hoped it was to add effect to the lie but he wasn't so sure. How would he feel if it were he being held by Charlie Nash? He'd be crapping himself. Courtney was probably doing the same. His stomach felt funny, guilt and fear creating an unpleasant mix. They were best friends, the three of them, but he couldn't ignore the awful relief that it was Courtney that had gone down the sheet rope first, and that it was Courtney that was now on the other side of that wooden door rather than him. *Depending on what it was they were sharing their hiding place with.* The thought rang out loud. *Maybe Courtney was the lucky one, after all.*

Something tickled the back of his neck, and the activity outside became simply a background buzz against the bright white of his panic.

"Let's get him over to Blane."

A foreign weight pressed into his shoulder and Craig

squeezed Leke's arm, needing something to stop him from pulling open the door and running screaming into Charlie Nash. *It was on him. Whatever it was, it was on him.* Air felt trapped in his lungs as he fought to breathe, his bladder tightening. The tiniest moan escaped from between his pressed lips, and then Leke was squeezing his arm back.

Craig waited for the spider's bite, or to feel those awful legs wrapping around his head. Neither came. Instead, the solid weight on him moved around to his other shoulder, light hairs tickling into his ear. His whole body trembled, the shivers making his teeth rattle. He couldn't stay still much longer. Not if all the lives of everyone left in the world depended on it. He wanted it gone. Off him. Dead. Tears pricked the back of his eyes and he hated them.

Outside, the voices finally moved away, the men talking among themselves over the scuffing sound of Courtney being pushed and dragged between them. The noise faded to silence.

Three sets of heavy breathing filled the noxious room as they waited a long minute to be sure Charlie Nash had gone.

"Something on me . . ." Craig muttered, urgency devouring his voice.

"Rat," Leke whispered back. "I can see it."

Rat. The word echoed in his uncomprehending ears, the letters slowly coming to meaning one by one, like a child forming its first word with bright alphabet pieces. Rat. He giggled, the sound less a laugh than an explosive release of panic. It was just a rat. An ordinary, dirty rat.

"Let's go." Leke's voice was low, as if for a moment he'd taken charge. He looked at Craig. Nodding, Craig let go of the wood and pushed open the door, shaking the creature from his shoulder as he stepped out into the damp air.

"Fucking rats," he muttered, his body shivering with disgust, his hands brushing at his shoulders in case perhaps some ghost of the animal was still attached to him. He glanced from side to side. There was no sign of anyone, but even out in the relatively fresh open, the smell of smoke was strong. Whoever was up there setting fire to stuff must be pretty much done now, and it would be just their luck that he'd choose the side they were standing in to come down.

"Look."

Nathan and Leke had followed him quickly out of the bin storage room, but were now both staring back inside.

"Those are some fucking rats." Revulsion wrapped itself in every syllable of Leke's words. Craig turned to look. Several pairs of bright eyes met his from the far reaches of the room. The arrogant intelligence in their shine made his stomach turn. The one that had been on his shoulder remained near the front of one overflowing cart, sitting up on its large haunches, its sharp front teeth clearly visible. Craig stared. These weren't just rats. These were something else.

"It's the size of a fucking cat." One hand brushed at his shoulder again, and he was sure the rat was watching and laughing on the inside. He kicked the door shut. The rats could think they were fucking clever. He still wouldn't put money on them if they came across the spiders. They wouldn't look so fucking cocky then.

"Rats like cats." Nathan smiled at his own rhyme.

Craig shivered and slowly unclenched his jaw, forcing his fear and anger to relax a little. "Come on." He trotted over to the far wall and peered around toward the garages. One was still slightly open, the one that Charlie Nash had been in. Staring at it, his heart leaped. Maybe there'd be guns or weapons they could take with them in there.

"I'm not leaving without Courtney." Leke's voice was firm.

"What?"

"I said I'm not—"

"I heard what you said." Craig turned. A long moment passed as the two boys stared at each other, Nathan's eyes darting from one to the other. "Look," Craig said eventually, "Charlie's left a lockup open. Let's get inside it, see what we can use and then talk about a plan to get Courtney back." Leke watched him suspiciously, and Craig didn't blame him. The lack of conviction in his own voice was obvious. How the hell were they supposed to get Courtney back? They didn't even know where Charlie had taken him. And even if they did, they had no chance of getting to their friend. The idea of leaving Courtney behind made Craig feel sick, but the idea of going after him was more terrifying. But Leke looked pretty resolute and Craig knew what a stubborn fuck he could be.

"Okay," Leke said.

"Maybe we should talk to those kids too."

Craig was so fixated on Leke, that it took a moment for Nathan's words to sink in. Slowly, both he and Leke turned to face the other boy. He was peering around the wall, not at the garages, but just off to the side.

"What?"

"Those kids over there."

Craig looked. Alongside the garages, like a mirror image of themselves, three white faces peered nervously out from the side wall. Two boys, maybe a bit older than they, and a thin man who was clinging to a bike.

"What the fuck?"

Nathan raised a hand and waved. The blond boy on the other side waved back.

"Oh fuck it." Craig nodded toward the older man and then pointed in the direction of the open garage. All three heads opposite nodded enthusiastically. Despite himself, Craig felt his spirits lift with the thrill of meeting new people. The more of them there were, the more chance they had of getting out alive. That's what he was hoping anyway.

CHAPTER SEVENTEEN

Crouched beside the wall of the garages, Harry could feel sweat running down his back in streaks thick enough to rival the rain. They'd been hidden there doing nothing but watching for over ten minutes, but his breath was only just slowing back to normal. He looked over at the nervous faces staring back at them across the sparsely graveled concrete and wondered if either Mr. Green or James were going to say anything at all about this new development. Other people; alive and organized, if not entirely friendly.

After everything that had happened so far that day, the discovery made him feel slightly dizzy.

Despite the teacher being only an inch or two in front, and the other boy so close behind that Harry was all too aware of his body heat, it seemed that during the stillness of the past ten minutes, the three companions were farther apart than they'd been since this whole madness started.

No one had spoken since Peter had been carried off by the monstrous spider. James had thrown up long and loud, bent double in the gutter until all that was coming out was spit. Mr. Green had simply stood in the exact spot he'd been frozen to throughout the attack and

stared at Josh's body, tangled up where it had fallen by
the bike. In the end it was Harry who had peeled off his
stupid yellow waterproof coat and laid it over the tiny,
broken body. He'd tried not to look at the hole in the
side of the bicycle helmet, its rough edges coated with
blood and small clumps of grayish pink matter that had
been forced out in a splatter, James's badly aimed bullet
making a mockery of its protection. He was glad when
Josh's head was covered.

They'd climbed back on their bikes, but no one had
spoken. James and Mr. Green were lost in their own
moments, and for his part Harry's head was empty of
words. There was nothing he could say that would even
touch the sides of their situation. Instead they'd pedaled
hard, Harry in the lead heading in the direction of the
plume of black smoke, sweating out their anger and fear
and grief. None of them kept a lookout for any danger.
During that ten minutes of speeding flight, Harry was
pretty sure that both James and Mr. Green were willing
the spiders to find them. They didn't of course. The
world hadn't changed that much. Fate and luck did the
choosing and whether you wished something on yourself had nothing to do with it. And anyway, he was
pretty sure that if the spiders had attacked, then the
other two would have quickly changed their minds
about dying. For most people, guilt only went so far.
He'd felt guilty watching the woman die from the bed-
and-breakfast window, but it hadn't made him rush out
to save her. His own life was too important and there
was no point in feeling bad about that. Not in this new
world.

For his own sake, his fast pedaling was simply to put
as much distance as possible between himself and the

memory of Josh's brains on the outside of his helmet. That they found the burning block at all was something of a miracle; Harry's sense of direction must have been working on autopilot because he had no memory of the journey until they'd come to a halt by a narrow alleyway at the end of a row of tatty houses and climbed off, wheeling their bikes across the broken surface of the uneven ground and coming out at the end of the long row of garages.

They'd been about to wander out into the open when Mr. Green had spotted the blond man emerge from the garage and yank down the black boy who was clinging to the sheet rope. There was nothing gentle in the way the man grappled with the teenager and pinned him down. It seemed safer to hide until that situation was over. He had a feeling that none of the men who marched the boy away would be too friendly to strangers. But the men had gone and now they had been found by these three boys who looked as scared as Harry felt.

Still without uttering a word, his feet followed Mr. Green's onto the drive, his body hunching over his bike as they jogged toward the slightly open door. James's trainers matched his pace, his front wheel threatening to collide with Harry's rear one. The three boys hidden opposite peeled away from their wall and trotted over to them, the two small groups suddenly a gang. Despite everything, Harry felt his spirits lift as they came to a halt.

The slightly chubby boy pushed his glasses up on his nose and frowned. "My coat is better than theirs are."

Harry waited for the boy to smile but his face was impassive, his eyes instead running over Mr. Green's and James's bright waterproofs. There was a long pause before James broke it.

"He has a point."

Harry was pleased to hear the familiar dry humor coating his friend's words, even if, when he turned to grin at him, he found that his eyes still looked pretty dead as they slipped away from Harry's gaze.

The other white boy snorted. "This is Nathan. You'll get used to him."

"I'm Harry. And this is James."

"Craig." He nodded toward the black boy who glanced furtively around them. "And that's Leke."

"Can we get inside now?"

"Sounds like a good idea." Harry was suddenly aware of the clipped tones of his own accent, compared with the rougher edges of their new companions' and felt an itch of embarrassment under his collar. The new kids might be younger than they, but he had an idea they might be a lot more street-smart.

His fingers gripped the rough, cool edge and hauled it upward. The metal screeched as it yawned open, like a seagull circling and announcing their presence to anyone or thing that might be looking. Above them, more glass blew out from the flats. Harry stared into the gloom. Mr. Green pushed his bike forward. The spokes clicked around, and Harry's eyes dropped to them. He saw the thin, tight line of string or wire and frowned. What was that? The wheel rolled through it, and he looked up, his mouth falling open, but unable to spit out the words quickly enough. *Trip wire*.

The air shook. He watched the boys around him flinch, the gunshot assaulting his ears as an afterthought, its sharp retort overwhelmed by another small explosion from within the block whose insides were consuming themselves in fire. Mr. Green spun, invisible hands turning him around on his heels in an awkward pirouette. Craig grabbed his tumbling body and dragged it inside.

They pulled the door down behind them, and crumpled into the quiet gloom.

CHAPTER EIGHTEEN

Charlie's nerves slowly tightened with each step he took on the short walk toward the smart new apartment block. The slowly turning internal screw had nothing to do with either the approaching storm that had started to growl above them, or the potential of a Whites attack. If anything he felt safer than usual from the latter. His eyes scanned the street as he pushed the young boy forward, keeping him trapped between the three larger men. Blanc had been serious about creating his citadel and it seemed he wasn't slow in starting.

His coat collar zipped as high as it could go, Charlie buried his head into its fabric to protect his mouth and nose from the rain. His unease refused to dissipate regardless of his attempts to shake it off. With what he could see around him, he should be feeling better. Blane was keeping everyone busy. That much was obvious. Along the top of the high wall that ran the full length from the back of the estate down to the edge of India Road, broken bottles covered every inch, sharp edges of thick glass rising skyward, ready to slash anything that might come heavily in contact with it. Charlie wasn't sure how effective it would be against the Whites but as a stopgap measure until it could be replaced with barbed wire, he figured it wasn't so bad.

On the other side of the street, three men strolled up and down, guns in hands, scanning the walls and space around them for any attack. In the road itself thick tires were spread at almost regular intervals, laid on their sides. Fires burned in their empty hearts, and the fumes of petrol and burning rubber weren't stopped by the rain from rising and finding their way to the men's nostrils. Charlie pressed his face farther into his coat.

He didn't recognize the men, and saw both Skate and Chokey peering suspiciously across at them too. Maybe they were new survivors who had just shown up, or maybe they were from the blocks. Either way, it seemed odd that Blane had just given them guns and trusted them on their own without him, or Skate or Jude watching them. It was more than odd. His feet paused, one hand automatically grabbing the back of the kid's jacket so he couldn't get too far ahead, and he stared. It was fucking wrong. Blane didn't trust anyone. Charlie was pretty sure he barely trusted him these days. Skate and Chokey turned.

"What's up, Charlie?" Skate looked as unhappy about the rain as Charlie felt.

He didn't answer, watching the other men. None of the three looked in the slightest bit bored, their eyes constantly moving and scanning the area. Charlie frowned. He'd run enough crews to know that at least one of them would have slacked off and been smoking or chatting. They looked stiff too; awkward and scared.

"What the fuck is that?" Chokey stumbled back slightly, almost knocking the kid into Charlie's arms. He pointed. "There. At the side of the house."

Charlie's eyes followed and when they found their

mark, his stomach turned. No wonder the men were behaving themselves so well.

"Seems you got your wish, Skate." His tongue was dry. "Looks like Blane's letting the Squealers out to guard." He watched the shiny, mottled shape as it scuttled sideways down the wall slightly, its red eyes appearing to be watching both them and the men guarding the street at the same time. Under control it might be, but there was madness in the angry, sharp movement of its squat legs, any fool could see that. As if hearing his criticism, it let out a high-pitched squeal of rage. Charlie's skin prickled with goose bumps.

"You feeling any safer?"

Skate stayed silent.

Feet thumped against the ground behind them, and Charlie turned to see Jude's thin frame catching up to them. He was slick with sweat and rain, but his eyes shone.

"Man, that was great! That was some fucking experience! That tower is blazing!"

"Where's Leeboy?" Jude's exuberance made Charlie's stomach turn as much as the sight of the Squealer had done. There was maybe a little madness in the younger man too.

"He's rounding up the men in the other tower. Blane wants everyone over at the new place. It'll be easier." His eyes finally found Courtney, and under the ash and grime that covered his skin, he frowned. "He's not the right kid."

"We know." Charlie felt the sudden urge to take Jude out, right there and then. The screw of tension was coiling slowly tighter and if he didn't get some breathing space soon it was going to snap. He needed to think about things, *really* think about them. But instead, here he was, just acting on impulse. His hand reached for the picture in his pocket and between his fingers it felt thin and fragile.

"He was the only one in there." Chokey unwittingly took on Charlie's lie and stopped him from having to repeat it. "The others have gone. I checked the building."

Jude shrugged. "Blane ain't going to be happy." His eyes darted to the wall, his grin spreading wide. "Holy shit, he actually did it! He fucking tamed them."

"Yeah," Charlie said, pushing Courtney forward and getting the group moving again. "How about that."

CHAPTER NINETEEN

Blane stared at the broken boy down on his hands and knees on the wooden floor. On either side of him his new guards hissed, the sounds turning into a soft, high-pitched wail, not quite the full ear-piercing squeal of earlier. They were calmer than they had been earlier. He'd sent Jude to pump some more shit into the flat and it was obviously taking effect. Even he had to admit that this group mentality stuff was freaky, but it was working in his favor. As long as two or three of the Squealers were kept mashed out of whatever served as their minds, then their calm filtered through to the rest. He smiled a little. Control one and you controlled them all. It was simple. And it seemed that as long as Janine was happy, then so were the rest.

He sniffed hard, a few more grains of bitter cocaine finding their way down the back of his throat and sending a delicious shiver down his spine. Janine. He had to laugh. She'd been his bitch before all this shit and now the freak still did what he told her. A dark cloud drifted across his buzzing mind. It was just like it always had been; as long as she was high, she was happy. He looked over at Charlie.

"Did you bring the stash over? You need to spend tonight cooking up some rocks, man."

The white man's face stayed impassive. "I got caught up with the kid. I'll get on it as soon as we're done here." His eyes passed over the creatures prowling on either side of Blane's chair. "Wouldn't want to keep the ladies waiting."

Blane grinned. Charlie always did have a dry fucking sense of humor.

"What shall I do with him?" Charlie nodded down at the kid, and Blane watched him for any sign of emotion. Charlie had been acting more distant than his normally reserved self over the past few days and it made Blane feel uneasy. Still, beating the shit out of the boy didn't seem to have bothered him. He lit a cigarette, pulling the smoke hard into his mildly numb mouth. Charlie was his oldest friend. He trusted him. He *had* to trust him, otherwise who else was there? One hand automatically reached to a creature at his side and his long, slim fingers traced out a train on its cool, slimy back. The Squealer trembled under his touch, perhaps a shiver of pleasure or just an automatic response, but either way something in that contact made him feel stronger immediately.

His anger with the boy returned. He leaned forward, his leather coat creaking.

"Now for the last time, where the fuck is your friend? The grass? Leke?"

The boy shook his head, long streamers of snot and saliva dribbling onto the expensive wooden floor.

"I told you." His voice was small and tired. "They left days ago. I don't know where they went. Said they were leaving the city." A sob hiccuped out of him. "That's all I know. I was too scared to go."

Blane sighed. The boy's tears revolted him slightly, but he liked the terror lurking beneath the sheer ex-

haustion as the teenager lifted his head, looking at
Blane and then the Squealers beside him with equal
fear.

"They're beautiful, aren't they?" Blane smiled, taking another long drag of his cigarette and blowing the
stream of smoke skyward. "Not like the others. The
Whites." The boy's eyes were focused on the spiders
now. Blane could see him taking in their red eyes and
angry, mottled skin. "These girls are meaner. They're
Squealers." He tossed his long dreadlocks over his
shoulder. "And they like their meat fresh."

The trickle of cocaine slid down the back of his
throat, numbing it further, and the shiver of pleasure it
gave him was heightened by the horrified sob that came
from the boy.

"I'm guessing you don't want to make a mess of the
penthouse," Charlie said, "but do you want me to take
him and feed him to the others? They might be high,
but that might not be a bad thing." He paused, looking
down at the kid. "They'll rip him apart slower."

"That doesn't sound like you, Charlie." Blane
watched his friend cautiously. "You normally like things
killed clean."

Charlie shrugged, his cool blue gaze meeting Blane's
directly. "I don't like grasses, Blane. You should know
that."

A giggle bubbled in Blane's chest. How could he not
have trusted Charlie? For a moment, despite the drugs,
he felt tired. There was so much to think about, so
much to do, and since he'd let a few of the Squealers
out, his brain had felt a little fuzzy every now and then.
He took a deep breath. But things were coming together and he was in charge. Shit, he was fucking God
now.

The kid was panting hard and Blane frowned. "Maybe. Maybe you should throw him in there with them."

He bit his bottom lip. Maybe the other kid was long gone, but if he killed this one then he had no chance of getting his hands on him. He wondered why it still mattered so much. After everything that had changed in the world there would be no trial. That much was for fucking sure. But the arrogance of the kid irritated him. That he'd thought he could take on Blane Gentle-King as if he were just some little player that didn't matter. It was a matter of pride. And the world might have changed, but Blane's pride was still the same.

"Tell you what," Charlie said. "Me and Chokey will go and work him over some more. Explain about the Squealers and Weights. Maybe that will jog his memory about the other kid. If he gives us something good, who knows, maybe we won't serve him up as dinner."

Chokey pulled the sniveling boy up from the floor. "Back down to the fourteenth for you."

Blane nodded. "Okay, do that." Feet scuttered beside him and a flash of pain shot through his head, gone almost before he'd noticed it was there. "And Charlie . . ."

The other man turned, already headed toward the lift. "Yeah?"

"Then get on the stash. We *need* those rocks, man."

Charlie smiled. "Be cool, dude. I'm on it."

Blane sat back in his chair as he watched the men leave, dragging the boy between them. His limbs felt heavy and he wondered if maybe it was too soon for another line. His arm dropped down to his left and as it rested on the abhorrent creature beside him, he was sure he could feel Janine buzzing in a dark space in his head.

* * *

What a difference a day makes . . . The old song lyrics had been going around in Charlie's head the whole time he'd stood in Blane's new pad. Was it really only that morning they'd spoken out on the vast balcony? Things had changed since then. The flat stunk, for one. And not just like Jude did of stale sweat and cheap cigarettes. Blane's new apartment stank of rot. The kind of rot that would soon be taking over the whole of London. Dead bodies and disease, that's what had filled Charlie's nostrils the minute the lift doors had slid open and from the way Chokey had flinched ever so slightly beside him, Charlie figured he'd smelled the same. It hung in every atom of the air around them.

Maybe the odor was drifting up from the pile of corpses burning outside, but Charlie didn't think so. It was too rich, the heavy sickly sweetness too clear to have crept up from outside. And more importantly, the apartment was smoke free, the vast sliding doors pulled closed. This hadn't come from outside. The stench was coming from those things . . . and Blane.

It had taken every ounce of internal reserve to keep his face impassive when looking at his best friend. Blane was high, that was obvious and no real surprise; he'd been high every day since this thing had started and Charlie had got him out of the nick. It was a concern, but it wasn't a surprise. What bothered Charlie was the greasy sheen Blane's skin had taken on, as if his pores were shedding fat rather than sweat in this new heat. There was something about it that reminded him of the Squealers and the Whites. He had the same slick appearance that they did, as if somehow his proximity to them was having a physical effect on him. Charlie didn't like it. He didn't like it one fucking bit. How could

Blane not notice the changes or the smell? He couldn't help but wonder if maybe wherever Blane's straight mind was, he wasn't a little bit terrified himself.

He took the stairs up to the sleek metal lift with his normal nonchalance, despite the urge he felt to run. The doors slid open as soon as he'd touched the button and letting out an invisible sigh of relief, he stepped inside. Blane's apartment disappeared and Charlie knew in that instant that he wasn't planning on seeing his best friend ever again. Enough was enough. The world had changed and Blane was changing with it and not in any way Charlie would have predicted, and if he didn't get out then he was going to lose his own fucking mind.

Even though they were only dropping one floor, the lift wasn't moving fast enough for Charlie. The kid standing between him and Chokey was crying, his chest pumping out low, soft sobs. Bruises rose up on his cheeks and chin and there was a cut across one eye. Charlie was pretty sure that by the next morning that eye would be swelled up so far he wouldn't be able to see out of it. If there were experts in these things, then Charlie was one. He didn't need a degree from any posh university. Plus, he'd inflicted most of those bruises himself. The fire had gone out of the teenager; that much was clear.

The boy had done well though. His mates should be proud of him. Knowing the truth hadn't stopped Charlie hitting him hard. He couldn't be soft; it would have showed, and anyway, if the kid had blurted the truth it wouldn't have mattered. They'd checked the block. There were no kids in there; whatever he said along those lines would just sound like a desperate lie. But he hadn't said a word, sticking to his original story like glue.

Charlie had hit him hard to make it convincing, but inside himself his stomach hadn't been in it. He just couldn't see the point. This wasn't business and there were too few people left in the world to fuck around with. With each blow he'd come to the realization that he couldn't fight it anymore. Maybe he and Blane weren't blood brothers under the skin, after all.

Maybe Blane's way was right if you wanted to still live in some kind of society. Charlie wasn't stupid; he understood that there would always be some on top and some underneath and a healthy dose of fear and respect helped keep the balance between the two—whether it was just the gangstas on the block or the whole fucking country with its government and police, but he was done with it. He couldn't live like this. And the idea of leaving the city and being on his own might scare the shit out of him, but the idea of staying scared him a whole lot more.

The doors pinged open and Chokey pushed the boy out into the sleek corridor. Charlie followed them. The city was dead or dying, there was no fighting that. Even those who survived would soon get sick from dysentery or cholera or all those other diseases that came from rotting bodies. Blane's citadel might survive for a while, but not forever. There were too many Whites for one thing, and once they'd stopped foraging on the survivors out in the streets, they'd find their way here. If Charlie was going to die and rot, then it wasn't going to be in this shitty part of London, which had taken all of his life so far. It was going to be somewhere where the air was fucking fresh.

They took the corridor in the direction away from where Jude was no doubt working as some kind of fucked-up zookeeper, drip feeding crack smoke to the remaining Squealers through his homemade contraption, and walked over to the third door. It was next to the apartment that Charlie had claimed for himself, but had no intention of ever sleeping in. Chokey pushed the door open, the lock broken from earlier in the day.

The boy stumbled over the threshold and into the blandly stylish hallway, Chokey shoving him roughly into the large open-plan living room, the right side of which opened out into a stainless-steel kitchen with brown lacquered cupboards.

"Nice pad," Charlie said, going over to the low sofa, and picking up a soft square cushion.

"Aren't they all?" Chokey laughed, pulling a futuristically styled dining chair out from under the glass table by the vast expanse of window. "And now they're all ours. Fucking great, isn't it?" Still grinning he placed the chair in the middle of the room and shoved the boy into it. There was no resistance, his legs crumpling under him as if they were made of paper. The boy's fight had gone. Charlie knew the look. He shook the cushion out and turned. The kid was in for a surprise though.

"Yeah." He smiled at Chokey. "Fucking great."

With the swift precision that had kept him at the top of the game for so many years, he pushed Chokey up against the wall, his own right knee tapping the back of the other man's and buckling it slightly. Before he had time to recover his balance, Charlie pressed the gun into the cushion against his chest and fired twice, the sound muffled in the padding. Chokey's eyes didn't even have time to widen, both bullets going straight through his heart. He was dead before he hit the floor.

Charlie stood back watching the body leave an untidy trail of blood on the magnolia wall as Chokey slid
downward. His lifeless legs splayed out in front and his
torso tilted, taking the streaks of red suddenly over to
the left. It looked like some kind of modern-fucking-
art shit. Charlie figured maybe the original owner
would have loved it. Art from real blood. Very Damien
fucking Hirst.

The kid's panting breath filled the open spaces of the
apartment, the panic in it climbing to the highest corners and cowering there. Chokey already forgotten,
Charlie turned to face him. The boy flinched.

"What's your name, kid?" Blane hadn't cared about
that when they'd been kicking the shit out of him in the
penthouse upstairs. Who the boy was didn't matter.
Just whether he knew where Leke Kudaisi was.

The damaged chocolate face stared at him and then
down at the gun.

"I'm not going to fucking shoot you. I just want to
know your name."

The jaw moved painfully and the boy spat out a word
along with a dribbled pink mess of blood and saliva.
"Courtney."

"Well, you probably don't need an introduction from
me, but I'll give it to you anyway." Charlie crouched by
the chair, his voice low. "Charlie Nash." The kid knew
his name, all the kids did. Blane and Charlie. Legends
in their own lifetime. He just hoped that hearing it out
loud might snap the boy out of his shock. He squeezed
Courtney's arm, his grip firm and steady.

"Look at me."

The boy did as he was told with his one good eye.

"I've had enough of this shit. I'm getting out." He
spoke quickly but clearly. They didn't have much time.

"Now you can come with me, or you can stay here and get your arse fed to those fucking freaky Squealers. It's up to you."

Courtney swallowed. "I'm coming."

"Good. Then let's go." Charlie stood up. "And let me do any talking. Just play along." He pressed the gun into Courtney's back. "You got it?" He winked. The expression was supposed to reassure the kid, but judging by the reaction it did anything but. He smiled. "Trust me, Courtney. If I wanted you dead, you'd be dead. Now let's get the fuck out of this madhouse."

Without looking back at Chokey, he steered Courtney out through the door and into the corridor. Their end was empty and Charlie's heart thudded. The gunshot had been muffled but not silenced and he had no fucking idea how sound traveled in this overdesigned and almost-empty building. He'd expected the two shots to at least bring Jude running, and his gun was ready just in case, but there was no movement. They walked swiftly in single file around the curve and toward the lift, Charlie pulling his second gun out from its place tucked into the back of his trousers and sliding it into his pocket. It was better to be safe than sorry. His feet padded softly, as if even that sound was dulled in the chic corridor, and within a few seconds they'd reached the lift. He pressed the call button and stood back slightly, looking to his left. Jude was crouched on the floor over his huge homemade bong, his head twitching slightly as he hummed. The dumb fuck had his iPod on. No wonder he hadn't heard the shots. Lights blinked above the doors signaling the machine's steady approach, and Charlie stepped forward and out of Jude's view.

The fool wouldn't survive long with that kind of relaxed attitude. Either a White would creep up and get him, or maybe even a Squealer, because if they were trained then Charlie was Mother fucking Teresa; and if it wasn't one of those then it would be Blane. Blane never could stand someone who didn't take the job seriously and he hadn't given many second chances back when he was *sane*.

A gentle ping sounded and the doors slid open. Charlie held his breath, but luck was with them and it was empty. He pushed Courtney inside and hit the ground floor button. Neither man nor boy spoke as the machine began its downward journey. The inside light flickered as they passed the sixth floor, for a moment plunging them into darkness and Courtney took a step closer.

"What's going on?" he whispered.

"I guess the electricity supply's going. Only so long those stations can run on their own." His heart thudded. The lights were back and the lift kept moving, but it was definitely a sign that things were going to get worse in the city. And suffocating in a dark, stuck lift was not on his list of ways to go. That's if they were lucky enough to be trapped there. If someone got them out then Blane would have far more inventive ways of dragging their deaths out. Before his imagination got too carried away with him, they came to a halt.

"Okay, Courtney. This is the tricky bit," Charlie muttered as the doors opened out onto the lobby. "Keep your head down and look as if everything hurts."

"Shouldn't be hard." Courtney's voice had more strength in it than it had upstairs. "Everything does hurt, thanks."

Leaving his smile on the inside, Charlie set his face in its usual cold expression and pushed the teenager out. He kept his pace steady. Up ahead he could see Blackeyes guarding the main entrance to the building. He wasn't worried about him. Like Chokey, Blackeyes was all brawn and no brain. He'd believe whatever Charlie told him.

"Hey Charlie! You okay, man?"

Skate's voice came from the left, and turning to where the lobby opened out, Charlie saw the other man standing behind the low desk designed for the building superintendent. In front of it stood three soaked and shaken strangers, one clutching his arm. The terror that was clear on his pale, chubby face made ~~Charlie~~ think it was a bite he was hiding. Whoever he was, he was already dead. He just didn't know it yet.

Skate frowned and Charlie steered Courtney roughly over to the other man. Talking to Skate was the last thing he wanted to do, but they didn't have any choice. Skate wasn't dumb like Blackeyes.

"What's going on?" Charlie flicked his head at the three newcomers.

"Between the tower fire and that fucking pile of bodies burning at the back of here, we're like a beacon for survivors. Had fifteen turn up in the last hour."

"Let's hope it's just a beacon for survivors."

"Nah. The Squealers will keep the Whites away. That's what Blane reckons."

Then it must be true. Charlie kept those words to himself. "Is that a clipboard?" He smiled, despite his itch to get the fuck out of the building.

Skate shrugged, his own smile embarrassed. "Yeah. Keeping track of who's where. How many people in each flat. I feel like I've suddenly got a real fucking job with paperwork and everything."

"If that's true then the world really is fucked up."

The three strangers watched the exchange without adding a word, fear and the rain having taken their curiosity.

"I've got to take this lot upstairs and give them a work detail for tomorrow."

"Work detail?" Charlie wondered just how much stuff Blane had been organizing without telling him.

"You know. Either building defenses or going out on supply runs. That kind of shit." He paused, turning away from the strangers slightly. "I wish to fuck a woman would show up. Just one, you know." He looked right into Charlie. "Just so we know they ain't all . . ." He didn't finish the sentence, but raised his eyebrows. The sentence didn't need finishing.

Women were the last thing on Charlie's mind. And as for the bigger picture, he figured that could wait until he was somewhere where his chance of surviving more than a few days was higher.

"I guess we just wait and see, mate." He shrugged. "Nothing else we can do."

Skate nodded, his hard veneer sliding back over his face, the moment passed.

"Where you going? The weather's shit out there, man. The storm's nearly here."

Charlie did his best to keep his eyes fixed on Skate's. "The kid reckons they had some kind of den at the back of the estate. Says that's where his mate may be hiding." He gave Courtney a shove, sending him to his knees and making all three of the new arrivals flinch. "I figure it's a pile of shit, but who knows."

Skate nodded. "Cool."

Charlie nodded his good-byes and felt the eyes of the newcomers following him as he steered Courtney toward the door. He didn't have to be a mind reader to know that they were each having a moment of revelation thinking that maybe this wasn't a perfect sanctuary, after all.

He nodded at Blackeyes as they pushed the heavy glass door open, but didn't stop to chat. From now on, all Charlie was thinking of was getting to the lockup and then getting in the car and getting the fuck out of there.

"Shit."

The rain was coming down in steady sheets now, driven into them by a strong, hot wind, and with heads down, both Charlie and Courtney had to lean into it to get moving. In front of him, Courtney wobbled slightly but there was nothing Charlie could do to support the weakened boy without looking suspicious. Still, they didn't have that far to go until they reached the side streets and at least there they'd have some protection from the wind.

The sky was dark overhead, the thick, angry clouds blocking out any hint of a summer's evening as they growled and churned, launching their wet assault on the changed earth below, and as they walked Charlie scanned the gloom for threats, human and otherwise. Heading down the side street, even the lit tires were struggling to keep burning in the downpour, chugging out as much thick black smoke as flames, the three men with guns staying well back.

Charlie looked over to the buildings. He couldn't see the Squealer. His stomach flipped. Where the hell was it? His feet slowing slightly, he peered around him. At the far end, where the street turned into a narrow alley leading to the blocks on the other side of the wall, a flash of purplish white shone in the darkness. It was on the ground. Courtney must have spotted it too because his feet slowed, Charlie almost stumbling into his back.

"Keep walking," he muttered. "Just keep walking straight past it."

The rain had soaked every inch of them within moments of stepping outside the apartment building, and despite now being out of the wind, Charlie could feel the constant onslaught of water weighing heavy in the fabric of his jeans and seeping under his jacket and into his shirt. Its warmth lingered, not growing cold against his skin like a normal rain shower would, and he had a horrible feeling that something in it was clinging to his skin. It stank too; greasy and rotten. As much as the rain revolted him though, it seemed that the Squealer loved it. The thing was stretched out beside the path, its crooked legs straightened out around it, with its bulbous body and head sections almost touching the ground. It trembled, turning around and around in fast circles, like a child spinning with excitement.

It paused as Charlie pushed Courtney forward, and for an awful moment Charlie felt its bank of crazed eyes watching him. His flesh pulled away from his skin, trying to withdraw inside him to somewhere safe, but he kept his feet moving, and refused to look down. His heart thudded with each step and even when they were several feet away in the alley, he half expected to feel the thing landing on his back and tearing at him.

His breath was ragged in his chest, and as the alley veered right, leading into the Crookston towers gardens, he stopped for a moment.

"Wait."

Hunched over against the wall he lit a reluctant cigarette and sucked in a damp lungful of smoke, enjoying the way its poison tingled through his veins. That was better. It made the rain taste better too.

"You want one?"

Courtney shook his head. "Don't smoke. Bad for football."

They walked side by side out into the courtyard. "Well, you may want to start. I think football season's over."

The path came out at a midpoint between the two blocks, and Charlie couldn't help but take a moment to stare. On one side, smoke still poured out of the broken windows and scarred surfaces of what had been his home all his life, and facing it, the second tower stood dark and still like a mourning relative. No lights shone out from its windows, the people moved over to their sleek new homes, and it felt to Charlie like he was standing in a graveyard on unhallowed land.

The grass ahead of them moved in waves and he frowned, pulling Courtney back before he stepped on it.

"Don't."

He stared into the dark, his eyes trying to focus. Something was surging across the square from the burning building to the abandoned one. He followed the line backward and grimaced.

"Are those rats?" Courtney breathed the question in awe and Charlie didn't blame him. Yes, they were rats, but not like any he'd ever seen before. These were huge, easily as big as cats, but with solid barrel bodies. The man and boy stood still, watching the exodus as it trickled out, the last few monstrous creatures finding their sanctuary in the empty building. Charlie let out a long breath.

"Come on. Round to the lockup."

Courtney was staring after the disappearing rats. "What's going on, Charlie? When did rats get so huge?"

"Who fucking knows?" Grabbing the boy's arm, Charlie forced him to a jog. "Maybe they were like that before all this. Maybe they've just come out of hiding. They'll be no fucking match for the Whites though. And they'll be crawling over this place soon enough. Now come on. We're nearly there."

CHAPTER TWENTY

Skate couldn't shake the feeling that had been bugging him ever since he'd seen Charlie take that kid back outside. Something was wrong. It had been itching at his insides all the while that he'd been sorting those newbies out in a flat on the fourth floor, and listening to their groveling thank-yous. He'd taken a note of their names, flat number and put a big star against Richard Armstrong to indicate a bite victim. At least the Squealers would be eating tomorrow easily enough.

He tried not to think about feeding people to the Squealers too much. It made him feel uncomfortable somewhere deep inside. But still, the Squealers were there to keep them safe from the Whites, and they had to eat. It was either sacrifice some people to the Squealers or be food for the Whites. Wasn't much of a choice really. And what the fuck did he care about Richard Armstrong? He didn't. But thinking about Mr. Armstrong's fate made him think about Brownie. About how the kid had screamed as those things dragged him away and that awful lost look that had filled his eyes. He didn't want to think about Brownie. The kid haunted his dreams. He was fucked if he was going to spend his waking hours thinking about him too.

He waited for the lift and turned his mind to other

things. That itch came back and with it Charlie. His foot tapped against the lush carpet. Something about Charlie taking that kid back to the block just didn't ring true and it was bugging the shit out of Skate. They'd brought the kid back and taken him straight up to Blane. Skate had gone back to organizing the move over and getting all the people allocated to somewhere on the lower floors, Jude had gone back to his post nannying the locked-up Squealers, and Chokey and Charlie had beaten up the kid.

The lift arrived and after getting inside, he stared at the buttons. He should go back down and see what was going on outside. Check everyone was doing their thing. He didn't press the G though, his fingers instead reaching for the 14. Skate knew he wasn't clever like Blane or as smart as Charlie, but he was ahead of most, and the one thing he'd learned over the years was to trust his gut. As the lift rose, he really hoped that this time his gut was wrong. The alternative . . . well, it wasn't good. The itch got stronger the more he pictured Charlie pushing that boy out past Blackeyes and into the rain. His eyes widened slightly, realization dawning. It was the rain that was bugging him.

Why would Charlie have gone with the boy out into that shitty storm? The rain was foul. It stank. And it was coming down hard, soaking everything it touched. And more than that, the blocks were all over now. There was no one on looking out for Whites; they hadn't left a single soldier there once the last of the people had been moved. It was dangerous territory.

He shook his head, his eyes darkening as the doors opened. Charlie wouldn't have gone out in the rain, and that was the bare-arsed hard fact. He'd have sent Chokey or Blackeyes with him. In fact, knowing Charlie, he'd have sent both. He might even have sent Skate along too. Charlie only ever took calculated risks. Charlie was cool and calm and thought everything through. Fuck, Charlie Nash was a fucking machine; never got angry, never impulsive, even when that shit went down with his bird, he just carried on without even talking about it.

He felt vaguely sick as adrenaline picked up its pace around his body. There was no way Charlie would have gone with that kid alone. No fucking way. He strode around to the Squealers' locked flat, cursing under his breath when he caught side of Jude. The skinny young man sat against the wall, his knees drawn up and eyes shut, swaying slightly to whatever music was pumping directly into his head. In one hand he held a thick joint, and as he raised it to his mouth, Skate delivered a swift kick to his ribs. The reaction was immediate.

"What the fuck?" His wide eyes stared in shock at Skate as he hauled himself to his feet, bent over to one side. He tugged the small speakers out of his ears. "That fucking hurt, Skate."

"You seen Charlie? Or Chokey?"

The other man shrugged. "They're not down this side. Maybe the other." He frowned, his words a little hazy from the strong drugs. "Weren't they dealing with that kid or something?"

Skate sucked his teeth, his disdain obvious. "You need to sort yourself out, man."

"What?"

Skate didn't stop to argue because he thought that if he did then he'd end up punching Jude hard, and once he started then he might not be able to control himself. He'd had an underlying coating of fear in his gut ever

since that first morning, but between Blane's plans and
Charlie's cool, he'd figured that one way or another
things might be all right for them. Now that fear was
raging.

He picked up his pace, jogging around the curved
corridor.

"What is it, Skate? What the fuck's going on?"

Jude jogged beside him, the thin man's light footfalls
like the echoes of his own. It pleased Skate to hear a
little of his own fear in Jude's voice.

"Hopefully fucking nothing. For both our sakes."

Unlike the lower floors where the flats were smaller,
there were only three large apartments on the other
side of the lift on the fourteenth floor. Skate pushed
open the door to the first one; Charlie's pad.

"Charlie?" He moved inside without waiting for an
answer, checking the bedroom and bathroom before
the vast living area. "Chokey?"

"Anyone there?" Jude hovered in the doorway.

"No. Next one."

He found Chokey within minutes. The man's eyes
were wide-open and staring into some space in the corner of the clinically smart flat, his head tilting at an
awkward angle from his body. Skate crouched down
next to him, fingers tracing the entry points of the two
bullets. They were almost next to each other, and Skate
had no doubt that they'd both gone straight into
Chokey's heart. No kid did this. Chokey wasn't bright,
but the kid wouldn't have been able to surprise him.

"Fuck. Oh fuck." Jude hovered above, shuffling from
foot to foot.

Skate looked up. "You didn't hear this? You're just
down the fucking corridor, Jude."

"I didn't hear, man . . ." Jude's voice had risen to a whine. "I had my tunes in, and I was smoking those bitches up to get them high . . ." His voice drifted off.

"Two fucking bullets to the chest." Skate stood up, shaking his head. Next to where Chokey lay punctured and dead, a cushion lay surrounded by the blood of its own feathers. "Even through a fucking cushion you should have heard."

The accusation was like acid between them, and Jude's shoulders crumpled. "I'm sorry, man, I'm really sorry. I didn't think. I didn't . . ." He looked up. "But who the fuck would have done this?"

Skate smiled despite the bile that rose from the pit of fear in his gut. "Don't you get it, Jude?" He paused. "Charlie. Fucking Charlie did this. He's taken the kid and run."

Jude gulped. "Who's going to tell Blane?"

CHAPTER TWENTY-ONE

The rain hammered loud against the metal door and in the darkness of the garage Mr. Green's face glowed pale, a sheen of sweat covering his skin. His thick fringe was stuck to his forehead and Harry gently pushed it up and out of the way, ignoring the heat that burned up through his fingers. The teacher gave him a wan smile from his propped-up position against the rough wall and Harry tried to return it, hoping his growing sense of hopelessness didn't show.

Mr. Green wasn't looking so good. The moment replayed in Harry's mind for the fiftieth time at least since the gun had fired. Why hadn't he called out or done something? It had all happened so fast, that was why. Just like all those life-and-death moments; they were over before you could do anything to stop them. In the first few moments after they'd opened the garage door and stepped in, it had all just been noise and confusion. Craig had dragged Mr. Green inside and Harry literally had to shove the rest in. Where James and Leke had looked ready to run, convinced someone was hiding in the garage, Nathan had stood stock-still, one hand at his glasses, all the muscles in his body so tense that he might well have been frozen solid, and Harry had to yank his arm to get him moving.

An eerie quiet had fallen with the metal door, and other than Leke's breathy exclamations of "shit" over and over, they'd not spoken more until their eyes adjusted to the gloom. Finally, James took off his waterproof top and tore strips from his damp shirt, and then Harry had pressed them into the teacher's wound before bandaging him up with the small stretchy roll from their pathetic first-aid kit. Mr. Green hadn't screamed or called out as Harry's clumsy fingers worked on him; his flinching body and small hisses of air were the only clue to the agony he was feeling. Harry had felt his respect for the teacher rising.

Unscrewing a bottle of water from his rucksack, he tipped some gently into the man's mouth. He swallowed it greedily. Harry tried not to look down. He'd done his best on the dressing but it wasn't good enough. The cream bandage had already turned to a slick black. The bullet had hit high on Mr. Green's right shoulder. Harry was pretty sure that in itself wouldn't kill the man, but the blood loss might. He peered at his watch, but the numbers were elusive in the darkness. How long had they been trapped in here. An hour? Maybe two?

While Harry had been tending to the wounded man, Craig had dismantled the rigged handgun with an ease that made all of Harry's years in the army cadets seem like he'd been in playgroup messing around with water pistols, and then, very carefully, taking a section of the garage each, they'd checked in the holdalls around them. Guns. There were a lot of guns. At least they wouldn't have a problem defending themselves. He just hoped their new friends had better aim than they did.

The storm had started to pound the air and earth harder after that, and each boy settling into his own space, they'd fought the sound of the unnatural rain that crept under the metal edge of the door by telling fragments of the stories that had brought them here. It was a careful dance of trust; Harry could feel that. Nathan said very little in his strange monotone voice, just that his mum had died. His nervous tics increased after that and Leke had taken over. Nathan had pulled a small book and pen from his pocket and intently wrote in it. Harry wasn't sure that anything he scribbled in this bad light would be legible, but it seemed to soothe the other boy.

Watching him, Harry figured there was more to Nathan's story than he was sharing. He was a strange boy; out of place with the others. Harry didn't blame him for not telling everything. After all, when he himself had quietly narrated the events that had brought them from their school trip to here, he'd left plenty out. Stuff that was private; that only he, James and Mr. Green needed to know. There were names he didn't mention: Josh, Peter, Christopher Watson. Those things could stay hidden for a while. Maybe forever.

Craig and Leke's stories were quieter. There were no dead soldiers and rummaging in the street. They'd been in their flats for the week, but they did talk about the men who had taken their friend and how dangerous they were. Leke stayed quiet for most of that, as if somehow he was guilty for them taking Courtney. Harry looked at all the young faces in the gloom. Was that their fate if they survived? To carry this guilt with them?

"How is he?" James asked quietly. Harry could only just make out the shine of his blond hair from where he sat in the corner, using one of the holdalls as a seat. They'd told him not to; one of the guns inside might go off and, as Craig had put it, blow him a new arsehole, but James had just laughed and said he'd take his chances with this one. No guns had fired as he sat down heavily on it, but Harry couldn't help but wonder if maybe his friend had some kind of death wish after what had happened with Josh even though it had just been a stupid, terrible accident. James would never say. He'd just pretend he didn't feel anything, rather than admit to feeling *something*.

He looked back at Mr. Green's pale face. "Not good. He needs proper painkillers and antibiotics. The aspirin from that stupid pack isn't going to even touch the sides." He paused. "We need to get him out of here, find somewhere he can rest up safely and mend. And we need a chemist."

"Oh, is that all?" James's sarcasm didn't need any facial expression to be heard. "No problem there then. Let's go."

"I'm being serious, James." Harry glared. "Stop behaving like such a dick."

"Oh hurrah, cub scout Harry is finally growing a spine," James bit back. "How do you propose we get him out of here in this rain?"

"I'm still alive, you know." Mr. Green cut through the boys' conversation; his voice paper-thin. He coughed, a wet sound that wasn't good, and then rested his head back against the wall with a heavy sigh. "We can't go out in this. The weather aside, it's getting dark out there. Nights aren't good."

"I'm not leaving without Courtney," Leke said.

There was a long pause.

"Blane's got him." Nathan's monotone made the statement as if it somehow made complete sense and answered all of Leke's concerns.

"I know Blane's got him. That's why we have to get him back. It's not his fault." Heat oozed from his words. "He's our mate. We have to get him back, don't we, Craig?"

"It's not that fucking easy, Leke. You know that."

Harry was glad they were in darkness. He didn't want to have to see the looks on the other boys' faces or for them to see the awkwardness on his own. He knew Craig was right. It wasn't that easy.

"Well, we've got all these guns. We can go in! They won't be expecting us!"

"Keep your fucking voice down!" Craig hissed. "I've told you. It's not that fucking easy."

"What Craig here is trying not to say," James cut in, soft and calm, "is that your friend Courtney is more than likely already dead."

"That's harsh, man." Craig's words were dull in the gloom.

"And it's not true!" Leke sounded close to tears. "I'm not leaving without him. I'll go on my own if I have to."

"This Blane doesn't sound like a man who's all about forgiveness," James continued. "He's probably killed your friend already, just because he couldn't get to you."

The dank garage air crackled with tension.

"If you don't shut it, I'm going to come over there and blow your fucking head off myself," Craig growled. "This isn't your fucking conversation. And what the fuck would you know about it anyway with your fucking posh-boy accent and perfect life? Would you leave your friend to die?"

Harry felt himself pulling in closer to Mr. Green's

sweating body. He hated confrontation, his stomach turned at the hint of a raised voice, and this was on the verge of getting nasty. Why couldn't James have just kept his nose out of it? Why couldn't he just do what they all wanted and shut up? If they were all honest, none of them wanted to go after this boy, probably not even Leke, but he had to get to it in his own time.

"Accents don't matter and there are no perfect lives. Not anymore." James's voice lilted softly, no hint of aggression. "Blow my head off if you want, I'm just trying to tell you it's okay. It's okay to leave your friend behind."

"Stop saying that, we're not doing that," Leke cut in, dull and lifeless.

"This isn't a film. Good doesn't win over evil. It's just an endless struggle to keep yourself alive. I'll give you an example." He paused and Harry heard him shifting on his canvas seat. "When we left the bed-and-breakfast this morning there were two more boys with us. Peter and Josh. They were just kids."

Harry's heart thumped. This wasn't to be shared. This was their thing. "James . . . don't."

"Shut up, Harry. They need to hear it."

"What happened to them?" The rims of Nathan's glasses glinted as he leaned forward. Harry was sure he had his notebook out, writing down whatever it was he found so important.

"They're dead. There's not a lot to tell. Peter, the youngest one, he got attacked by one of the spider things as we were coming down the main road. We weren't looking properly. We were all too busy watching the fire over here and wondering what it meant. By the time we turned around it was obvious he was in trouble. Not just him, all of us. There were two more coming to attack down the side of the building. To give Harry his due, he started shooting straightaway. Killed one of the other ones. Josh didn't have a gun. He was fourteen."

Harry closed his eyes, squeezing back the tears. He didn't want to listen. He didn't want to think about it.

"He'd been scared since day one but it didn't stop him running in to try and save Peter. He was pulling at the thing's legs, and he got bitten, but he didn't stop. Mr. Green over there was in the best place for a shot, but he was frozen, just staring. I had a handgun and I honestly thought I had the spider right in my sights. But when I pulled the trigger it wasn't the spider I hit. Instead I blew Josh's brains out. Right through his cycle helmet."

There was an awful bleakness hearing the words delivered in such an easy, conversational tone. "The spider took Peter, probably back to the park. He'll be hanging in one of their trees now. Maybe alive. Maybe dead. Perhaps somewhere in between. We never went to find out."

"Jesus fuck," Craig breathed.

"That's not the same thing. That's not the same thing at all," Leke said. "You tried to save them."

"And failed very miserably," James answered. "I've got another story for you. A few nights ago we heard a woman in the street."

"A woman?"

With that one word, woman, James had everyone's attention, and squeezing Mr. Green's hand, not sure if the teacher was even still conscious but knowing he would hate hearing these stories as much as Harry himself did, Harry wished he had the guts to get up and shoot his friend himself.

"Yeah, a real live one. Still with legs and arms and long red hair."

Harry remembered the glory of that hair and the small hard-on he'd had in those first few moments of seeing her. There was something precious about that memory before *the bit that came after*, and James was destroying it.

"She was drunk and out in the street. Maybe she was immune to whatever made the others change, who knows. But that's not my point. My point is that we sat in the house and peered through the curtains watching until those things came and killed her." His voice was thoughtful. "If this was the movies, then one of us would have sacrificed himself for the greater good of the world and rescued her. After all, she was a real healthy woman, and I should imagine that there aren't a lot of those still around. In some people's eyes, she was way more valuable than any of us were." He paused, and despite himself, Harry found himself listening. James had that about him. He could drive you mad, but he could command a crowd. Charisma, that's what James had, by the bucket load.

"But she wasn't more valuable than us in *our* eyes. And that's all that counts really. So what I'm trying to say is that it's okay to be selfish. It's okay to leave people behind if the alternatives don't look good. It's the new way. It's the *only* way, if you want to live."

"And the alternatives really aren't good, mate." Craig's voice was low. "There's something me and Courtney didn't tell you two. We didn't want to freak you out."

"What?" Leke sniffed too hard for there not to be tears behind it. Harry liked him. Where Craig seemed hard and street-smart in a way that made Harry slightly nervous, Leke seemed *good*. It was the only word he could find that fit. Maybe James was right about selfishness being the only way forward, but if there were no people like Leke left, and even Nathan with his strange tics and way of looking at things, then what was the point?

"We saw something out the window last night. It was Blane. And he had these things with him. Like the white spider things, but different."

"What?" Harry opened his eyes, drawn into the conversation. "What do you mean he had them *with* him? And how were they different?"

"They were smaller. Their color was funny. It was hard to see cos it was dark. But Blane had four of them around him, like they were fucking guard dogs or something. They were just walking. And Charlie was following behind. Blane said he'd trained them."

"Trained them?" James's voice was edgy. "How? Because if we knew that—"

"There's no way to fucking train them," Harry cut in, the rare swear word hard in his mouth. "You saw what they did to Josh."

"Yeah, I think you're right." The whites of Craig's eyes shone in the gloom as he looked around. "You can't train those fuckers." He shook his head. "And these ones . . . they didn't look tame. They just looked like . . . I don't know . . . like he'd made some kind of deal with them." He shrugged. "Like I said. They were different. But I doubt they were any less mean."

There was a long pause.

"Fuck." James's word seemed to sum up the whole group's feelings.

"Yeah, fuck." Craig leaned back against the wall. "So as much as I'd willingly go up against Charlie and Skate and the boys to get Courtney back, even though it would mean getting my own head blown off cos we've got no fucking chance of managing it"—he let out a long sigh—"I just can't face those things as well, Leke. I just can't."

There was a long silence after that.

"There was a woman," Nathan said at last, and there was almost the slightest whisper of wonder in his monotone.

James laughed gently. "Yes, there was. Maybe there's a chance we won't all die virgins, after all."

Harry flushed and was glad for the darkness. Nathan was probably going the same color. Maybe Craig and Leke had both slept with girls but judging from the quiet that followed James's thought, he figured maybe not.

"Speak for yourselves." Mr. Green's husk of a voice drifted into the conversation. "I've had plenty in my time."

Harry snorted, the laugh exploding in his nose before he'd realized it was coming. On the other side of the garage Nathan giggled; a tight, controlled sound that was out and gone in a moment. Craig shook his head.

"That's so sick, man. Teachers don't have sex." He sounded amused though.

"That's what you think." Mr. Green pushed his words out. "They're at it like rabbits."

More giggles filled the dark space, and Harry was sure that even Leke was smiling.

"Well, as much as I realize that revelation might have spoiled everyone's appetite's, I've got some biscuits and crisps and stuff in my rucksack. If we're not moving

just yet, then we may as well have something to eat."
James turned, hunkering over in the shadows and the
sounds of zips undoing filled the room. Eventually, sitting back on the holdall that had become his domain,
he passed around two tubes of Pringles and some chocolate digestives. Harry hadn't realized how hungry he
was until the first handful of curved crisps crunched in
his mouth.

He rummaged in his own pockets and tugged out a
partly melted Mars bar. The crisps and biscuits would
be no good in Mr. Green's already-drying mouth, but
the chocolate would be fine. The wrapper undone, he
held it in front of the man's mouth.

"Just some water."

Harry shook his head. "You need to eat. You need
the energy." The teacher's eyes met his, and Harry saw
pain and fear alive in the dark, dilated pupils. He
thought about what James had said. About how survival
and selfishness were everything.

"You need to meet us halfway, sir." He held the chocolate bar out. "You'll need your energy if you don't want
to get left behind."

Mr. Green's mouth opened and he took a large bite.

By the time the food was gone, the gloom outside
was settling into an early dusk, the wind and rain lashing the heavy metal door, forcing it to rattle in its old
and rusty frame. The small strip of air at the bottom no
longer brought any light with it, just a warm draft that
smelled rotten. Craig fished around in one of the bags
in the middle of the room and pulled out a gun and
then rummaged for a box of clips. He loaded the gun
with ease.

"Anyone else want one?" His voice was low. They

were all spooked by the aggressive weather and the falling night. No one needed reminding of the dangers that were out there.

Harry shook his head and then remembered that the gesture wouldn't be seen. "No thanks. I've got one."

No one else spoke. "Suit yourselves. It's me and Harry guarding tonight then." He paused. "We'll leave at dawn."

CHAPTER TWENTY-TWO

"Don't move! Don't fucking move!"

What the fuck? The words attacked him before the garage door had even screeched up on its runners and Charlie's hand instinctively reached for his own gun. Who the fuck was in here?

"Don't shoot!" Beside him, Courtney held his arms out wide. "It's me! Don't shoot!"

Crouched and ready to attack, Charlie peered into the silent darkness, and above the sound of the wind and rain that beat at them, ragged breathing pumped out its own rhythm as if the concrete room had its own heartbeat.

Eventually, someone inside shuffled and got to their feet, coming forward to take a closer look.

"Courtney?"

The thickset blond boy peered at them cautiously. Charlie didn't recognize him, but then he'd never taken much notice of the kids on the estate. Not until they got to be old enough to be useful. Maybe this one wasn't a Crookston kid. He had eyes that would harden though, when he got older. There was already an edge in them visible to anyone who knew the signs. Charlie was pretty sure that if pushed this kid would have fired the gun. He might not have hit the target but he would have shot. The boy beside him nodded. "Yeah. It's me."

"Fuck, we thought you were dead."

"Nearly was."

"Your eye is fucked. What the fuck did they do to you?"

Charlie peered over his shoulder, a distant sound tugging at him. Surely they couldn't be found out already? He frowned.

"Well, this small talk is very sweet, but we need to get the fuck out of here. And now."

More figures shifted, and as Charlie's eyes grew accustomed to the gloom, he saw several shiny pairs staring back at him.

"We can't move our teacher. He won't be able to walk far in this weather." Following the voice, Charlie found its owner. He definitely wasn't from the blocks. Charlie didn't need to see his face to know that. It was all in that cut-glass accent.

"He got shot coming in here. A booby trap."

The accusation in the teenager's voice was clear, but Charlie let it wash over him. How the fuck was he to know a bunch of kids would wander into the stash? You couldn't control all the variables, and he wasn't going to choose now to start feeling guilty about stuff that he couldn't manage. His eyes wandered over the pale, sweating man propped up against the wall. It could have been worse. He could have died. Thinking of what lay ahead of them, Charlie amended that thought. Maybe it would have been better if he had died. The last thing they needed was hauling a wounded man around. He looked at Courtney.

"Who the fuck are these people?"

The boy shrugged.

"They're with us now." The blond stared at him, and Charlie felt the challenge in it and it almost made him smile. Little fucker had balls, he'd give him that. He crouched by the teacher, scanning his shoulder. It was bad, but it wasn't terrible.

"Your lucky day. We're not walking. I'm going to drive us out of here." He looked up at the posh kid with the untidy mop of dark hair. "But we've got to go now. If you stay here, you're dead."

The man looked up at the boy. "I think we'd better do as the man says."

"Good plan, teacher."

"Andrew Green."

"Okay, Andy. Do your best."

Charlie got to his feet. Three other boys had stood up: a tall, blond, good-looking kid with a rucksack, a geeky boy with glasses, and then . . . his eyes rested on the black boy with tight plaits against his head. The kid's eyes wouldn't meet his and instead slid away to the walls and floor, his shoulders slouching, doing all he could to make himself invisible. Leke Kudaisi. The kid Courtney had been prepared to die for. Just like he and Blane when they'd been kids. His jaw tightened and a knot of something between guilt and sadness formed in his stomach. He and Blane were done. There was no going back to that now.

He nodded at the blond boy with attitude. "What's your name?"

"Craig."

"Grab one of those holdalls. One with guns and ammo in. Each of those has fifteen handguns in it. We shouldn't need more than that." He watched the boy as he hauled a bag up. The one with the raw coke in it was in the far corner so that was safe and he didn't even think about taking it. Blane would need the drugs to boil up and keep those fucking Squealers under control. And it wasn't like they needed it for anything. Maybe Green could use some for his pain, but it was a road that didn't go anywhere good. He'd seen it too many times. If the teacher survived getting out of the city, then they'd find him some proper drugs. Until then, he was just going to have to put up with the pain.

"We should take all of them." Leke finally spoke.

"No room." He stared at the boy. "And I won't leave them unarmed."

"Oh, you're all heart, Charlie." Craig's words dripped with dislike.

Charlie stepped up close to him. "I'm still Charlie Nash, boy. And trust me, if you piss me off enough, I'll have your kneecaps gone before you can even get your gun out." He felt better when the kid shrank back slightly. Boys needed to know their place next to men.

He looked back at the bedraggled group and then thought about the space in the Merc. It was going to be a tight squeeze. "Bags'll go in the boot. Craig and Leke share the front passenger seat. You others in the back. Got it?"

They nodded.

"Good. Then let's go."

As he stepped out from the shelter of the garage door the rain swirled around him, carried on a wind that seemed to blow in all directions at once. He ducked his head, checking the others were close by, and with one handgun gripped and ready to fire, he jogged toward the Mercedes parked at the end of the row of garages. As he tugged the keys from his jeans pocket, a human wail cut through the sound of nature's torrent. His feet slowed to a halt, his eyes scanning the darkness. What the fuck was that?

The anguished scream came again, carried on the wind. Somewhere in it was a plaintive cry for help, the words slurring as the shriek took over. Whoever it was, it was human.

"Don't stop. Keep going!" Charlie ignored the hissed words from one of the kid's behind him. The screaming was coming from the courtyard. He trotted around to the side of the building and the others had no choice but to follow.

A dark shadow of a man staggered out from the entrance of the opposite block, his feet stumbling onto the grass. Something hung from his arms and his trouser legs, the weight obviously heavy. Charlie stared. Leeboy. It had to be. He'd been clearing out the second block. Must have been doing a final recce that the place was empty. Surely he wouldn't have been in there alone? He wasn't that stupid. Maybe whoever he'd been with was already dead inside. That made more sense. His stomach twisted as the man fell to his knees, dragged down by the creatures that swarmed on him.

"What are those things?" The posh blond boy stood alongside him, his eyes wide. "Those aren't the spiders."

More dark shapes ran from the building and leaped onto Leeboy's form, one landing on his back and forcing him forward. The screaming stopped suddenly.

"Rats." The word came out of Charlie and Craig in unison, equal horror in both voices.

"Those aren't rats," the posh blond boy said. "They're too big."

"They're rats. We saw them in the bin room."

"Yeah," Charlie added. "And we saw them on our way around. They were running into the other building."

"Jesus."

"Don't think he can help." Taking one last look at the midnight mass that swarmed over Leeboy's form making his dead body twitch as they tore at it, Charlie turned away and headed for the car. There was nothing they could do for him, not that he would if he could apart from maybe put a bullet in the man's head to end it quickly, but if they didn't move fast, the rats might come after them. And if the rats didn't, then it wouldn't be long until the Whites were finding their way to the abandoned blocks.

The yellow sidelights flashed as he squeezed the key ring and the group hurried forward, even the injured teacher keeping up the pace. As the two boys clambered into the front seat, Leke sitting on Craig, Charlie shoved the backpacks and the holdall in the boot and then held the back door open to ease Andrew Green in.

"You okay?"

Despite how pale his face was and the way his breath came in uneven hitches, the teacher nodded, flinching slightly as the dark-haired boy slid in from the other side.

"Sorry, sir. We're short on space."

"It's okay, Harry. Just get everyone in."

It was more than a squeeze. The geeky kid with glasses sat on the posh blond boy, his legs stretching through the gap between the front seats, his feet on what should have been Charlie's armrest. Courtney twisted his body to the side to fit in, and Charlie padded around and closed the door on him, before getting in himself.

The engine purred into life. "Keep the windows shut. Even if it stops raining." He looked into the rearview mirror at the crush of people in the back. None of them were in a position to fire if the car was attacked and even if they were, Charlie wasn't sure they wouldn't just get him in the back of the head. Fucking great. When he'd thought he just had Courtney coming with him, getting out had seemed easy. Now he felt like some kind of group leader on a school trip. Maybe as soon as they got somewhere safer, he'd leave them and head off on his own.

"Um . . ." The dark-haired kid, Harry, thumped the back of his seat. "I can see some lights. I think someone's coming."

"We need to get out of here." Fear ate into Leke's words.

Charlie didn't linger. Keeping the headlights off until they were back behind the block, he drove slowly out over the uneven and badly maintained road, feeling every familiar dip and hole in its surface for the last time. The windscreen wipers skidded back and forward against the glass fighting the onslaught of water and wind, and despite the overwhelming urge he felt to push his foot to the floor, he eased the car out on the road, keeping the speed down. If they crashed here, Blane would be on them. Slow and steady was what he had to stick to. He turned to the right, peering out into the dark as he guided the car down the middle of the street. As the Crookston blocks disappeared into the night behind him, he didn't look back. That life was over.

He didn't take the main road down to the river. It was the best direction to be going in for heading out of

London, but it would take them past Blane's new base
and he wasn't going to risk that. Plus, he was pretty sure
that the burning bodies would be blocking the road.
Easy access to his "citadel" would not be something
Blane would want. Instead, he turned inward through
the residential streets of the borough, keen to be hidden
from anyone who might be following in the maze of
houses, but also trying to keep them headed up to the
A13, Newham Way, which if their luck held they could
follow all the way out to the suburbs of East London
and then the quiet of the coast. It wasn't a great plan,
but it would do.

It was hard keeping track of where they were though.
Streetlights flickered on and off, some roads brilliantly
lit and others lying in darkness as the night hesitantly
crept up to claim them. Water poured across the slick
surfaces of tarmac, pools forming where drains clogged.
For every road they managed to make their way down
successfully, there were two he had to reverse out of and
try another.

"This is way worse than this morning," Harry
breathed.

"Looks like a day is a long time in London." Charlie
kept his voice low. "Everyone's trying to take charge."

They fell into silence after that, the boys all staring
wide-eyed out of the smeared windows . Wreckage lay
in every direction. A car was turned on its side, the glass
panels smashed. Household items littered the pavements and trailed into the gutters. Charlie couldn't help
but look as they cruised slowly past the devastation. It
was an odd array of past normality that presented itself.
A DVD player hung over the curb next to a large, soft,
embroidered cushion designed to sit elegantly on a sofa,

but to rarely be used for comfort. A food processor poked out from behind a parked car, its accessories spread across the road like spilled guts.

The car rolled past and turned a corner. There were no smashed windows or angrily launched pieces of human debris in the next road and Charlie found the inconsistency disturbing. Where was the logic? The occasional street was perfect as if nothing had changed at all and the past week or so had just been a bad dream, and where the rest were wrecked. He wasn't sure if the houses had been broken into and looted by other survivors or simply attacked by the Whites. He swerved around a motorbike lying at an angle in the road. Its headlight was still on, and he had a feeling if he touched the engine it would be warm. The rider wouldn't have just abandoned his bike. Not in this weather. If he'd skidded off and was injured they'd see him, but there was no sign. The Whites had taken him. It was the only realistic explanation. He saw his own thoughts reflected in the fear on Craig's and Leke's faces beside him. Both boys leaned into the window to peer at the tops of the buildings around them. Strands of webbing coated them like an early snow.

"This shit is not good." Courtney's whisper echoed around the cramped car and sent a shiver up the damp hairs on the back of Charlie's neck. He couldn't disagree. They should have been on the A13 in minutes. He had been days earlier when he'd gone to the warehouse. But now . . . now it was all different. They were in Whites territory. How many women had lived in these streets? Hundreds? He couldn't shake the thought that maybe banks of those angry red eyes were peering hungrily down at them from the tops of the buildings and the insides of houses. Maybe there were some human ones watching also, hiding behind the curtains, too afraid to come out and thinking that the strangers in the car were fools to take to the roads in this storm and on the edge of night.

"We'll never get out on the roads," Craig said. His voice was void of emotion, the statement purely fact. Charlie couldn't find an argument against it, and it seemed like no one else could either.

"Anyone got any suggestions?" He turned on the air-conditioning and set it to full before lighting a cigarette. His jaw ached with tension and he could feel it spreading down into his shoulders. He needed something. The lighter clicked loudly and he took a deep breath of the hot smoke, exhaling toward the vents. It didn't really make much difference, the car quickly filling with the pungent scent. No one answered.

"Well, I guess we just keep going then." He took two more drags on the cigarette before stubbing it out, his voice dull. They were fucked if they didn't come up with a better plan.

"Water." Nathan mumbled the word from his cramped place half in the back of the car and half in the front. Charlie peered out at the rain.

"Yeah, mate. You're not wrong. There's a lot of water."

The boy in the back pushed his glasses up on his nose and swallowed. After a labored effort, he said the word again, with more emphasis. Charlie stared at him and then returned his attention to the dangerous road surfaces. Nathan was right. The water was getting worse. If this rain kept up then some of the streets would be mini-rivers by the morning. Lightning flashed and moments later thunder cracked overhead, rolling for several long seconds before fading, the storm defying any wish they might have for it to move on. He sighed.

James suddenly leaned forward. "What about a boat?"

"What do you mean a boat?" Charlie eased up on the accelerator, slowing the car. He glanced in the rearview. The posh blond was smiling. All heads in the cramped space had turned to look at him. Even Green.

"My dad's got a boat at the O2 marina. He keeps it there for corporate entertaining."

"What kind of boat?"

"A bloody good one. Fifty-footer. A motor cruiser." James paused and then smiled. "And I know where he keeps his spare keys."

Charlie felt his heart leap slightly with sudden hope. If they had a good boat they could head up the coastline. "You know how to work it?"

The boy nodded. "And I've got a seamaster certificate to prove it. We just have to get there."

Excitement crackled in the smoky air, passing from one person to the next like electricity.

"We could go up to the north of Scotland. Maybe set up some kind of camp on one of the islands off the coast."

"Scotland might not be a bad idea." Charlie fought the smile that threatened his face. He'd never been north, but in his mind's eye the place was wild and mainly uninhabited, all beautiful green mountains and fresh lakes. It could work. If they could get there. "Did you say the O2 Marina?" He shook his head a little. "It's not going to be easy getting there. Have you taken a look at the Millennium dome recently? The whole building is crawling with Whites."

"Whites?" Harry frowned.

"The spiders. The Whites are the normal, ugly, dangerous fuckers. The Squealers are the junkie ones."

"The trained ones," Courtney added.

"Yeah, if you want to call it that." Charlie's jaw tightened. "He just has what they need, that's all. I don't fancy anyone's chances when he can't give them the crack anymore. If the crew have any sense they'll shoot the fuckers. Anyway, that's beside the point. It's going to be fucking hard getting to the boat. The O2 is crawling with Whites."

Craig shrugged. "Look around you, Charlie. The whole city's crawling with them."

"We'll just have to be very quiet and very careful." Green's voice was weak, but at least he didn't sound feverish. "Maybe find somewhere to hide out near there until dawn when they're at their quietest."

"So how are we going to get there? Try and get down to the Blackwall tunnel?"

"Canning Town to North Greenwich." Nathan didn't move as he barked out the words. "One and a half miles in a straight line underground."

Leke twisted around in his chair. "You want us to go through the underground?" He stared at Nathan. "Are you mad? The trains won't be running. We'll have to walk the tracks. In *the dark*."

"One and a half miles in a straight line." Nathan repeated himself as if it was the most sensible thing in the world. Charlie stared at him. And it was.

"Canning Town station's only a couple of streets from here. And he's right. It's the quickest way."

"Oh great." Leke shook his head. "Oh, fucking great. We're basing our plan on Nathan."

Charlie raised an eyebrow. "I can drop you back with Blane if you'd prefer."

Leke peered over. "You're not even funny."

It was enough to make Charlie laugh.

CHAPTER TWENTY-THREE

Blane stared into the open garage and then back at the space where the car had been parked with the same sense of disbelief he'd felt since Skate had come up to the penthouse and told him there was something he needed to see. This was not right. This couldn't be right. Charlie wouldn't do this. Charlie wouldn't fucking dare. He wouldn't . . . Black rage stormed behind his eyes, eating up the words. Even when Skate had nervously shown him Chokey's body, so expertly dispatched that it had to be Charlie's handiwork, he didn't want to believe it. Charlie wouldn't betray him. Charlie had *never* betrayed him, not through all the fucking years since they'd been kids. Blane Gentle-King and his right-hand man, Charlie Nash. Kings of the Crookston blocks.

His flesh simmered. A scream was building in the pit of his soul and tingling through his body. He wasn't sure if he could contain it much longer. If Charlie could leave him, then how could he ever trust the others? What would they make of it? What was Skate thinking now? His heart tore at itself with anger and grief and a whirlwind of memory.

Having left Skate and Blinka back at the new block, it was Jude and Blackeyes he'd brought with him, and as he internally exploded, they both kept their huge torches pointing away from him and away from the three Squealers that skittered and pawed at the ground around him as if they were feeding from his rage.

Blood dripped from the rags of flesh hanging from their mandibles and the suckers in their bellies. As they'd come into the blocks, the beams of light from the torches showed a mass of huge rats swarming on the grass. They'd run, but not fast enough, and they were no match for the Squealers who were on them in an instant, ripping apart the writhing furry bodies as the others fled.

In search of some kind of comfort, Blane looked down at the creatures that prowled around him. The splatter made their purplish mottled coloring more intense, strands of ligament and meat dangling from the suckers on their underbellies. Janine hadn't taken part though; instead she'd stayed trembling by his side as he strode toward the back of the burned-out building, ignoring the screeches and squeals coming from the massacre, not even turning his head down against the rain.

He felt her hard, spindly leg brush past his as she scuttled up the front of the closed garage next to Charlie's lockup. Even if she'd been covered in traces of blood and meat like the others he'd still have known which one was her. It was as if they had some kind of connection. He tried not to think about it too much, but wondered if it was strange that he was fonder of her now that she'd changed than he had been when she'd just been a skinny little junkie fuck.

Jude spun the beam of his torch into the garage sending a large pool of yellow light forward. It hurt Blane's eyes after the relative comfort of the gloom. The constant buzz of cocaine in his system wasn't getting rid of the strange headache he'd had all day, which throbbed deep inside his brain. Even before this chase over to the blocks and the rage that burned inside him, he'd been sweating. Maybe he was coming down with something; he didn't have to look in a mirror every five minutes to know he wasn't looking his best. His skin was tinged under this strange greasy liquid that was oozing from his pores, and his eyes were bloodshot. The rain clung to his skin as it landed on him, following the contours of his face and creeping under his clothes, its warmth and his mingling in the damp, the foul stench of the heavy water almost as overpowering as the sourness of his sweat.

Staring into the empty garage he bit hard on the inside of his cheek. If he was ill, it could wait until later. He had some more personal fucking business to take care of now. Jude stepped out of the rain and into the dark concrete room, the wide beam of his torch moving from side to side as he peered into the bags that were scattered inside.

"Hey." He turned and grinned, his wide smile bright. "It's cool. He's left us loads of guns, boss." He shook his head. "Charlie must be going soft, man, leaving all this shit behind."

Blane didn't smile back. His nerves were wound so tight he was pretty sure he could feel some snapping. Fucking Charlie, trying to do the right thing. That's what this was. Like he was fucking patting Blane on the head or something. And what the fuck did Blane care about the guns anyway? There were always more guns, and the guns came second to the Squealers. While they had those under control, then they were pretty much safe. It wasn't the guns he was freaking out about, it was the drugs.

Was he the only one with any fucking brains?

The rain beat heavily into the ground around them, washing away any evidence of the Mercedes's tire tracks. It wasn't even Charlie's fucking car. Jude's grinning face was too much for him to bear, and the scream starting as a growl in his chest, Blane waded into the garage, the tails of his leather coat and his dreadlocks both flying out behind him. He yanked the torch free from Jude's hand and shoved the thin man back out onto the gravel drive, happy to see him stumble and nearly fall, his eyes wide.

"What?" Jude whined. "What the fuck did I do?"

His ears deaf to any sound but his own roaring rage, Blane tore at the bags, the light swinging erratically as he discarded the holdalls in heaps, his eyes glaring inside before tossing them and their cargo ruthlessly to his right or left. The growl was growing to a shriek of rage, but he was so lost in his task that if it wasn't for the sprays of saliva that touched every open canvas bag, he wouldn't have even heard himself.

"Where's the fucking drugs? Where are the fucking drugs!" Heat burned his face. Charlie wouldn't have done this to him. He wouldn't. Why the fuck would he leave all these guns and take the drugs? What kind of sick joke would that be? Charlie *knew* how important they were.

Guns clattered around the walls and hard floor of the garage as he cast them aside, tipping the canvas holdalls, going through each again, his words turning into simply a howl of rage as the obvious dawned on him.

The drugs were gone. Charlie had brought eight kilos of pure cocaine over from the warehouse stash. It would have been enough to keep the Squealers high for at least a week. Plenty of time for the boys to have gone back and cleared out the rest. Tears of frustration pricked the back of his eyes. Fucking Charlie. Why hadn't he brought all the gear with him and left the guns behind?

The small wrap of coke that he'd been working his way through all day burned in his nose leaving a bitter and dissatisfying aftertaste in his dry mouth. There was none left for him. And there was none left for *them*. His stomach churned slightly and for the first time since he'd been a boy, Blane Gentle-King felt vulnerable. And it was Charlie's fault. His best friend, brothers under the skin, Charlie fucking Nash.

It took a moment before he realized Jude and Black-eyes were both staring at him. He panted hard, finally standing still in the center of the mass. Something skittered to his left and swinging the torch around he saw Janine creeping inside the garage and scuttling up the wall toward the ceiling. Her bulbous body looked much larger in the confined space than it had outside, and Blane shivered.

"Did you say the drugs are gone?" Blackeyes's voice was low and Blane felt the tension creep from the other man to himself. His stomach tightened.

"Fucking Charlie Nash." Jude shook his head and spat on the ground. "We need to make him pay for this, Blane. This fucking disrespect. He can't do this to you, man."

Blane's and Blackeyes's gazes were locked on each other. Jude might be a dumb fuck and not realize the dangerous nature of their situation, but Blackeyes did. Blane could see it in the horror growing in the whites of his eyes.

"Jude." Blane spoke softly. "Shut the fuck up."

"Sure, boss. I was just saying . . ."

His words drifted off as the two Squealers squatted outside, rose up a little, their bodies trembling with a noisy hiss that rose like the whistle of a kettle, unable to sustain any noise that didn't result in an awful squealing. From inside the garage, Blane watched the heavy drops of water bouncing off their slimy, discolored bodies as they twisted in circles, spinning erratically on their awful legs. Jude pulled inward, tucking himself under the overhanging garage door.

Blackeyes opened his mouth to say something, but the words never had time to form. The two Squealers leaped, one from each side, and as he tumbled to the ground under their weight, all he could utter was a terrible shriek.

They tore him apart with swift brutality and Blane could only watch, his brain frozen and stomach turning to water. Blackeyes didn't scream for long, but Blane wondered if that was because one of the spiders had ripped out his tongue rather than because he was no longer feeling anything. Flesh and clothes tore and the dark gravel soaked with blood. Blane stared at the soles of Blackeyes's trainers as his legs bucked and trembled, banging out a silent beat on the road beneath him, kicking faster than any man should be capable of.

Something tickled at his face, and he brushed it away. It was sticky against his fingers. More irritated his forehead like a feather tracing its shape against his damp skin. Shivering with disgust but still focused on Blackeyes's awful demise, he raised his hand again. This time, the soft strands coiled around his arm, tugging it downward, back to his side.

What the fuck? Suddenly Blackeyes didn't seem so interesting. He slowly looked down. Even without the torch, the sheen of the silky ropes was visible as they slid over his legs and around the back of his long leather coat. They were so delicate he couldn't even feel their movement through his trousers until they pulled in tight, forcing his legs together. Panic thumped in his chest. Real panic, for the first time since this whole mess had begun.

"Janine?" He spoke softly. "Janine, we can sort it out. We can get the drugs back. We can get more . . ." Something dropped from the ceiling and landed behind him with a soft thud, sending a hot breeze across the back of Blane's neck. He didn't turn around. He wasn't sure that he could. It couldn't end like this. Not after everything he'd done. It couldn't. It wouldn't.

Jude was staring back at him, the horror of their situation now clear in the trembling of his body and Blane willed the dumb fuck to pull out his gun and start shooting.

"Janine, honey . . ." His arms were trapped against his body, and before he could finish his sentence, he felt the hard, spiky legs wrap tight around him. Finally, his legs crumpled under him as white panic took hold, punching his anger out of him. More webbing shot around his legs, pulling his knees up tight into his chest, squashing them there as the Squealer tugged him into her underbelly. Tears pricked at the back of his eyes and he lifted his head.

Jude stumbled backward. So focused on Blane, he didn't look behind him. He didn't see the Squealer waiting there, front legs raised, thin strands oozing from the tips and sliding along the ground seeking out the skinny young man. As something cold trickled into his spine, Blane figured he probably had enough breath to scream a warning. To give Jude at least a fighting chance of blowing the brains out of the fucking monster before it was on him. He didn't though. If Blane was going down then so was Jude.

The Squealer leaped and only as it spun the young man around did he finally get off a couple of shots. They landed firmly in the spider that was using Black-eyes for dinner, the creature crumpling dead as Jude dropped the gun.

"Oh god, help me . . ." Jude finally wailed. His brain foggy, Blane figured they were past that. He fought the urge to giggle, and scream and cry. There were two lines left in the wrap on the glass table in the penthouse flat. He wished he'd taken them now. What a waste.

As Janine scuttled over to the various abandoned bags and sacks, her mandible clacking hard, she hovered over one. Blane felt her tremble running through him. He found, as the strange numbness crept into his lower body, that he could feel a lot of Janine. He could feel the madness of her mind and the sheer power of her rage. As she pawed the ground and leaped away, following the invisible tracks of the car and the scent of the drugs she so badly needed, Blane realized just how badly he'd underestimated her.

CHAPTER TWENTY-FOUR

Courtney's face ached as he stepped out of the Mercedes and into the storm. But then again, so did his ribs and most of his body. He wouldn't be surprised if somewhere inside him there were cracks and bruises that in normal times would have him in bed or on the sofa for at least a week if he'd done them in football. He winced shutting the door behind him, the sudden movement causing his chest to wail. He had to give it to Charlie, he could throw a mean punch.

The boot slammed, and with a quick glance around to check there were no obvious signs of danger around them, Courtney followed the others over the road to the vast entrance to the modern station. At least all the streetlights seemed to be functioning in this part of town. Maybe it would keep the Whites, as Charlie called the normal spiders, away. He doubted it, but at least they'd be able to see if any came near them.

His legs resisted his insistence on running and by the time he was on the pavement he was panting. If he was honest he just wanted to sit down for a while and cry. A couple of hours ago he was pretty sure he was dead, and now everything had changed. It was too much to deal with.

"That's not a good sign." Leke pointed upward.

A few thick strands of webbing coated the hard lines of the roof, dipping as they stretched over to the sign declaring they were at Canning Town, the name printed in white on the blue strip running through the middle of the red circle of the iconic London tube sign.

"Doesn't necessarily mean anything." Mr. Green was leaning heavily on Harry. "They might have been here days ago."

His weakly delivered words didn't fill anyone with confidence, Courtney was pretty sure about that. "We haven't got any other choice," he added, looking over at Nathan. The boy's eyes looked strange, his glasses coated with thick streaks of rain. "How far did you say it was?"

"Mile and a half. Less as crow flies."

There was something reassuring about Nathan's monotone delivery, even if Courtney was sure the weird boy was panicking just like the rest of them inside.

"Let's do it then."

Charlie led the way through the unshuttered entrance. "And stay alert. Guns out."

Leke hung back waiting for him as they walked up the stairs and into the station.

"Hey, Courtney. You okay?"

"Sure."

There was a long pause. Without turning to look, Courtney knew Leke was licking his lips. He always did it when he was nervous. Leke had been nervous a lot over the past few months.

"We were going to come and get you. You know that, don't you?"

They stepped through the entrance and out of the rain. Light from the streetlamps outside crept through the large atrium-style glass ceiling that ran the length of the ticketing hall, past the barriers and down to the stairs. It sent slanted shadows across the marble floors and as pricks of light danced behind his eyes as they adjusted to the gloom, Courtney glanced over at his friend.

"We wouldn't have left you there." Leke's eyes slipped away. "You know that."

"I know that." Courtney nodded. Their feet clicked on the pale marble floor that matched the walls. At least that reflected whatever light made its way inside. It was definitely less gloomy in the building than it had been in the growing night outside. Leke's feet splashed slightly. The rain had made its way in though, small patches of damp pooling here and there. He smiled at Leke and the other boy returned the gesture, with obvious relief. He knew Leke was lying; he could see it written all over his face. Leke's eyes never had been able to lie. It was something that had got them into trouble too many times at school. His guilt was always obvious.

Courtney looked up at the atrium. Maybe there was a crack in it. Maybe the Whites had sat on it too heavily. The rain shouldn't have crept this far into the building.

"Are we okay?" The sadness in Leke's voice made Courtney smile softly.

"Course we are. We'll always be okay." His voice echoed softly, bouncing back at him from the walls.

And he meant it. If it had been Leke who Charlie and Skate had dragged off instead he wasn't sure he'd have gone after him. Not after seeing Blane with the Squealers.

Ahead of him, Harry turned as much as he could manage while propping his teacher up. He frowned. "Where's James?"

Courtney turned and looked back toward the entrance. "James?" He couldn't bring himself to shout, the slow dread that lived in the pit of his stomach roaring awake. The older boy had been just behind them fiddling with his backpack. Had a White got him? He glanced at Leke, his thoughts and fears reflected on the other boy's face. A shadow loomed into view above them and for a moment his heart stopped, before roaring into life again.

The blond boy sniffed hard and then stared at the faces glaring back in the gloom.

"Jesus, James," Harry said. "You scared the crap out of us."

"I was just checking there was no one following." He grinned and the edges of his smile twitched. "Don't be so chicken!"

No one laughed.

"What do you think, should we stay here and wait until morning or keep going?" Craig looked around the huddled group standing under the atrium. James's foot tapped on the slick floor, his head glancing from side to side. Courtney stared at him. He seemed agitated. Maybe that was the way he showed his fear. Or he was just excited about the whole thing and that was just crazy. Harry seemed okay but there was something off-kilter and a little wild about James that made Courtney feel on edge. But it was the posh kid's boat they were heading for so at least until they were out of London, Courtney figured he'd keep his thoughts to himself.

"We keep going," Charlie said. "It's only a mile or

so. The longer we stay outside the more we increase the danger."

Just thinking about the boat made Courtney itch to be on it; the excitement at the prospect of being safely on the water, battling with his fear of what might happen on their way to the marina. That mile and a half seemed like an eternity after the shit they'd seen in the streets.

Nathan pushed his glasses up on his face, staring at the row of turnstiles ahead of them. "It's going to be dark in the tunnel."

Stepping away from the group, Harry leaned the teacher back against the clean walls, stretching out his arms. "It's dark everywhere."

"Don't get his blood on the wall, Harry!" James fired the words out and then peered back at the entrance. "It might bring those things." He wiped his nose with his sleeve.

"James, if they can smell his blood, they'll bloody smell it anyway. It's not as if it's the best-dressed wound in the world."

"He's right. Calm the fuck down." Charlie lit a cigarette and stared at James until the boy's eyes slid to the ground. Courtney was glad Charlie Nash had the same effect on the posh boys as he had on the estate ones. They needed someone to be in charge. James pulled a pack of his own from his jeans pocket and lit it with a trembling hand.

"I was just thinking aloud. That's all. I'm sorry."

"It's going to be dark in the tunnel," Nathan repeated.

Courtney looked past the barriers. "He's got a point. It's pretty dim up here, but down there it'll be pitch-black. We won't be able to see anything." He looked over at Craig. "It'll be like being blind."

"Shit."

Without thinking, Courtney found himself looking over at Charlie for an answer.

The man sucked on his cigarette, the glowing end blazing as the air around them grew a shade darker. Night had fallen. "There's got to be some fucking torches or something around here somewhere. Health and fucking safety." He looked around them, his eyes falling on the guard's office past the automatic ticket machines. He slapped Craig on the arm. "You come with me. The rest of you stay here. Courtney, you and Leke keep your eyes on the entrance; Harry and James, you watch the turnstiles and stairs. You should have plenty of time to shoot if you see something."

The handgun felt sweaty and awkward in his grip, but Courtney felt a lot happier with it than he would without. He stared at the mouth of the building that seemed to yawn wider as if inviting the terrors of the outside to come and seek them out. He swallowed hard. When had he suddenly grown such an active imagination?

He tried not to see spindly legs creeping in every shadow, but his nerves twitched, his eyes darting in every direction and focusing on nothing. It didn't help that one was very nearly closed, and try as he might to keep opening it despite the pain, it wouldn't be very long until he was limited to seeing out of only one. He lifted his hand and gently touched the bump that rose huge above his cheekbone. As soon as his fingers brushed it, he flinched. He hoped they didn't have to run for it. Between his eye and the ache in his chest that hinted at a cracked rib or two, he figured he'd never be able to keep up. He glanced over at the teacher who'd sunk down against the wall. It could be worse. There was still one person in the group he could outrun. The thought left a bad taste in his mouth and he was glad when Craig's shout interrupted it.

"The room's locked. We're going to shoot the lock off."

Even with the warning, the sharp blast of the shot made Courtney and Leke both jump. The echo bounded around the walls, ricocheting to each pocket of people and relishing in its own brief existence.

"Well, if the spiders didn't know we were here before," James drawled out the words as if he really didn't care, "they probably bloody do now."

Nothing moved in the shadows though, and a few moments later Craig and Charlie were back with three heavy torches.

They moved quietly and climbed over the turnstiles, both Harry and Charlie helping the wounded teacher. Courtney leaned on Craig's shoulder and hauled himself over. It was embarrassing. He should easily have been able to hurdle it. He grimaced as his legs bent into his chest, relieved when he could jump down and straighten them out.

"You okay?" Craig frowned. "Your face looks pretty mashed up."

"I'm okay. My ribs hurt." He paused. "I'm doing better than that other bloke." Ahead of them Green was doing his best to get down the stairs, but he was pretty much being carried by the two on either side of him. They took the wide steps quickly, eager to catch up. Darkness chased at their heels.

"Maybe we should put that torch on."

Craig shook his head. "Charlie said we should wait until we get in the tunnel. Says we don't know how much battery power they've got left." He paused. "Seems weird taking orders from Charlie Nash."

Courtney shrugged. "He's beat the shit out of me, but then saved my life."

"Doesn't that freak you out?"

"No, not really." Courtney sniffed, and his swollen eye finally closed. "He was just doing what he was told until he saved me. This is the real Charlie. And I feel safer with him with us than I would if he wasn't."

"Maybe. But I still want to give him a good kicking for what he did to you. And what he would have done to Leke."

"Those days are done, Craig. Let it go." His face cracked into a wide and painful grin. "Anyway, I'd like to see you try."

Craig smiled back. "I'd get him when he was sleeping."

The stairs finally led down to the open-air platform, and Courtney could feel the breeze. It was cooler than it had been now that night had fallen, but it was still damp and warm.

"You'd have to. And even then my money would be on Charlie."

They stepped out into the night and shivered as the falling rain embraced them again. On the other side of the tracks a fence rose high protecting the line from any foolhardy or drunk teenagers who might decide to run down the steep embankment and play chicken with the trains. As one the group turned their head to the left, peering at where the track disappeared into the tunnel a hundred yards or so away. For a moment no one spoke. Anything could be in there.

Charlie went first and climbed down from the platform. Suddenly he seemed very small, and Courtney hastily joined him. The platform looked strange from the lower angle, and despite its sleek and angular look, the design barely ten years old, it seemed to Courtney like it were a relic from a distant civilization. Even looking at the signs hurt his heart. It all meant nothing. Destroyed without even noticing.

He turned away, and walked with the others toward the tunnel. Their feet crunched in a steady rhythm on the wet shingle until eventually they stopped at the entrance. The wind whistled through it, ghosts of life tickling Courtney's ears as he stared into the darkness. It was as if the wind and rain were mocking them. His stomach flipped with the prospect of a mile and a half in that darkness.

"What if there's a train in there?" Courtney muttered.

"A train will be the least of our worries," Harry said.

"It's only one stop. Straight under the river and then we'll be out at the marina."

"The O2 arena," Leke added.

"Yeah." Charlie flicked on his torch, and Harry and Craig did the same. "Let's worry about the arena and what might be living on it once we've got through the tunnel. Deal?"

Leke nodded. "Deal."

The beams from the torches were strong, each sending out a wide shaft of bright white light, and suddenly the black void in the tunnel was visible, at least for a few feet ahead of them. Courtney's heartbeat slowed slightly. Maybe they'd be okay in there. A mile and a half wasn't far really.

"Let's go then." Charlie peered around at them. "And keep close to the side. We'll take it in turns to cover the rear."

Courtney nodded, but Charlie had already turned and started into the tunnel. With a deep breath, Courtney followed.

CHAPTER TWENTY-FIVE

Blane's mind drifted as the creature carried him through the storm, her body protecting him from the rain. She ran as if he didn't weigh a thing, unhindered by the loss of the legs that were holding him so firmly against her underbelly. He wondered why he wasn't dead yet. The thought was almost idle and he couldn't help but think that maybe something in his system was subduing him. He should be panicking. He should be screaming for help, not that either would do him any good.

She had inserted something inside him, he knew that. He could feel the cold against his spine; wrapping around his vertebrae. That was something he didn't want to think about too much. The idea of her being inside him, locked onto his delicate nerves and fiber, just the tiniest squeeze able to paralyze him or worse; it was enough to drive him to panic whether she was pumping some kind of calming drug into him or not.

Warm water splashed into his face from the vast puddles forming on the road whose tarmac was only a few feet away. Occasional light glinted on its surfaces, reflected from somewhere far outside of Blane's limited vision. He let his eyes blur out of focus and concentrated instead on the events inside his body. Strange things were happening. He could feel Janine through the thing that was in his back; at first it had been a mere irritating buzz as if a fly were trapped inside his own empty skull, but with each step the sensation had changed and grown. As she was controlling him through the physical link, he realized that he could slip a little inside her. His mind crept slowly forward, gently nudging his way inside, an invisible intruder. She was too focused, too intent, to notice him.

He could feel the completely alien nature of the creature she'd become humming into his own veins. There was so much coldness. His veins filled with an empty ache of centuries of waiting somewhere deep and cold, hidden in a vast ocean until the earth cracked and bubbled and set the eggs free. He saw other planets devastated; wrecks of beautiful and abstract civilizations cloaked in webbing. His mind almost cracked with the enormity of the images that roared into his mind and he pulled back, leaving the creature's subconscious and reaching for the shallower surface. Her anger bubbled as she traced the path of Charlie and the boy. Mentally, he frowned. *More than one boy.* Their individual scents filled his head, and he could feel their fear and their sweat, and below that he could almost taste the sweet copper of blood, and the bitter tang of cocaine.

There was more than one mind at work here though, and he could feel the others locked up back in the flat. They were flooding their sense of smell into Janine, enhancing her own tenfold. He could feel their impatience; their itch, the growing need for a fix. It wasn't too bad yet but in a matter of hours they would be going crazy. He shivered slightly, not sure if the sensation was physical or only in his own mind. They were crazy already, these things. Janine would rip him apart if her addiction wasn't fed.

Beyond the ugly insanity that formed at the edges of the thing's mind like a stagnant black cloud, he could sense more. A collective that was bigger and stronger. He could feel their revulsion at the Squealers. He could feel their strength, the clarity of their shared thought, and he felt a terror in the core of him. The Whites. The pure breed. They'd been right. The Squealers had kept the Whites at bay, but not because the Whites were afraid . . . they simply wanted nothing to do with the "different" ones of their kind. The Squealers' mental potential was crude and limited next to the Whites'. The Squealers were outcasts. He almost smiled but thought that maybe the numbed muscles in his face wouldn't quite manage the expression. Just like in life, Janine was still an outsider. A misfit. Nothing had really changed at all.

Blane could hear the feet of the second Squealer as it scuttled in Janine's wake, and was glad he couldn't see it. He didn't want to have to look at Jude wrapped into her underbelly. He was scared to. Jude's physical state would be a reflection of his own, and if he was going to even have a chance of surviving this then he needed to keep his sanity. And some hope. He let his mind settle somewhere beneath the thing's conscious. How much of Janine was left in there? If the thing had a collective memory of its race's past, then maybe it had a residue of its host too. It had felt like that from the outside. How much of Janine could he find from the inside? He settled somewhere just below the raging surface of the creature's thoughts and waited. He'd controlled the bitch for years. What was to stop him from doing it now?

The liquid forming in the armpits of Skate's T-shirt had nothing to do with rain or heat and everything to do with the panic that was slowly pulling strips off him from the inside out. He had to fucking keep it together. He had to. Maybe he shouldn't have told Blane about Charlie until the morning. Things were quieter in the daylight. Safer. He should have known Blane would kick off. But then if he'd left it overnight, all of Blane's anger would have been directed at Skate himself and with the way things were that might have ended with him being as dead as Chokey, and maybe not killed so swiftly. Blane had got edgy over the past week; shit, they all had, but there had always been something a little crazy about Gentle-King and now he was sure he could sometimes see the glow of that madness shining right in the center of Blane's hazel eyes.

Shit, it was all fucked up. He leaned back against the smooth corridor and shut his eyes, listening to the thumps and thuds of the Squealers as they threw themselves at the walls and doors. He needed to hold it together and stay calm.

The door shook in its hinges, and then the flat fell silent. The moment had passed. But how long would it be before they thought to throw themselves at the thick glass windows? Skate doubted it would take them long to crash through that. Then they'd be out. And angry. He swallowed hard. And they'd be hungry.

Sweat clung to the cracks in the palms of his hands. Where the fuck was everybody? Leeboy had gone with some other bloke to check that everything useful had been retrieved from the second block, but he hadn't seen either of them since and it wasn't like Leeboy not to check in. He mentally added walkie-talkies to the never-ending list of supplies they were going to need if they had half a chance of making this block secure.

Not wanting to be around when the Squealers started up their racket again, he took the lift back up to Blane's penthouse. Without the huge character of Blane filling it, the vast open spaces seemed desolate and cold, even in the damp heat. There was no comfort to be found here, but with nowhere better to go, Skate sat down on the leather couch. Traces of cocaine glittered on the smeared glass surface of the coffee table. Shit. He liked to get high as much as anyone, but he'd learned from Blane and the others that there was a time and a place. Charlie Nash didn't even touch anything harder than weed. But now Charlie was gone and Blane was out there somewhere high, and with some fucking Squealers in tow. Nothing about it felt good.

His head ached as he rested it in his palms. He didn't want this responsibility. Blane, Jude and Blackeyes should have been back by now. They'd only gone over to the garages to check Charlie's stash. Ten minutes max to get there, ten minutes of screaming and shouting and then ten back again. Half an hour. They'd been gone an hour and a half. With only himself and Blinka of the main crew still around, that firmly made Skate in charge.

Maybe they should send a couple of people over to the blocks to check. Even as he thought it, the suggestion faded. Five people had gone over to those blocks and none had come back. Why would it be any different for anyone else who went out there?

He sighed. Night was fully upon them now, and the

dark was dangerous. He had only one real choice. He had to lock down the block for the night. There'd be someone on the door so if Blane and the others got back they'd get inside fast enough. They'd go over and check the blocks in the morning. It was all he could do. Standing up, he lit a cigarette and cursed Charlie Nash before heading back downstairs.

CHAPTER TWENTY-SIX

Craig's shoulder was starting to ache and in the dark he could hear his own heavy breathing echoing back at him from the boy on the other side of the teacher. Mr. Green was pretty skinny, but with every step he was getting weaker and becoming more of a dead weight hanging between the boys. He didn't complain though, even though Craig was sure that gunshot must really fucking hurt. The worst they heard was the occasional groan if they stumbled over the uneven ground, and those were normally followed by a weak apology.

His gun dug into his hip as he walked, but he didn't want to stop to move it. Harry had his army semiautomatic out, and Craig's free hand had the torch. He was surprised that he was okay with it. But then he was surprised to find that he was starting to like Harry. He was a bit awkward and soft, but he'd carried Mr. Green all the way, and Craig had a feeling that he would never have left the man alone in that garage when there was a chance of getting him out. He wished he felt the same about the other one, James. He could just make out the blond boy's moving feet in the unsteady beam of the torch.

"What's your mate's problem?"

"James?" Harry's low voice was breathless.

"Yeah. He's fucking twitchy. Is he on something?"

"No. Just the odd bit of puff."

The phrase sounded funny delivered in Harry's clipped, upper-class accent. He never thought of posh people really taking drugs. Maybe some of those city boys, but not people like Harry and James.

"James is just . . ." Harry hesitated. "Well, he's just James. You haven't met him at his best."

Craig thought about how James had been behaving and thought maybe Harry was wrong. It looked to him like James was on the pills of speed or something. He was too edgy. Even in this situation where they were all fucking edgy.

"Maybe. You two just seem a weird pair to be friends."

Harry laughed softly. "Yes, I suppose we are." The humor slipped out of his voice and disappeared into the darkness. "I just like him. I can't help myself." He paused. "And you and Nathan don't seem likely friends either."

"Nathan's all right. But we were never friends before this." His stomach twisted slightly. "We were always pretty fucking mean to him, actually. Treated him like a freak." He paused. "He probably didn't deserve it. He's different, but he's no freak."

They walked another minute or so in silence, Craig's irritation at James vanishing into his own guilt and grief for the past, all the lost friends and family crowding in at the edge of his sanity. He wanted to shake them away, but their ghosts filled the gloom. Afraid that he might panic completely, he concentrated on the man beside him whose limp and sweaty arm dragged across his shoulder and strained on his neck. James's feet were almost out of view. They needed to pick up their pace or they'd fall behind, and it wasn't as if the rest of the group were going at any great rate, each of them carefully picking out their steps in the filthy blackness that threatened to swallow them whole.

His arm knocked into the wall on his left and the torch beam lurched around the tunnel while he steadied himself. On the other side, Harry's feet stumbled and for a moment Craig felt the weight drag through the injured man and thought all three of them might fall, before the extra pounds disappeared and he found his footing.

"Sorry," Harry breathed. "Tripped."

"My fault. Knocked the torch."

A low, wet moan drifted toward them from a few feet ahead, and they froze. James stopped too.

"Who was that?" Leke's whisper came out of the darkness. "Who the fuck was that?"

No one answered. Cold dread trickled from Craig's gut down to his bladder.

The sound came again; weak and full of despair.

"That is not good," James drawled and Craig felt the urge to kick him in the back of the legs. That was what irritated him. He always sounded like he just didn't give a shit. It was fake and Craig fucking hated fakes.

"Charlie?" Despite himself, it was the grown man's voice he wanted to hear.

"It's coming from ahead. Sounds human." Charlie sounded at least fifteen feet or so ahead of them. They really had fallen behind. He swallowed his panic.

"Wait," he whispered, hoping his fear wasn't overly obvious. "Stay where you are. We need to come to you."

James and Leke ahead, they shuffled forward until they reached the others and huddled against the wall, listening to the soft sobbing moan that drifted and danced around them.

"Everyone ready?" Charlie asked. "Whatever it is, I reckon it's not that far ahead. Be fucking alert. And keep those torches on the center of the tracks."

No one spoke, the increasing beat of his heart filling Craig's ears.

"Can you manage him?" Harry whispered.

"Yeah. I think so."

Harry slipped out from under Mr. Green's arm, his hand holding the gun, ready to shoot if he had to and while the others focused on the awful noise, Craig just concentrated on getting one foot in front of the other while carrying the teacher.

"Sorry about this." The words were almost nothing in his ear, and it took a moment before Craig realized Mr. Green was speaking.

"Don't worry about it. It's fine."

"Maybe you should just . . . put me down. Might be for the best."

Craig's heart squeezed and he gritted his teeth, surprised by the tears that threatened to blur his limited vision. His arms didn't seem to ache so much in that moment.

"No fucking way," he muttered.

"No fucking way, sir, is what I'd prefer, young man." The teacher laughed weakly.

"No fucking way, sir." Craig smiled and there in the darkness of the tunnel, for just a few seconds, everything was okay. Fucked up but okay.

It didn't last.

"Oh shit." Charlie stopped.

"Fuck."

"Holy fuck."

"Is that . . . it can't be . . . are they . . . ?"

Craig raised his head from watching his feet and stared into the tunnel. With four torches all beaming into the same location the space was filled with light. Craig's mouth dropped open.

"Oh fuck," Leke moaned. "We can't walk though this. We can't. What the fuck is it? What the fuck?"

"Food store," Nathan said, matter-of-factly.

And he was right. Stretched ahead of them, for as far as the torchlight went, and Craig was pretty sure for a long way farther than that, the ceiling of the tunnel was covered in thick strands of white webbing, a mesh of the stuff so interwoven none of the man-made cables or concrete above was visible. Cocoons hung in rows of three or four, each one five or six feet long, the webbing bound tight around the obviously human shapes. The moan came again from somewhere a few feet to their left.

"Don't tell me someone in there is still alive." The horror of what they were seeing must have revived the teacher somewhat and Craig felt his shoulder and arm relax and rise in delicious relief as Mr. Green stood up straight, taking his own weight.

The moan came again and this time Craig was sure he heard words in it.

"Heeeelp meee."

Leaving Mr. Green against the wall with the torch, he picked his way around the others to Charlie. "Should we take a look?"

Without speaking, Charlie ducked between the first two hanging sacs, and Craig followed, turning sideways to avoid touching them. He grimaced. They smelled rotten. Sweet. It was like old women's breath and it made him flinch. He stayed inches behind Charlie, terrified that if he lost sight of him then he'd be trapped in this field of bodies forever, stumbling through their lines and searching for freedom, the cocoons closing in on him until eventually smothering him. It was stupid. He knew that the others were only a few feet away, their torches easily picking them out in the dark, but he couldn't shake the feeling that he and Charlie had stepped into another world and if they weren't careful, they might never get out of it. For the first time in a long time, Craig felt like a kid. Nothing street-smart would help him here. This was the stuff of nightmares.

"Look at their faces," Charlie whispered.

Craig did as he was told. He felt immediately sick. The cocoons had lashed around the bodies, some with their legs tucked in at their knees but the arms still visible at their sides, others as if the victim had simply stood and let the creature do its terrible work, and under the solid webbing the shapes of hands or fists or knees were obvious. He dragged his eyes up. The heads were different though. Although also coated in thick strands the mouths and noses were uncovered. He frowned. What the fuck was the point of that? The answer screamed somewhere at the back of his mind, but he ignored it.

Charlie raised the torch. The small parts of skin visible around the person's lips were blue and purple, as if he'd been beaten so hard every part of him was bruised. Was that what the rest of their skin looked like under the thick white coating? Craig's eyes widened. Had the mouth just moved, ever so slightly?

"What the fuck?" Slowly, he raised his hand and held it in front of the open lips. His nerves tingled, seeking out a change. And there it was; just the softest hint of fresh warmth tickling his sweating palm. Craig slowly counted out the seconds in his head. Nearly ten had passed before he felt it again. For a moment he thought he might actually throw up all over the trapped thing in front of him, acid bile surging up his chest. He swallowed hard.

"I think he's alive," he whispered. "Only just. But he's breathing."

The mouth and nose didn't react to his words. If the person was alive, he wasn't conscious, and Craig was glad about that. The moan drifted to them again. Someone was though, and both his and Charlie's heads flicked left. The voice was right beside them.

"Heeelpp . . ."

Craig reached past Charlie, the instinct to pull the man down overriding the revolted fear that gripped him. They had to free him. They had to. The idea he was fucking alive in that shit . . .

Charlie pushed his hand away. "Don't touch it."

"What?" Craig felt his old loathing for Charlie Nash rear up inside. "But he's fucking alive in there."

"Just wait."

"What's happening? What's going on?" Harry's whisper snaked its way through the bodies. Both Charlie and Craig ignored it, Charlie pulling a cigarette out of the packet in his pocket. Craig stared. What the fuck was he doing?

Instead of lighting it as Craig expected him to, Charlie carefully held out the cigarette, touching it very gently against the cocoon. Nothing happened. The man moaned again, and Craig saw his black tongue flick out between his discolored lips. They needed to do something quickly.

"Can we help him now?" he hissed.

Charlie didn't look at him; instead he threw the cigarette to the ground and pulled out his gun. He tapped it firmly against the man's chest twice. The whole cocoon trembled and strands broke free and swiftly stretched out to trap the gun, slithering over it in an instant. Charlie jerked his hand away, leaving the weapon behind. Within seconds it was covered in white; a deformity against the smooth lines of the dying man's body.

Craig stared, panting. If he'd touched him; if he'd tried to yank the man down as he'd planned, that stuff would have been all over him.

"Jesus fuck," he mumbled. His breath came ragged and fast.

"We can't help him." Charlie's voice was cold. "Don't think we can even shoot him without risking getting that shit on us."

The man's sobs increased. Whoever it was trapped inside there, he could hear them; Craig was suddenly very horribly sure of that.

"You want to just leave him like this?" Craig's mouth was dry. "You're sick, Charlie."

The older man stared at him. "No, I don't want to fucking leave him like this. But we don't have a fucking choice, and I'm taking that decision on me so no other fucker has to feel bad about it. Now do you get it, you stupid little fuck?"

The hissed anger and frustration filled the small space between them.

Craig wasn't sure if he'd feel worse if Charlie had actually punched him in the face than just snarling at him like that. He'd always thought he was pretty tough himself, and maybe he would be in a few years' time, but standing there in the dark he realized he had a long way to go until he was anywhere near as hard as Charlie.

"Now come on. Let's leave this poor bastard to die in peace."

The torchlight guiding them, Craig stayed close to Charlie's back. Although there was plenty of space for them to move between the cocooned people, now that he'd seen what could happen if he touched one too hard, Craig wasn't taking any chances of accidentally stumbling into one. Only when they were beside the small huddle on the other side of the tracks did he step away from Charlie.

"Nathan's right. It's a food store." He paused. "Don't touch them. The webbing's kind of alive. It'll grab you."

"I think I may have a problem in that department." The weak voice came from a few feet away, and the huddle turned as one, shining all four torches at the wall.

Mr. Green was leaning where Craig had left him resting just a few moments before. He raised a half smile, his eyes squeezed shut behind his glasses. "You're blinding me."

Craig lowered his torch and the others did the same. It had been better when they'd all been pointed at his face. He'd looked normal then. Webbing snaked down from above, clinging to the walls in wispy strands, thin and ethereal rather than the thicker cords that held the cocoons hanging along the track lines. His torch paused at the teacher's shoulder wound. The tiny threads slid over his body and disappeared inside, worming their way under the badly fitting bandages and into the wound.

"At first I didn't realize." The four torches danced over Mr. Green's face and body, highlighting each terror as the man spoke. "Then I tried to move and couldn't. They're in my hair, I think. I'm stuck here. I think they're wrapped around my legs too."

A quick glance confirmed it was true. Craig said nothing. His heart beat hard against his chest and he stared at something and nothing in the torch's beam. He couldn't look at Harry. He couldn't look at anyone. They hadn't seen the man in the cocoon and the fucking color of his skin. That was going to happen to Mr. Green, and it was his fucking fault for just leaving him there. The torch wavered as his hand shook.

"We'll get you out of there. We'll get you out of there." Harry stepped forward but James pulled him back. The blond boy's face was pale.

"You heard what Craig said. You can't touch that stuff."

"But there must be a way. There must be." Craig looked up to find Harry staring at him as if he had some miraculous answer. His stomach shriveled further into the pit of his gut.

"It's not often I agree with James." Mr. Green hiccuped a tired laugh. "In fact, I think this may be the first time on record that I can say he's one hundred percent right." He looked up, squinting at them all. "Isn't he, Charlie?"

There was a long pause. "Yeah. I'm sorry."

Craig's heart squeezed, tears biting angrily into him. "But I said I wouldn't fucking leave you. I just said it. I won't fucking leave you. Not here." An arm came around his shoulders and he shook it off. It came back again and this time squeezed tight. It was Leke. It had to be. Only Leke was like that.

"Well, I'm afraid I'm the adult here," the teacher said softly. "And where I'm from that means you have to do as you're told." Mr. Green's head lolled forward slightly, the effort of speaking tiring him, but it was held firmly by the grip of the webbing that had weaved into his thick hair.

"Don't think of it as you leaving me behind. More that I'm choosing to stay."

"How can you be so fucking calm?" Craig's spit flew in a wet rage into the dark space between himself and the teacher. It didn't make sense. It wasn't fair. They'd come so fucking far, they must be over halfway through the tunnel by now.

"I'm tired. I'm injured. And I'm very, very weak." He smiled. "And now I need you all to go, so I can get on with what I need to do."

Charlie stepped forward and gave him a handgun. They didn't speak, the teacher gripping the handle. "I need to do this before the stuff gets my arms."

A squeal echoed down the tunnel, chasing their invisible footprints.

"What was that?" Harry whispered.

"Fucking Squealer," Charlie muttered. "It's Blane."

"Blane?" Craig found himself spitting out the word at the same time as Courtney and Leke. He thought he heard Nathan echo it in his deadened tone a nanosecond behind them.

"You need to go," Mr. Green said.

"Fuck." Charlie pushed the boys into a line. "Keep to the walls. Don't touch them or the cocoons and stay together. Just keep moving. And Harry, give me that army gun."

The boys paused and Harry handed over the weapon.

"What are you doing? Aren't you coming?" Even James sounded freaked out by the wails coming at them from the darkness.

"Trust me, I'll be right behind you. Now move."

The group disappeared into the gloom, but Craig hung back, his torch creating a single small beam, insecure in its battle against the solid blackness.

"Charlie?" the voice called loud. "Are you fucking down there, Charlie? I want my drugs back, man!"

Craig's blood chilled. It was Blane. But he sounded funny. His voice was different; there was a hiss in it that had never been there before. The words sounded unnatural.

Charlie ignored it, taking the torch from Craig and placing it at Mr. Green's feet, angled outward into the awful field of bodies. "Can you manage the semiautomatic?"

"I think so."

"Good. Take out what you can before you do what you have to. Don't worry about these people. They're dead already."

The teacher nodded. "But I think you should take this." His free hand worked its way into his pocket and pulled out what looked like a grenade. "We got it from the army truck. Don't want to bring the bloody tunnel down on your heads."

Charlie took it, squeezed the teacher's hand and then Charlie had Craig's arm, pulling him along in the gloom. The dark swallowed them in moments, leaving Craig to trust his luck in the blackness and trying not to think about the man they'd left alive behind them to die alone in the dark. When the next squeal wailed at his heels, however, all thoughts of anything but his own survival were gone.

Andrew Green leaned back against the rough wall. He didn't really have much of a choice so what was the point in fighting it. A thin strip of webbing tickled as it crossed his neck, pinning him into position. It didn't concern him overly much and he figured if he stayed still it wouldn't tighten. Not too soon at least, and within moments the squealing creatures coming down the dark line would be here anyway. His finger wrapped around the trigger making sure that whatever the webbing did in the next few seconds, he'd still be able to squeeze. He hoped he'd hit one of the Squealers. He'd definitely kill a few of the poor men trapped in the cocoons. If he fired fast enough in all directions it was likely he'd do some damage before it was time to turn the gun on himself.

He searched his feelings. Death was coming. That was a certainty. It was coming for him in a destroyed world in the bowels of the earth. And it was very likely that something new and vicious would eat his body when it was done. It was too surreal. Maybe that's why he found he didn't feel very much at all. Maybe if he was dying on a clear sunny day and knowing he was leaving his wife behind for extra years without him, years that he couldn't share, then maybe there'd be a tinge of bitterness. But his wife was gone. Dead before him, a parasite having fed in her and on her, and changed her into something he loathed and was pleased to leave behind when the time for the school trip came around.

Maybe if he'd been on a burning boat, trapped like others had been in his navy days, facing a fiery death, then maybe he'd be more afraid. But those days were gone and any men who had survived alongside him were too old to fight this new threat. Maybe if it was anywhere other than here and now then he'd feel that deep-seated panic and the coming nothingness. As it was, all he could see was darkness, and he was already surrounded by that.

At least he would go out fighting. The next squeal made his ears vibrate and his mouth dried. He *hoped* he'd go out fighting. Feet scuttered toward him, too many to be human, but bringing with them a rasping heavy breath. He gripped the gun and peered into the thin stream of light. A strip of webbing tightened across his forehead, pulling up his eyebrows and widening his stare as if in preparation for what he was about to see.

The creature crept forward along the tracks, its body half in the light, flashes of its purplish skin and sticklike clawed legs cutting through the yellow torch beam. Underneath its belly, Andrew Green made out the figure of a young man wrapped tightly in webbing. The man's head turned to the side, his dulled eyes reflecting Green's own horror, both men condemned to a slow and painful death and recognizing it in the other. The thing carrying the black man squealed, and Green was sure he saw the trapped face stretch wide in a silent scream as it did so.

This wasn't the man who'd called after Charlie. He was pretty sure about that. There were more feet scuttling in the darkness and appraising the situation ahead. The man they were all afraid of, the one who had supposedly tamed the Squealers, was behind somewhere.

Still, Green decided, you had to start somewhere. Gritting his teeth, he squeezed the trigger. The tunnel exploded with noise and color as bullets sprayed, and somewhere beyond that, behind his flinching eyes, Green could hear himself yelling as he waved the gun from side to side, peppering the tunnel with death. What he was shouting for, he didn't know, all the rage and anger and grief pouring out of him, his screams merely a backdrop to the fireworks of the semiautomatic's thunder. As the cocoons twisted and turned and fell to the ground under his attack, the strands of deadly white silk came to life, desperate to recapture their lost prey. Something crept into his open mouth, diving down his throat. His scream stopped, his finger releasing the trigger. He tried to close his lips but the feel of the webbing at its edges revolted him.

For the first time, he felt the edge of fear. Not of death, but of the stuff that was so clinically finding its way to the very core of him. The tunnel fell into a hushed silence, and he surveyed the damage in the small area that was visible. He'd hit one of them, he knew that. A trainered foot lay at a funny angle under a heap of almost purple, the rest of the body eaten up by darkness. He smiled. Somewhere up ahead, toward the exit that he'd never see, a squeal shrieked. He'd been right. There was one more, but taking care of that was up to Charlie now. He'd done his bit.

He sat in silence for a moment and stared at the darkness. How bad could death be? Everyone did it. Children, animals, plants. Everything. And yet, he found his hand hesitating on the gun. Something moved in the dark on his left. An angry hiss spat at him. All the activity had brought the spider back to its store, and as the bank of red eyes shone like lasers as it approached, Andrew Green remembered that there were some things a lot worse than death. He tilted the gun upward and under his chin and without a moment's pause, pulled the trigger.

The darkness was complete.

CHAPTER TWENTY-SEVEN

Finally, the end of the tunnel came into view, and pushing Craig forward Charlie picked up the pace. He'd felt the boy flinch when the gunshots had started behind them, but he hadn't said a word. Craig was a good kid and he was tough too. If the world hadn't changed, Charlie would have got him working for the crew and trained him up. Now they all needed training up, and fast, if they were going to survive out there.

A squeal echoed in the blackness behind them, and Charlie's stomach twisted. Fuck. Green may have taken something out in his last moment, but he hadn't got them all. Craig's feet moved into a sprint, and Charlie didn't slow him down. They needed to get the fuck away from here. The huddle of lights was clear and within moments the group was together again. Hot air burned his lungs as he panted.

"We heard the shots," Leke whispered.

"What happened? What . . . ?" Courtney hissed.

"Mr. Green's dead." Nathan answered as if the events were obvious. Charlie stared at him. The kid was strange, that was for fucking sure, but he wasn't stupid.

"Turn the torches off." Standing in the mouth of the tunnel as they were, light beamed in from the strip lighting that ran the length of the platform and up into the station. This part of London was all rebuilt and new. Maybe their circuits were working better than back at Crookston. For a moment he couldn't picture his old flat. The blocks already seemed like a lifetime ago, every moment spent staying alive feeling like a year. Fuck, he wanted a cigarette.

"There's still one behind us, isn't there?" Harry's eyes were red and Charlie figured he'd been crying in the darkness of the tunnel. There was no shame in that.

"At least one. We need to move as silently as possible. Stay close to each other and keep armed and your eyes open. James, you know where this fucking boat is, so you're out front." He paused. "If we don't stay silent, we're dead. We've got to creep under the walkway by the arena to get to the marina. When I saw it this morning, the Whites were all over it."

The boys stared back at him, and slowly nodded.

"We got it," Craig said.

"Good. Then let's get the fuck out of here."

After shoving the boys and their bags up onto the platform, Charlie climbed up. James was already trotting in the direction of the way out sign, the others following in a line. He wondered how long they'd hold it together. Down here, in the bright light and with the garish blue and red lacquered walls of the modern station, everything was quiet and normal, but no matter what they'd all seen since this shit kicked off, he doubted they'd be ready for the whites that covered the dome. Fuck, he wasn't sure he wouldn't panic himself. On his own, he'd have a good chance of survival. He was pretty sure about that, but guarding this bunch of kids? Fuck only knew.

He gritted his teeth and followed them around to the long escalator that would take them to the surface. The metal steps were stubbornly still as if they, unlike the lights, were clever enough to have figured out that their services would no longer be required for the foreseeable future. They creaked as the group strode up them. Charlie glanced behind. So far, so good.

Climbing the steep stairway, taking them two at a time, they finally arrived at the vast entry hall. A solitary handbag sat discarded in the middle of the floor between them and the ticket barrier as if its owner had just dropped it and walked away. Maybe she had. He'd seen the state of half the world's population just before they changed. Fat and stupid and mean summed it up. Whoever had owned that bag had started disappearing long before she died. He pushed a random thought of Lucy out of his head. She was dead and gone. And so would he be if he let himself get distracted.

He vaulted the barrier and took a deep breath. Up ahead, Leke looked like he might throw up. Leke wouldn't have taken the beating he'd dished out to Courtney. Leke would have broken on the first punch, but he was a good kid. Sometimes the bravest people were the most scared. Nodding at James to start the journey outside, he smiled wryly at himself. He was fucking beginning to like these kids. What the fuck was that about?

"Charlie?"

The voice drifted up from the bowels of the station, only the still and silence allowing it to be heard. *"I'm coming, Charlie! Sssseeee you ssssoon!"*

Courtney turned and with his one working eye wide, whispered Charlie's thoughts aloud. "What the fuck is the matter with his voice?"

Charlie raised a finger to his lips and then pushed the boy forward. He didn't want to think about Blane's voice. He didn't want to think about the Squealers. They had enough to deal with getting past the fucking Whites that had taken up residence on the dome. Anything else that was coming they'd have to cope with as and when.

The wide-open space outside North Greenwich tube made everything on the Canning Town side of the tunnel seem small and cramped. There was no road or houses or abandoned cars, just a vast walkway designed to cope with the thousands of visitors expected at the dome each year. It was empty, rain pounding its cream surface into a dark brown. All along the side of the station and leading up to the huge white circular building barely two hundred meters away, a clear hard canvas protected half the wide path. James kept under it as he led the group at a steady jog, protecting them at least a little from the blast of hot rain and wind that raged in the sodden air and battered angrily against it as if trying to punch through to reach them.

With each step the dome grew, peering over the wall at them as they neared the edge of their protection. Despite every nerve in his body telling him to keep his eyes down, Charlie's eyes tilted. In the brightness of the outdoor lighting, the yellow poles reached skyward from the curved surface, rising high above their heads. He'd been here once before, with Lucy, and in the mass of people the structure had been impressive, and now it seemed almost overwhelming. And fucking terrifying. Ahead Nathan stumbled, righting himself before he hit the ground, and the others slowed. It wasn't only Charlie who had looked up. It was impossible not to.

At the edge of the smooth wall they paused. Beyond

it there were no hiding places, but at least there were no more lights. Normally the whole area would be lit up at night, the bulbs of various colors running up the sides of each of the yellow poles and covering the surface, making the building a beacon to any on the river, but it seemed that whoever was the last to leave the dome had made sure they flicked off the light switch on their way out the door. Or maybe the Whites had damaged it somehow. Either way, the darkness would help them. He looked up again, and swallowed. It didn't look like the Whites had their minds on food.

"What the fuck are they doing?" Craig breathed.

Webbing stretched across the network of wires running between each pole and its base, thin and thick ropes and strands creating almost a huge cradle. It was filled with Whites. He'd been expecting them and horrendous as they were, that wasn't what had stopped them all in their tracks. It was what the spiders were doing.

"The rain," he whispered. "Maybe something in the rain."

The creatures lay on their backs, shiny legs waving in the air, writhing as the water poured over the awful suckers that made up their underbellies. They were a mass of hissing white, some of the spiders barely visible against the building's surface, only their glazed eyes betraying their presence as they rolled and twisted in what looked like ecstasy as the rain fell onto them. Their skin glowed with pure vitality compared to the mottled color of their squatter cousins, the Squealers, and Charlie could understand perhaps why they were revolted by them, if he was capable of understanding anything at all about these clinical, alien creatures.

He stared across the gloom toward the glittering

Thames whose silky black surface seemed to taunt them with its proximity. Fuck it. They needed to move. Prodding James, they slid as a line, into the night.

His feet seemed to thump heavily into the ground as he ran, the fifty yards between them and the pier and the marina on the other side stretching too far into the distance. His vision of the world shook, watching the kids' backs jerkily bouncing up and down in an unsteady rhythm with his own breathing, which roared in his head. Water splashed up from the ground and flooded from above, soaking Charlie's clothes and skin. He fought to keep it out of his mouth. It tasted wrong, and seeing how the Whites were reveling in it could only mean that it was probably no fucking good for him. Surely they must have been spotted. How could the Whites not have noticed?

Up ahead, Harry glanced over his shoulder. Charlie waited to see panic rise up in his eyes, but beneath the fear there was only relief. In the corner of his own eye the O2 arena curved away. They'd reached the pier.

James grinned. "It's that way. Two minutes and we're there."

"*Charlie!*"

The scream was part word, part squeal as it cut through the tempest that howled through the dark night, and the huddle froze. Slowly, Charlie turned.

"*Charlie fucking Nash! I want my fucking drugssss!*"

Charlie stared. He couldn't help it. Just in front of the end of the station wall, Blane was clearly visible. The thing carrying him scuttered and scrambled forward in an uneven line and then rose up on its hind legs, exposing Charlie's childhood friend. Webbing lashed him to the underside of the beast and with the water raging around them he thought of that film about the whale and the obsessed captain drowned covered in ropes against its back. Blane was like that. Strapped in. And maybe worse. Even from thirty yards he could see Blane's hazel eyes were glowing slightly red. What was that thing doing to him under that webbing? Was his skin turning purple like the men in the cocoons had been? Surely just being attached to that thing would drive you mad. But then Blane had been pretty much on his way to a kind of crazy before this night.

"The dome." Nathan didn't need to say any more. Charlie glanced up. The Whites were coming out of their trance, a few flipping over onto their bellies and up on their feet. Their red eyes were focused now, looking down at Blane and the thing holding him. It wouldn't be long before they turned their attention to Charlie and the boys.

"*I want my fucking drugsssss!*" Blane screeched again. His dreadlocks blew around him in the wind, a halo of snakes.

"I don't have his fucking drugs," Charlie muttered, confused. "I left them. What's he done all this for?"

"I've got them." The small voice lacked all hint of its previous arrogance, and Charlie turned to see James holding out the four packs. One had a tear in it.

"I didn't think . . . I just wanted to feel better. I didn't think." The boy was almost in tears, but Charlie still fought the urge to wring his scrawny neck.

"You dumb fucking kid. You dumb . . ." He couldn't finish the sentence. There were no words to cover the sheer frustration and rage that simmered under his skin. "Give me that," was all he could manage. "Now get to the boat. Get it started. I'll catch you up."

"What are you going to do?"

With his free hand Charlie felt for the grenade in his pocket. "I'm going to finish this."

"I'll come with you," James said. "I'll cover your back."

Charlie stared at him. "I don't fucking think so. You've done enough. And you're the only one that knows which fucking boat it is."

"Charlie!" Courtney elbowed him. "Quickly."

"Go!" Charlie pushed at James and Leke herding the others between them. "Get that fucking boat started."

As soon as the boys were running, Charlie turned back. Blane and the Squealer had moved farther forward and were level with the dome. Neither seemed to see the Whites that hung over the edge and back, hissing. Maybe they did; maybe their need for what Charlie had was stronger. He walked forward a few steps. His heart raged against his chest, but he kept his pace even.

"Looks like you're in trouble, Blane," he called into the rain. "Now who's the fucking trained pet?"

Two Whites dropped to the ground between them, and four more behind Blane and their deformed relative. Charlie's mouth dried. Who was he kidding? He had no chance of getting out of this alive. The first White hissed, its smooth front section twisting as the bumpy bank of eyes looked at Blane and then Charlie and then Blane again. Its mandibles clacked sharply together like soft machine gunfire. Charlie forced his legs to move. He needed to be closer. The White leaped.

Before he could react, three shots cut the air and the creature's eyes exploded into one mess as it collapsed. Courtney stepped up beside him, the gun raised.

"I thought you might need a hand."

Despite his battered face and chest, Courtney stood tall.

Charlie didn't take his eyes from the growing number of Whites that were undeterred by their fallen cousin. They moved slowly as if waking up, and they were curious. He could feel it. Whatever they were going to do, it had to be quickly.

"Thanks, kid." He paused. "Sorry about the face."

Courtney snorted. "Don't make me smile. It hurts."

"This what you want, Blane?" Charlie held up one bag of the white powder, letting the other three fall to the wet ground at their feet. "You need to get high? That going to make everything better?"

As Blane screamed, the creature squealed, dropping back down to its squat position, and as it lowered ready to charge, Charlie could clearly see the four Whites gathering behind it. He eased the grenade out of his pocket.

"Get ready to run."

Somewhere behind them, an engine fired into life. Raindrops beat at his face, making his skin prickle. And then the Squealer leaped, the still moment broken. Charlie launched the bag of drugs at it, the plastic tearing on its mandibles, and the Squealer twisted, its attack distracted, the drugs coating both it and Blane underneath, confusing both with its sudden ingestion. Charlie forgotten, the thing rolled, coating itself in the white powder before the rain could wash it away. Blane's smooth face was powered white and as both felt the effect of the pure cocaine, they trembled, the Squealer's body pulsating in delight.

The Whites didn't hesitate. Sensing the mutated spider's defenses were down, they pounced. For a flash of a second Charlie saw Blane's eyes widen, and then he was gone, covered in the bodies of the attacking Whites. The air was filled with a squeal so filled with pain that Charlie almost felt sorry for the thing. Almost, not quite. He hoped Blane had soaked up that powder. He hoped his mate was going out high.

Courtney fired again, the first shot missing a White that turned to them, but the second taking a chunk out of its body. It crumpled, hissing and snarling, writhing between them and the dome. Charlie looked up. The place was alive, the rain forgotten, the Whites righting themselves and scurrying along the various coils of foul webbing to reach the edges.

Charlie pulled the pin and using all his strength threw the grenade. He watched it twist and turn through the dark night air, before disappearing into the melee of sharp limbs and smooth bodies.

"Run!" He grabbed Courtney's arm, turning him. "Run!"

Pulling his gun from his pocket as he moved, Charlie's arms pumped the air as he counted down in his head, his eyes already flinching from the blast. They had to get some distance between them and that side of the dome. His feet curved around to the darker side. Up ahead, the lights on the boat shone like stars on the river. They had to fucking . . .

He felt the *whump* of air in his back. It threw him forward and knocked his breath to the ground, his body arriving in a heavy thump a moment after. The explosion rocketed through his ears and rattled his brain and the night was suddenly alive with light. He rolled onto his back and stared up. The roof of the dome was burning, a blaze of howling, hissing flames. Parts of it broke away and leaped to the ground, but the creatures burned just as hard there as they did on the roof. He pulled himself to his feet.

Courtney lay a few feet behind him, slowly starting to stir.

"Come on." Charlie's words sounded funny in his ears, deadened like he had a cold. "Let's get to the boat."

The boy sat up and turned to smile. His swollen eye had split, a trickle of blood dribbling into the rain. "That was amazing. That was . . ."

Charlie wasn't listening. His eyes stared and although his mouth moved he knew it wasn't going fast enough. There was something behind Courtney. He needed to shoot. He needed to shoot the fucking thing, but his gun hand was empty, the weapon lost as the blast threw him to the ground. The White loomed out of the fiery backdrop, all the rage of its race glowing in its eyes as it hissed forward, no caution or fear, but at full speed.

"Courtney!" He spat out the word. It was all he could manage and it wasn't enough. The White leaped and landed full on the boy's chest. Courtney's smile fell.

"Char—" There wasn't even any fear in the start of the word, his surprise too complete. And then the spider was gone.

Charlie stared as it rounded the burning building, leaping away with such speed it was almost as if Courtney had just vanished, and then his eyes finally spied the gun barely five feet away. Grabbing it, he emptied the chamber into the night, his own scream adding to the cacophony of the burning building and its dying contents and getting lost in the storm. It wasn't fair. It wasn't fucking fair.

"Charlie!"

His name drifted at him but he ignored it.

"Charlie, come on! Come on!"

He stared at the desolation around him for a moment longer, before, with an empty heart, he forced his legs to jog down to the waiting boat.

CHAPTER TWENTY-EIGHT

Skate's hands trembled as he lit his cigarette. He concentrated on every trace of smoke that poured into his lungs as he sucked in. The heat felt good in his throat and mouth. The acrid, familiar taste filled his taste buds. Smoking. You couldn't fucking beat it. He thought that maybe he should roll up a mother of a sinsemilla joint and burn it up. Get himself so high he'd throw up. And maybe he should, and if there was time, then maybe he would. For the moment though, he figured he'd just settle for a fine Marlboro.

The electric had gone off fifteen minutes ago. He wasn't sure why, because from where he stood on the balcony it seemed that streetlights were blazing in most parts of the city along the water's edge and over in Greenwich and the rest of the south. He drew in another strong lungful of smoke. Despite being partly protected by the awning on the deck, the smoke was edged with the bitter taste of the rain. Still, it was better being outside than in. Inside, he'd heard the screams and yells coming from below as soon as the power went. And they weren't screams of surprise. Something was in the building. Something that might be more intelligent than they'd first thought.

It was ten minutes ago that he'd heard the glass

smashing below. He didn't need to go and look to see what it was. The Squealers were out. He just knew. Maybe he wasn't as bright as Blane or Charlie, but he wasn't fucking stupid. As soon as the lights had gone off, he'd known that something had come for them. Listening to the shrieks flooding the building, it sounded like the Squealers from elsewhere in the city had come to find their own. Maybe they'd been waiting in the wings all this time, until whatever weird communication they had going on let them know that the men were no longer useful and it was time to come and feed.

How the fuck had he got into this? Why the fuck hadn't he just got the fuck out after what happened to Brownie? He should have just tooled himself up and headed out of town, before the Whites and Squealers had found their feet. Why did he always have to follow someone else?

He stared out toward the burning O2 arena. The lights had gone out just after that had gone up, the small explosion clearly audible in the night. He'd gone out to look as the building plunged into darkness. It was still ablaze now, even in the heavy rain.

Lights flickered on the black ribbon of the Thames and his brow furrowed as his eyes picked out the small, flashy cruiser slowly creeping along the water's surface, its engine chugging healthily. He couldn't see any people on board, but he knew in his soul that Charlie Nash was among them. Fucking Charlie Nash was always going to make it. He pulled harder on the cigarette, but it brought little comfort and he pretended that the tears that stung the back of his eyes were simply raindrops.

When something landed with a soft thud on the decking from the roof above, he didn't turn around.

* * *

By morning the storm had passed and the river was coated in a mist so deep it seemed as if they were steering through clouds. No one had spoken much in the hours that had passed since leaving the marina. They'd taken it in turns to sleep in the sumptuous cabins below-decks, but no one could do more than doze for an hour or so. They'd been through too much to simply switch off, each needing to slowly let go of their grief and loss and terrible fear before their bodies could relax.

James clung to the helm, steering them through the fog with his eyes as empty as Charlie's heart had been while watching Courtney ripped away from the ground to fuck only knew where. For a while he'd wanted to rip off James's head with his bare hands, but as his anger faded into dull grief, Charlie figured the posh kid had to carry it all inside and that was punishment enough.

He stood outside, listening to Harry's voice steadily cutting through the eerie silence repeating the message over and over. *They were heading north, to one of the islands off Scotland. They'd send coordinates when they found somewhere safe. They were children. They were going to try and set up a clear colony. Any other survivors please head north and join us. Bring supplies.* And then he started again, his voice clear and crisp and tired.

Charlie listened to the gentle slosh of water against the smooth side of the boat. They didn't even know if the radio was working. It was all static and white noise, and although they'd thought at times they could hear someone saying something about being under the Tower of London, it was gone again in a moment. Still, Harry insisted on sending the message. And maybe he was right. Maybe someone would eventually hear them.

His eyes burned with tiredness and his back hurt

from where the blast had picked him up from his feet and thrown him to the ground. He needed to lie down but thought that maybe if he did, he'd never get up again. His hands buried themselves deep in his jacket pocket and brushed against a thick edge of paper. It was the photo. He pulled it out and stared long and hard at those two childish smiling faces from a lifetime ago. In the gray dawn light, the hope and happiness in their twinkling eyes still shone out at him. He sighed. Holding out his hand, he let the picture drop. It floated on the surface for a moment, those faces looking up at him, and then mist swallowed it up. He was glad. Those days were gone.

It was a new dawn.

✂

☐ **YES!**

Sign me up for the Leisure Horror Book Club and send my FREE BOOKS! If I choose to stay in the club, I will pay only $8.50* each month, a savings of $7.48!

NAME: _____

ADDRESS: _____

TELEPHONE: _____

EMAIL: _____

☐ I want to pay by credit card.

☐ **VISA**   ☐ **MasterCard**   ☐ **DISCOVER**

ACCOUNT #: _____

EXPIRATION DATE: _____

SIGNATURE: _____

Mail this page along with $2.00 shipping and handling to:
Leisure Horror Book Club
PO Box 6640
Wayne, PA 19087
Or fax (must include credit card information) to:
610-995-9274

You can also sign up online at **www.dorchesterpub.com**.
*Plus $2.00 for shipping. Offer open to residents of the U.S. and Canada only.
Canadian residents please call 1-800-481-9191 for pricing information.
If under 18, a parent or guardian must sign. Terms, prices and conditions subject to change. Subscription subject to acceptance. Dorchester Publishing reserves the right to reject any order or cancel any subscription.

GET FREE BOOKS!

You can have the best fiction delivered to your door for less than what you'd pay in a bookstore or online. Sign up for one of our book clubs today, and we'll send you *FREE* BOOKS* just for trying it out... **with no obligation to buy, ever!**

As a member of the Leisure Horror Book Club, you'll receive books by authors such as **RICHARD LAYMON, JACK KETCHUM, JOHN SKIPP, BRIAN KEENE** and many more.

As a book club member you also receive the following special benefits:
- **30% off all orders!**
- **Exclusive access to special discounts!**
- **Convenient home delivery and 10 days to return any books you don't want to keep.**

Visit www.dorchesterpub.com or call 1-800-481-9191

There is no minimum number of books to buy, and you may cancel membership at any time.
*Please include $2.00 for shipping and handling.